SURE–DART

Sure-dart Witnesses the Battle of the Sea Monsters

[*Page 312*]

SURE-DART

*A Story of Strange Hunters
and Stranger Game in the
Days of Monsters*

BY

FREDERICK H. COSTELLO

WILDSIDE PRESS

PREFACE

IN this story I have taken a few liberties with what are generally accepted in the scientific world as facts, and so I suppose some explanations are desirable. The greatest liberty I have taken is with regard to the introduction of human beings into the story when the period is so very remote. The period is that called by geologists the Secondary, and the particular part of it is toward the close of what is termed the Cretaceous. As far as our knowledge goes at the present time, this is a date several hundred thousand years earlier than the coming of man. But I desired to introduce human beings to make the story more interesting, and I felt a greater right to do so because there was nothing in the condition of the earth at that time which would have made it impossible for human beings to live and flourish. In fact, the conditions were more favorable than in some of the inhabited parts of the earth now.

Another bit of license is that relating to the animals and birds. I have introduced a few rather earlier than some authorities would allow, and have detained others on the stage, so to speak, a little longer than perhaps there is scientific authority for. But I believe that this matter is of slight importance, and the more so because specialists are by no means agreed as to the dates, and because all our absolute knowledge is comparatively limited.

Beyond this, I think the story follows the lines of accepted fact and conclusions. Thus Colorado, with its great fresh-water sea; with its strange forests of mingled palms, oaks, beeches, yew-like conifers, and cycads (which were like palms crossed with gigantic ferns) with its hot, steamy days, and its tropic nights, when a moon bigger and brighter than we have ever seen looked down on a world that would have made us gasp by its strangeness — these are brought on our stage faithfully and without exaggeration.

And neither are those seeming nightmares, the monsters of the story, exaggerated. I have spoken "by the card" when I have asked to step out before us the lizard as big as a small house, and that could have pulled a man out of the upper branches of a moderately tall tree; that other lizard creature bigger than any elephant, but that looked somewhat like a hideous caricature of a rhinoceros; and yet again, the creature nearly as big as the last, that had a part of its brain substance in its rump, and a spiked tail that could have switched once and dashed a man into a bloody pulp.

Then there are faithful pictures of the smaller creatures — the toothed birds, the bat-like lizards which stretched nearly twenty feet across the spread wings, and the turtles as big over as an old-fashioned tavern table.

But I am raising too much of the curtain. I will make one more explanation and then let it fall. In giving names to the monsters and other wild creatures, I have invented in behalf of the human characters such as are simple and would naturally be suggested by the looks or ways of the creatures themselves. It would hardly do to proceed on the line of reasoning of the old lady who said that she did not marvel so much that the remains of ancient creatures had been discovered as that science had found out also their names. However, to be more informing, I have inserted a list of the modern names of the principal creatures.

FREDERICK H. COSTELLO.

BANGOR, MAINE, *July 1, 1909.*

CONTENTS

CONTENTS

ILLUSTRATIONS

MODERN NAMES OF CREATURES
OF THE STORY

DEATH-BEAST . . . . . . Ceteosaurus, or "monster lizard." One American variety is also called tyrannosaurus rex, or "tyrant king lizard." It is likewise known as "terrible lizard." It was a large, flesh-eating dinosaur.

THUNDER-BEAST . . Atlantosaurus, or "gigantic lizard." A dinosaur of the brontosaurus or "thunder lizard" family, and the largest land animal known.

GREAT STALKER . . An American species of the iguanodon, called thespesius or "marvellous." It is also called claosaurus. It was a vegetable eating dinosaur.

LITTLE STALKER . . A smaller variety of the thespesius family.

MARSH-HOPPER . . The smallest known dinosaur. It was a thespesius on a diminutive scale.

THREE-HORNS . . . Triceratops. A dinosaur somewhat like a rhinoceros. It was not carnivorous.

THORN-TAIL . . . Stegosaurus, or "backlered lizard." One of the strangest-looking of the dinosaurs.

FISH-SNAKE . . . . Plesiosaurus or elasmosaurus. A marine monster with a long, snake-like neck.

GREAT KILLER . . . Mosasaur, or "Meuse River lizard," a kind of lizard-crocodile.

GREAT FLIPPER . . Archæochelon, or "primitive turtle." An enormous turtle.

SPEAR-TOOTH . . . A moderately large, very voracious fish, with a huge head and teeth like sharp spikes.

WORM-TAIL . . . . Archæopteryx, or "primitive bird." A strange bird of the Jurassic period, but possibly surviving to the Cretaceous, the period of the story.

TERROR BIRD . . . Brontornis, or "thunder bird."

BIG BEAST-BIRD . . Pterodactyl, the "finger-winged." A kind of flying lizard, with enormous wings.

SCAMPERER . . . . Hyracotherium. The ancestor of the horse. He does not properly belong to the period of the story, but to a time later.

SURE–DART

Sure-Dart

CHAPTER I

HUNTING TERRIBLE GAME

THE boys did not talk much as they went along. It would have been dangerous, for the enemy just beyond had good ears; and then, it was not the way of the people of that day to talk for the mere sake of talking.

They stopped just short of the last ridge and looked back. It was a matter of prudence — a prudence taught them by grim experience. One of the two was only fifteen, and the other two years younger, yet both were old in the dreadful kind of knowledge that a hazard like this called for. It was such a hazard as would have excused doubt and hesitation in the bravest man, to say nothing of a boy.

But that will have to be explained later. Just now they were making sure that they were safe thus far, and that there was no danger of a surprise. The enemy beyond the ridge had come up from a valley to the left, and who could say that others of his kind might not come trailing along after, but keep on around the hill, instead of turning off into the little valley? In that case they would be caught in a trap, with one enemy before, and one or more in the rear.

But as they looked they saw nothing of any new danger. The countryside seemed quiet, and only what they had already observed and accounted for came within their range. There were other ridges right and left, both climbing higher till they cut out the full bigness of foot-hills, and just above the surface of the lake were the bald, yellow spots of low chalk cliffs. In other directions these fell away till they ran themselves out in the marsh levels, or straggled in little grave-mound shapes back to the two great horns of the far-reaching woods.

The boys turned back again after this one look; the older said a single low word to the other, and began to crawl on hands and knees toward the low crest of the ridge. It was not far, but at the rate he went it must take some minutes to reach it; meanwhile the other boy lay down almost flat, and with Indian-like patience waited. He laid three long, flint-headed darts close by his hand, and made sure that a small stone axe was safe in his leather girdle. He was stripped either for fight or flight, for his only clothing — unless one reckons the belt — was a leather breech-clout. The leather both of this and the belt was of a peculiar sort, and looked more like alligator skin than ordinary leather. He was a savage, then, but yet not an Indian. What he was and what the other boy was (they were dressed and armed alike) will very soon appear.

While the first boy was worming along toward the top of the ridge the other looked back again and along the sides of the slope. He still saw nothing that troubled him, and nothing even that was out of the commonplace — the commonplace to him. It will be worth while to stop a moment and see whether it will seem wholly commonplace to us. To begin with, let us see what region this is. Now we start with something to think of, for this is the eastern part of the present State of Colorado. Yet the lake below, after escaping from the arms of the two little headlands, widens and reaches out till it is lost everywhere on the sky-line! Nor could an eagle, if he should rise to the region of thin air, raise the land boundary!

But there are other things to see, and no farther away than the shores of this unaccountable lake. There are the trees and other vegetation. It certainly seems as if there must be some mistake here. For down there, rising from the midst of strange, rank ferns and huge, unfamiliar canes are what can be none other than palm trees. They are not tall, but robust in trunk, and they seem at home, so to speak, in the company of the rank, tropical growth about them. To be sure, the trees that we should naturally look for are not wholly wanting, for there are what resemble modern yews, and some fine-leaved trees that at least look like willows, and on the slopes of the ridges, higher up, are low oaks and beeches. Yet mingled with these again are alien forms of cedars, and some strange cycads that seem to be in part palms, and in part a kind of gigantic fern.

But still again, to look along the banks of the

lake. It is only late spring, and early in the morning, and yet the half-clouded sun has a hot sting,
and a little, steamy mist rises from the dank borders of the lake. The faint puff of a variant
breeze, too, from that direction, brings with it a
mingling of tropic scents, spicy and yet rank,
and a whiff from the overcrowded and dying vegetable growths. In a moment some of the tall
reeds by the northern shore wave, and then bend
sharply down, and out of the heart of them walks
a living creature. It walks, and somewhat like a
man, for it comes along on two legs, and with
a kind of waddling duck-gait. Its great hind
legs slap along, and its little fore ones hang down
limp. It stands ten feet high to the top of its
coffin-shaped, earless head, and its thick, tapering
tail drags after it ten feet more. It certainly looks
somewhat like a kangaroo, and yet repulsively
unlike one. For another thing, it has a comparatively smooth skin, though broken into lizard-like
scales, and it is gray on the upper part of its body
and white the length of its belly.

After a struggle with the absurdity of saying
so, one would call it a monstrous lizard, but with
the perversion of an upright carriage, and with
legs like a kangaroo's.

And this seeming flight of the imagination
would go not a whit beyond the truth, for this
strange and puzzling monster, amid strange and
puzzling surroundings, *is* a lizard.

But as the waiting boy is neither disturbed nor
amazed at such a sight as this it is evident that
it is not strange to him. Are there still other
sights that he is looking dull-eyed at, but that, as

we make them out, set us to staring, and almost to gasping? What is the monster lizard himself at this moment looking at?

The cove, toward which the monster is heading, is shoal at this point (the great lake itself is not relatively deep), but there is a drop, or hole, near the immediate shore, and the water is deeper there, and it is toward this spot that the creature is looking.

No wonder! The almost smooth surface of the water ripples, and then breaks, and up into sight flashes a dusky, longish object that in an instant takes shape as a huge snake. Its head is rather large for what so far appears to be its body, though thin at the jaws. Up it still rises, straight into the air, until — how long, in horror's name, can the creature be? The head is more than twenty feet clear of the water now, and unless the monster is standing on its tail, which would be out of the question — but what is this? The length of body has run itself out, indeed, but in the name of all that is strange, how? It has ended in another body that is as thick as a small whale's, but with two seal-like flippers that at this moment show a little out of the water, and gently beat up and down.

Perhaps ten seconds of this suspense, the lizard watching the — call it the fish-snake, — and the newcomer seemingly looking that way, as if questioning him, and then something new happens. The long, upraised neck curves gracefully down, the jaws fly open, and the head dives under the water. It comes up instantly, and in the jaws is a shining and flapping fish. With a little beating

of flippers, the great body turns and heads lake-
wards, and the neck droops till it is almost level
with the water. More paddling, and the creature
heads down the channel, and goes steadily out
to the broad water. There it slowly sinks and
vanishes.

The giant lizard at this starts along again and
keeps on till he splashes down into the water. His
business is commonplace, after all, for when he
is a little way out he stoops and drinks. This
done, he turns and waddles off among his reeds
and ferns.

There are other strange sights down there,
only it would take a nearer view to bring them
out; meanwhile, the creeping boy on the hill-slope
is on the point of uncovering a sight more amaz-
ing still. It will be better worth while to follow
him.

He shuffled along relatively fast, though he did
not rise from hands and knees, and was not long
in reaching the final little crest of earth that
crowned the ridge. Then, ever so cautiously, he
raised his head and peered over.

There was a sharp slope down to a little ravine,
and beyond that a rise to another ridge. In fact,
the surface of the land just here was like the
monstrous furrows of some giant's ploughed field.
Across the ravine, on the opposite rise, was the
thing that the boy was looking at.

It may well be called a thing, for it was like
nothing that any living human being of our day
ever saw, and more like some hobgoblin of a
dream. It stretched out longer than an ordinary
dwelling house, and rose, at its curving rump, to

the height of a New England farm-shed. Its
bulk in the middle was greater than any elephant's, and its huge tail at its beginning was
bigger than a sugar barrel.

The head was no longer than a horse's, but the
mouth was split up much farther, and as it opened
it showed great, tiger-like teeth. The upper lip
— if it may be called a lip — bent down and
ended in a kind of bill. There was a horn a foot
long on the snout. The long, snake-like neck
ended in a little rising hill at the fore shoulders,
and from there the back rose still higher to the
hind-quarters; then the monstrous tail ran down
another slope to its pointed end. All along this
curving back, and to the very end of the tail, was
a little saw-tooth ridge. Hair does not belong to
reptiles, and this one had none. Instead, the
whole body was covered with close scales, green-
ish on the upper part, and almost white below.
The relatively short fore legs ended in frog-like
hands, with short claws on the fingers, and a claw
a foot long on the thumb. The huge and long
hind legs tapered down, and finished in great
bird-like feet. Each toe of the foot ended in a
claw as long as a sickle. These claws cleared the
ground a little, as the monster stood on all fours,
and so preserved the sharpness of the terrible
points.

This, then, was the strange something that the
two plucky boys were spying on, and yet held in
such dread. It is easier to understand the dread
now.

The creature was just at this moment turned
a little away from the boy. Its head was down,

and it stood lumpishly, and with its low-set eyes half shut.

Backward crawled the boy and did not stop till he was well below the crest of the ridge. Then he stood up and ran swiftly down the slope.

The other boy saw him coming, and rose. Like the cool little hunter that he was he said nothing, but merely looked his question.

" He 's going," with a grin, was the answer. " He has eaten every bit of the carcass."

This brought a responsive grin.

" He is n't down yet? "

" No, but drooping. I did n't see anything of the others."

The questioner picked up his darts. In bending down to get them he seemed a trifle awkward. It was because one foot was a little deformed, and the leg a bit shorter than the other.

" It is a first-rate beginning, Hop-foot," went on the older boy. " Even if the others don't get the poisoned stuff now they probably will another time. It is good news to carry home."

" Yes, it 's good news," assented Hop-foot.

They started down the hill, and Hop-foot went on:

" It is ten moons now since the last death-beasts came up from the farther lake shore. It looks as if they were dying out. Don't you think they are, Sure-dart? "

" Yes, they must be," answered Sure-dart, " and in fact, the old hunters are beginning to say so. It will be fine when they and all the others of the kind die out. There will be things enough left then to worry us."

"But they are mainly water creatures. For instance, fish-snake, and spike-tooth, and the destroyers. Fish-snake, too, does n't bother us very much."

"There are some others, and you forget the birds. What about the terror bird? I had rather fight some of the beasts than him. Then there is the big beast-bird. If he comes along in the night, and you are out by yourself — I 've got one scar that matches his teeth."

"Yes, he 's bad," assented Hop-foot. "So, too, are some of the others. But what I meant was, we don't have so much trouble from these creatures as our tribe used to. Look at the safety-holes all around the lake, and up here in the hills. My father says that when he was a boy people were using them all of the time."

"Oh, that is so, and your main idea is right. But, Hop-foot, there are things worse than the beasts and birds. Those don't know much. Human creatures are worse. Look at the way things are just now. If the Fishers are really coming, and if our people don't beat them, then maybe we shall wish we were fighting the beasts. We shall all stand a good chance to be roasted and eaten."

Hop-foot soberly nodded.

"Yes, that is so. But perhaps the story of the war-party is not true; if it is — " his black eyes lighted — "my father will know what to do."

Sure-dart nodded in turn.

"Big-axe is a great fighter," he said respectfully, "and my father put him higher in that than any other headman we ever had. Besides, he is cunning, and a good trap-layer. But you know," he went on more soberly, " the Fishers fight well, too, and they far outnumber us."

" Well, Sure-dart," said Hop-foot, undisturbedly, " I am not going to worry. I think we shall have good news from our party, let what will be the matter. When Big-axe led the Rock-people against the Cane-dwellers, you know what happened. We did not have to hide in the safety-holes, as if the death-beasts were coming."

He smiled proudly, showing a splendid set of teeth. The jaws that held them were long and strong, and went well with his muscular if rather thin arms, and the play of other muscles over his broad back and thick shoulders. He was hardly so tall as the average American boy of the present day, and he was a bit full at the waist for our idea of power and beauty, but nevertheless, he was a wonderful boy. His strength was great for his age, and his wind and general endurance were far beyond what we expect to find even in our most robust boys. His face was by no means stupid, either, for all that the forehead was low, and the skull retreating. His eyes were bright, and his general expression alert, and there was a kind of manly composure in his look. His hair was jet-black and coarse, and flowed down over his shoulders; and his skin, except for a deep coat of tan, was yellowish white. More than any other people that we know of he resembled a Laplander. He looked brighter and more energetic, however. One other thing in his appearance deserves mention. His body was wonderfully hairy. The black hair grew like a bed of moss on his chest, and ran in ridges down his arms and legs, and out upon his hands and feet.

Sure-dart in most ways resembled him. He had the same kind of complexion, and the same sort of powerful, hairy body, with relatively thin arms and a bit of portliness, and with a deep chest. He was a little less stocky, but a bit taller, and was rather quicker and more supple in his movements. His face, too, was a little more comely,— judged by our standards,— and seemed to show a somewhat keener intelligence.

His weapons were the same as Hop-foot's — a small, stone-headed axe, and three flint-headed darts. The darts were about two feet long each, and were adjusted for flight by some bits of split reeds placed vertically at what we should call the feather-end. The points of these darts showed some discoloration, and it was to be noticed that both of the boys handled the little missiles carefully. In fact, they had kept them, till within a few minutes, in a kind of case, or quiver, this made of the lizard skin (looking like alligator skin) already mentioned.

" No," said Sure-dart, in response to Hop-foot's remark, " it is certain that we did n't have to go into safety-holes when the Cane-dwellers made their raid. We beat them, and those that we did n't kill we made slaves of. It ended the Cane-dwellers. I only hope —— "

He stopped, and his look changed. He happened to be walking on a little crest of ledge, and from there could see over a small spur of rocks, and down into a winding valley. This valley led back to the furrowed ridges whence the dying horned monster had come.

" Run! " he shouted, jumping off the ledge and whipping his darts into their sheath; " the other death-beasts are coming! " He wheeled to the left, and started at a run along the hill-slope.

Hop-foot lost a little color, but he, too, stopped long enough to slip the poisoned darts into their sheath. No wise man or boy would plunge along such footing with these death-dealers exposed; and on the other hand, this experienced hunter knew better than to throw them away. He understood what it would mean to be shut up in a little hole in the ground with no help nigh, and these raging beasts outside. They would quiet down after a while, but would not leave, and unless some weapon availed there would be left but a choice of deaths.

One might have thought that a family of monstrous kangaroos, with the weight of elephants, was coming! The huge legs lifted the massive bodies in great jumps, so that the dreadful heads were twenty feet in the air. Stones as big as a man were knocked out of the way, and bushes were crushed like grass. As if they had caught the scent or the sight of their prey, the creatures put out their vast strength, and by the sheer force of it hurled their great bulk along, and over the side-hill level to the very shadow of the outcropping rock that the boys were passing.

Sure-dart was ahead, but in spite of the danger he was not running his best, for he lagged a little for Hop-foot. The lame boy was simply doing marvels in the way of speed. He hopped, skipped, and jumped along, and gave Sure-dart little margin for waiting.

Now, one of the three monsters — the largest — was within the length of its body from Hop-foot. Sure-dart looked once more backward, groaned, and made one swift dart into the shadowed mouth of a safety-hole.

The crashing monster seemed to jet its hot breath after him, and with its thunder fairly made the ground shake.

Hop-foot must be among the things that were.

CHAPTER II

SURE–DART plunged on into the little cave till he came to the end. The distance was not more than twenty feet, and none too far to seem clear of the pursuing horror. It is to be remembered that the monster had a long, lizard neck, with a range from the body of several feet.

The boy leaned against the wall for an instant, getting back his breath and steadying his shaken senses. He had no hope whatever for Hop-foot, for he felt sure that the giant beast had overtaken him, and this could mean but one thing. The monster, clumsy in a certain way, was still unlikely to miss such a plain target, and therefore Hop-foot was now no more than a shapeless welter of blood, flesh, and bones. One lurch of the great mass upon the little squirming body would make it well-nigh as if it had never been.

But now the moment of weakness and helplessness had passed, and the hardy barbarian turned from the wall, and looked toward the mouth of the hole. His ears, like his eyes, were again in full action.

The opening was half blocked up, and the light inside was reduced to dusk. There was no need to ask why. A fishy and musky smell drifted in, and something that looked at first glance like a huge hammer, with a very long, crooked handle, was at the moment swaying up and down in the dimmed light. Not to be mysterious, the death-beast was crowding up close to the mouth of the hole, and just at this moment was thrusting his head inside.

Sure-dart took a second look, and noted the distance to the swaying head. His eyes took on a hard gleam; he slipped a hairy arm to the case at his side, and drew out one of the little spears. Without hesitation he walked forward a few steps and raised the dart. The beaked head stopped its swaying, and the mouth opened redly and shut again. The monster certainly perceived him now, if he had not before, and was preparing to make an effort — who could guess the measure of it? — to reach him. Sure-dart took one more step, stopped, and brought his right arm still farther back.

The light almost vanished, for the monster had crouched, bringing his body more exactly against the hole, and was beginning to use his mighty claws. He was trying to enlarge the opening.

The boy's eyes steadied, he swung forward a bit, and then back, and with another forward swing the dart left his hand. It was cast with a skill that came of long practice, and with a force far beyond the seeming power of his arm.

He had aimed for a bend of the long neck at a point perhaps two feet behind the head. The skin was not extremely thick here, and the outside scales not firm enough to resist the strong impulse of the dart. But in fact, the boy had cast the weapon with such force for another reason than merely to pierce the skin and scales; he wanted to reach with the poison as many blood-vessels as he could. He knew that these cold-blooded reptiles were hard to kill, and that even the strong poison on the dart would not take effect at once. Indeed, cases had been known where the smitten creatures had held out long enough to starve the cave-hider into coming forth, and then had killed him. Sure-dart could not count on help from friends; the greater number of the able-bodied men of the caves were still out on their expedition, and the few that were left with the boys, women, and small children could not be counted on to meet such enemies as these. Besides, the boy knew that he and Hop-foot were in a sense to blame for the present situation. They had stolen away to look up the fate of the poisoned monster, when prudence required them to wait longer, and take no such chance. Even if the other monsters made a descent on the dwelling-caves (which was unlikely, for the crea-tures, thick-headed as they were, had learned better than that), then retreat to safety was easy. The dwelling-caves were relatively large, and were provided with food and drink sufficient for a short siege of any kind. The Rock-people, as they called themselves, had learned this piece of precaution by deadly experience. So Sure-dart felt that he must get himself out of the scrape if he could, and must not bring destruction on his friends in an effort to help him.

As he let the dart go he bent forward eagerly and watched the result. At the very moment that the dart left his fingers the creature slightly turned its head, and the end of the long snout stuck out into the track of the dart. The little missile glanced from the horn-like beak, and fell harmless to the ground.

Sure-dart, trained though he was to bear disappointment, scowled, and fetched a little sharp breath. One of his three chances was gone.

The great lizard was perhaps annoyed by the little rap on its nose, or it might have been excited to new exertions by the nearness of its prey, for here it made still greater exertions to enlarge the hole. It pushed against the rocks, wriggled, and dug sideways with its claws. Some of the smaller rocks gave way and let a little more of the straining body through, but the rest held. The greater part of the beginning of the cave had been dug through the solid rock, and even the mighty strength of the great reptile could not start it. The Rock-people had guarded against just such enemies, and by dint of great labor had hewed and dug away with their flint tools till they had made a safe gate-way. They had one thing in their favor, which was that the rock was of a lime formation and so was not the hardest kind to work.

Sure-dart watched the labors of the monster with a derisive sneer. He was not at all worried about the outcome. The danger for him lay in quite another direction.

For a few minutes longer the giant reptile kept up its wriggling, digging, and clawing. It had the dull perseverance of creatures of this kind, and its wind and endurance seemed to have hardly a limit. But at last it relaxed a little, and again began to reach out its head, its mouth angrily opening and shutting.

Sure-dart saw that another chance had come. The target was once more a fair one. He stepped forward, poised a dart, and again put wonderful force and deftness into its flight.

This time there was no armored snout in the track. The dart struck half-way down the uplifted neck and sank its whole head in the flesh.

The boy gave a little snarl of triumph (his expressions of this kind were little better than animal noises), and flashed out his splendid teeth in a grin. Coolly he drew the remaining dart and waited for another chance.

Though the monster's nervous organization was of a dull kind, so that the pain of the wound could not have been great, it was still sufficient to give him a little surprise and add considerably to his irritation. He drew his head back, broke out in a queer kind of hiss, and then made a new and stronger effort to reach his tormentor.

It was still in vain, but this time the effort was so mighty that one loose piece of rock that weighed tons was lifted from its place, and the creature raised itself under it, and actually stood with the enormous weight on its back.

It was only for an instant, and then the giant settled back under the load, and half sprawled out, as before. There had been little real danger, for it was out of the question for the creature to advance while sustaining such a load, and even if he had, he must have brought up against the solid rock of the two sides of the opening.

Nevertheless, what he did was sufficient to give the boy a decided start, and take the confident look out of his face.

What next? Sure-dart had no doubt that he had given the monster its death-wound, and so it seemed unwise to give him the remaining dart; he might need that for one of the other beasts. On the other hand, the present enemy might last for hours, or even till the next day, and after that he might settle down where he was and die, and then how was Sure-dart to get out? He had lost his little flint-headed axe in his flight, and there was nothing left with which he could cut through the huge carcass. The war-party that was abroad might be gone two or three days, and in case the other monsters should linger, no party that could be raised from the cave settlement would be strong enough for a rescue. It was true, as a further matter for consideration, that the death-beasts had sometimes been so galled and intimidated by a few poisoned darts that they had lost their courage and beat a retreat.

Sure-dart had been trained to make quick decisions, and he made one now. He was resolved to take his chances on trying to finish his present enemy.

Without hesitation he advanced to within two paces of the outreached head. Here were some small pieces of loose stone, and he threw several at the extended snout. This irritated the creature, and he broke out again in his sputtering sort of hiss. As before, he finished with flashing open his red mouth. Before he could close it the arm of his pygmy foe went up and jerked forward,

3

and a dart shot fairly between the open jaws, and lodged somewhere in the gaping throat.

Then, to be sure, there was a twisting and smashing. The armored head swung this way and that, the fore feet struck out, and the writhing of the enormous body again made the overhead mass of rock start.

Sure-dart laughed, and cut a caper.

" That time I did it."

He turned around, walked back a few steps, and calmly sat down. He was prepared to await developments. It was with the patience that went with his savage training.

The time of waiting proved to be short. The monster, stung at last, and bothered by the shaft of the dart, began to retreat. It backed till it was clear of the cave; then it lay down and began to paw at its mouth. Sure-dart now had a chance to see the other immediate surroundings, and found that at least one of the other monsters was still there. This creature, smaller than the one that had been besieging him, had been standing behind the other, and seemed to be awaiting his turn. As the big beast backed away and cleared the opening, the smaller one walked up and poked his head in at the hole.

Sure-dart did not stir, but simply looked at the beast. He believed that it was his wisest way to remain quiet and excite the creature as little as possible. If his first foe should go away, the others — unless they were angered — would probably follow.

Perhaps five minutes went by. The wounded beast was still pawing at his mouth, trying to get out the dart, and the other nosed around the entrance, but made no effort, as the first had done, to force his way in. But at the end of this time Sure-dart heard a new sound. It was one that made him start, and in a moment leap excitedly to his feet. The noise was that of human voices.

He listened, and the sounds came nearer. He clapped his hands to his mouth, and sent out a high-pitched, peculiar cry.

Almost like an echo, a similar cry came back. At that the nosing monster, showing uneasiness, backed away, and left the mouth of the hole entirely open. Sure-dart, his eyes shining with hope, boldly ran forward. He continued to within two paces of the entrance, and from there glanced out, and down the hill.

Marching up from the bottom were over twenty ' men, their ranks bristling with spears. At their sides were likewise cases of darts, and rough flint axes and knives, and the greater number carried canoe-shaped shields. Other than the difference in weapons, they looked like Sure-dart and Hop-foot on a larger scale. In a word, it was the war-party that had gone out three days before, and now, for some reason, early returned.

But Sure-dart knew that he could not look for deliverance just yet. The fighting party, strong as it was, would not march directly on the three monsters. Experience had taught them quite another way. In a moment the lines fanned out, and the party divided, one division going to the right, and the other to the left. Here Sure-dart lost sight of them, but he could still follow them in his mind. He knew that they

would scatter still more, till each seemed to be
acting independently. But this would not be
really the case. Every little group would pick
out a safety-hole, and all the others would take
notice; then the men nearest the monsters would
close in, and all would suddenly let go a flight of
darts. After this there would be a general scat-
tering for the holes. By arranging in advance
the parties would be divided among a good many
holes, so that it would be out of the question for
the monsters to besiege them all. As soon as the
creatures had made a rush (which was their
way), those men in the holes not watched would
come out, and as soon as near enough, would let
go a shower of darts. Of course the end, after
this, would be merely a question of time. Nor
could the monsters, even if they were a long time
in yielding to the poison, starve out the men.
Some holes would still be unwatched, and those
in them (this was done where the attacking party
was smaller than at present) could steal out and
go after reënforcements, and thus any hole where
the men had been long cut off from food could
be relieved. The stupid giants always wheeled,
on an attack in the rear, and gave chase to the
new enemies.

Yet after all, Sure-dart was agreeably disappointed. The first monster had begun to feel the
working of the poison, and in a few minutes he
wheeled, and slowly shuffled off. The other two
hesitated, but then followed, and in another three
minutes the hindmost had disappeared over the
first of the southerly ridges.

Stoical as the boy was, as he peeped out and

saw the last great rump sinking out of sight behind the ridge, he gave a yell of triumph and delight, and leaped out into the open. The men, who were not very far away, came running forward, and there was a din of cries and eager talk.

The speech of the day was confined to a very small vocabulary, but there was a good range of grunts and clicking cries, and on this occasion all seemed to make the most of them.

But above the noise one man quickly made himself heard. He was over six feet high, and so almost gigantic for one of that day, and his figure was relatively well proportioned, and showed signs of great strength. His face was rather attractive, and his look was bold and keen. He was perhaps forty-five, and there were a few gray hairs in his long locks and in his short, spiky beard. He carried, besides spear and shield, a long and very broad-bladed axe. This was slung over his massive shoulders. About his forehead was tied a string of white objects that, on near inspection, could be seen to be human teeth. This man not only raised his voice above the others, quickly silencing them, but spoke directly to Sure-dart.

"Where is Hop-foot? Was he not in the hole with you?"

The joy and relief faded out of Sure-dart's face. Where, indeed, was his friend? This was Hop-foot's father who was asking. In the suddenness and tremendous relief of the deliverance, Sure-dart had for the instant forgotten the terrible disaster.

As Big-axe spoke, Sure-dart glanced once sick-heartedly around. To be sure, the crushed body was not immediately in sight, but it could not be far off. A little to the left of the hole, and where Hop-foot had probably been overtaken, was a low mound, with a hollow on the farther side, and with some trampled-down bushes partly over both; here doubtless was the place. Without answering Big-axe, Sure-dart stepped that way. He parted the bushes at the top of the mound, and jumped back with a cry.

His eyes stared like a crazy person's. Then he whirled, and leaped bodily over the mound, sputtering out something unintelligible as he did so.

CHAPTER III

THE FLIGHT TO THE HILLS

WHAT he saw was certainly startling. There was a break, or cleft, at the bottom of the little hollow, and out of this was sticking a white bone, the top making a bobbing motion.

But this was merely what he had seen at first, and not on the second look. What he had discovered then was a hand grasping the bone, and an arm following the hand up farther out of the cleft. The hand was smaller than a man's, and was evidently using the flat bone as a kind of shovel to dig away some loose earth. This earth had fallen down into the cleft, which itself looked as if recently broken wider and deeper, most likely by the foot of one of the rushing monsters. Sure-dart dropped on his knees, calling out: " Hop-foot! Hop-foot! " and pulled away the tangle of inside bushes and clutched the extended hand.

Out of the cleft then, with a little starting scramble, climbed Hop-foot. Or he did not exactly climb out, though he started to do so, for Sure-dart gave a mighty pull, and almost at the same moment Big-axe was beside him, with two great hands clapped under the climber's arms. It seemed as if other hands swarmed over too, and helped, for the boy finally came out into light in the very midst of the jabbering and delighted crowd.

The chief showed the restraint over his feelings frequently observed among savages, for he merely patted the boy once on the head, and then began to ask him questions. How had he come into the hole? What were he and Sure-dart doing here? How did they draw on themselves the fury of the death-beasts?

Hop-foot boldly "faced the music," though perhaps he was encouraged by the probability that this time there was no whipping in store.

"Sure-dart and I came up to see whether any of the death-beasts had eaten the poisoned meat," he said. "We found that one had eaten it, and started to go back, but on the way we forgot about the beasts, and the three that were not hurt came around the low ridge and charged us. We started for this safety-hole, but before we could get there — before I could — they overtook us. I jumped one side and threw myself flat, just as you, Big-axe, once told me to do, and the first monster almost went by me. But before I could jump up and get another start he swung around and stooped to grab me. I thought I was as good as between his teeth, but just then the ground under us both began to sink, and he lurched back, and I tumbled through. I did n't go very far at first, but as I brought up I put my hands out and found a little side-cleft, and I crawled into that. All I thought of then was getting as far away from the death-beast as I could."

"Lucky that the country just about here has these honey-comb places," interjected Big-axe.

"The rest of it is this," concluded Hop-foot: "I stayed in the hole till I heard your voices, and then I started to come out. By that time, I suppose on account of the thrashing about of the heavy creatures, some dirt had fallen into the hole, and a bush had likewise settled down into it. Along with the dirt came down the big, flat bone, and I took that to help in digging out. You know the rest."

" You should not have left the caves," said Big-axe, sternly, " and but that I think you have been punished enough I should give you a turn with my belt. Sure-dart, you did wrong likewise; but I think that you, too, have been sufficiently punished. You may tell your mother, therefore, that she need not send you to me to be whipped."

Sure-dart looked a little sheepish, but he managed to hold up his head (he was helped by the thought of the work he had done with his darts, and knew that his coolness and success would eventually be recognized), and nodded respectfully when the chief had finished.

" Something was the matter with the biggest death-beast when it left," here observed one of the warriors. " I half thought I saw the shaft of a dart sticking out of his mouth."

Sure-dart's eyes lighted, but he merely smiled. The observant chief noticed the look.

" Your darts are all gone. Did you plant one of them in the beast's mouth? "

" Yes, Big-axe."

A murmur of admiration ran around. Full well the listeners knew what nerve it took to go close to that awful mouth and drive a dart into the right spot. The neck of the death-beast was supple, and often stretched beyond what could

have been guessed, so that more than one confident hunter had been nipped by the great bill, and
twitched under the monstrous feet. Or now and
then the bill itself, or a few of the outermost teeth,
had scraped down a poor fellow's head, and this
had generally cut through skull and brains. Besides admiration for the boy's skill and pluck,
the listeners felt greatly relieved; another death-
beast was surely doomed, and thereby a great
service done to the valley.

The last bit of harshness faded out of the chief's
look.

" You have done well. After this I shall reckon
you as a warrior, and call on you if there is need.
But we are losing time. If the Fishers should
after all march on us, we should scarcely have
time to prepare for them."

He made a sign, the whole band fell in behind
him, and all started at a sharp trot down the hill.

Meanwhile their families, left behind, had
grown anxious, and all but the very infirm and a
few of the small children had left the caves, and
come as far as the foot of the hill. A shouting and
piping up of relief broke out as they saw the whole
unharmed party coming down, and there was a
rush to meet them. As soon as everything was
told there was another tumult of rejoicing, and
Hop-foot came in for congratulations and Sure-
dart for praise. His foster mother, Scar-face
(so called because of a great scar down one cheek,
the work of a terror-bird), held her head high
with pride, and Gentle-hand, the young wife of
the chief, and mother of Hop-foot, admiringly
clapped him on the back. Even Bull-head, the

son of Big-axe by his former wife, and a cross-grained, surly fellow, condescended to contribute an approving grunt.   Little One-ear, the only child of Scar-face, and who was the remaining member of her family, wormed his way to where Sure-dart stood, and in silent pride and admiration gripped one of his fingers.

Sure-dart relaxed a little of the gravity with which he had received the compliments, and smiled down at the boy.   The little fellow was a pet of his, and was in fact a bright, lovable child, but physically was below the standard of the ordinary cave-children.   He was small and rather delicate, and his head was too large for his thin body.   He had lost one of his ears, too (from a grazing blow from the same great-toothed bill that had disfigured his mother), and this added to his rather queer and unusual look.   He was now ten, but no larger than most cave-boys of seven.   As he was so delicate he wore, besides the ordinary breech-clout, a kind of sleeveless shirt.   This, as if in a spirit of vengeance, was made of the skin of one of those ravaging birds. Scar-face herself, fired by revenge, had helped to bring this creature down.   From the tree where she had stationed herself she had flung a dart, and it had struck the raging monster squarely in the breast.   But Scar-face, like most barbarian women, had been trained to self-reliance, and in her case beyond the common, for she had early lost her husband and her older boy.   Both had been killed in the Cane-dwellers' raid.   She was large for one of her race, and, though portly, was both strong and quick.   She had the animal-like marks of the men, for a growth of hair ran down her shoulders and arms, and came out in little tufts on the backs of her hands. She was not more than forty, and her black, coarse hair did not show a thread of gray. She was dressed in much the same manner as the men, but a kind of short petticoat (made of the skins of two " scamperers " — what they were will be seen later) was added to the other dress. Her great cataract of hair nearly covered the upper part of her body.

After a few moments the little excitement spent itself, and Big-axe, raising his voice, said that they must be about some important matters; on that they all trooped down, and stopped in front of the chief's cave. This was their usual gathering-place when anything of importance was to be discussed.

It will take but few words to show what this cave looked like, and it will stand as a sample of all, only it was a little bigger than the others. It was partly natural, and was partly the work of tools. It went back into the hill-slope perhaps forty feet, and at the end was rounded out and enlarged. The room here may have been thirty feet in diameter. The passage leading to it was some six and a half feet high, and not over five feet wide. There was a great, roundish stone just at one side of the outer entrance, and this was for a door. It was to be used in case of particular emergency, such as war, or an invasion of some of the smaller monsters. For several years, however, there had been no trouble from the latter source. The beasts, big and little, had learned that it was well to keep away from these black-haired creatures who walked upright, and could spit out some kind of mysterious death.

For further safety another large stone had been hauled into the passage, and was made to serve as an inner door. This stone was in regular use; for notwithstanding the greater general safety, as compared with former days, it was still the course of prudence to lock one's inner door. There was nothing that deserved the name of furniture in the cave. In opposite corners were piles of dry rushes that served for the two beds,— one for the chief and his wife, and one for Hop-foot,— and near one wall was a largish, flinty stone, flat on the top, and showing the marks of blows, or a good deal of hard rubbing. This was the food-stone, and was so called not because food was eaten from it, but because the harder kinds of food, including marrow-bones and some sorts of nuts, were cracked on it. This cracking was done with a stone, either large or small, as the case required. Several of these stones, conveniently shaped for the hand, lay about. With the exception of some clumsy flint knives, they completed the entire kitchen outfit. There was no fireplace, for these people had not yet learned to cook their food, and all they knew of fire was the dreaded sight of it when it burst forth from some of the nearer volcanoes, or shot out of the ground in the midst of an up-tearing earthquake.

There were a few lizard skins, and a few skins covered with short hair. This remainder of the family wardrobe was hanging on pegs driven into the back wall, and near the grown folks' bed was a little pile of weapons. These were of the same sort as those already noted. There was nothing in the shape of a bow, for that had not yet been invented.

One other thing remained that ought to be noticed. It was a small, hollow stone, set in a high niche in the wall. It contained only a darkish, rather thick liquid. But they did well to be thus careful of it, for it was a powerful poison, and was the kind often used in dealing with the death-beasts. It was made by mixing the juice of a certain lycopod (a flowerless plant, some species of which secrete an inflammable powder) with the juice of a kind of swamp berry. This compound was rubbed over a freshly killed lizard (one of the big, vegetable-feeding kind), and the bait put where a family of flesh-eating dinosaurs would be likely to find it. In the recent instance the straying of the little herd of death-beasts toward the caves had been reported, and Big-axe had personally prepared and placed the poisoned carcass. He had been called away then by what seemed a greater danger, and had ordered the people left behind to keep close to the caves, and in no case to go in the direction of the westerly ridges. It was disobedience to this order that had come so near costing the two adventurous boys their lives. They were so full of curiosity about the movements of the enemy that they had stolen away, meaning, however, to be careful, and planning not to get far away from the safety-holes. They were now aware that they had still something to learn about these giant foes.

It should be explained, in speaking of this

method of dealing with the dinosaurs, that the poison put on the carcass of the lizard was not the same as that used on the darts. The first was a stomach poison, and would not be likely to work effectually in the blood; that used on the darts came from quite another source. It was obtained simply by thrusting the points of the darts into some kind of carrion. - A dead lizard, especially of one of the smaller varieties, was as often used as anything.

As to the other caves, smaller, as already stated, than the chief's, they mainly ran in an irregular line along this low, chalky ridge. That of Bull-head, his oldest son, was twenty paces or so to the south, and Scar-face's was about the same distance to the north. There was a general slope from the whole tier down to the cove, or small lake, though there were some little ridges, like ploughed ground, and a few masses of out-cropping rock.

There were ten or twelve small " dugouts " drawn up on the strip of beach, and this was the entire navy and merchant marine of the tribe. They would hold but two or three persons apiece, and were used only for inshore fishing. The Rock-people were willing to leave to the Fishers the supremacy of the seas. Of these Fishers it might as well be said now that they lived on the south bank of the Great Lake, perhaps fifty miles from the cave-village, and in numbers considerably exceeded the Rock-people. They counted up about three hundred and fifty, and mustered over sixty fighting men. This was double what Big-axe could raise, even reckoning one or two boys, including Sure-dart. The Fishers had skin-covered small boats, similar to what we know of the ancient coracles, a little fleet of fair-sized "dugouts," the largest capable of holding six men. Long-spear was the headman, or chief, of the Fisher settlement, and he was as tall as Big-axe, and nearly as heavy. He was also younger, being only twenty-four, or twenty-five. Since the Fishers had settled on the lake shore, which was not more than a hundred years before, they had proved troublesome neighbors, and it was seen that they would sooner or later make war on the Rock-people. Under the fierce and ambitious Long-spear it looked as if the time were at hand, and Big-axe and his men had accordingly made their preparations. The recent expedition was a kind of scouting party in force, Big-axe having in mind a possible ambuscade, or perhaps a sudden dash at the enemy. He hoped it might be when the foe was off his guard. He was disappointed in this, for a march of over twenty miles, and some lingering afterwards, had not disclosed a single Fisher. Evidently the crafty Long-spear was not quite ready.

What Big-axe had now in his mind to say was that they must prepare to leave the caves, and retreat to the hills. There, among rocks and cliffs, and in a place that he knew of, they might defy the Fishers. They could take their most valuable belongings, except the canoes, with them, and those they could hide.

As soon as all were quiet he told them this, and his fighting men, some of whom already understood the plan, immediately commended it. This was sufficient, for in that age might alone governed, and women and weaklings were supposed to have nothing to say.   In a time so short that a single modern family could scarcely have packed one ordinary trunk the whole village had gathered up its belongings and was on the move.

CHAPTER IV.

HARD PRESSED

A MILE or so back of the rather low ridges on the west the hills proper began, and these straggled on, with some valley and morass between, for eleven or twelve miles. After that was a great high, and almost dry plain, and then the vast blue masses of a seemingly endless line of mountains. Here, as far as the Rock-people knew, the world ended, for not one of them had ever ventured so far. The peaks and valleys might be the home of new and terrible creatures, and they were sure that there were perils of another kind. The peaks sometimes, as seen from the westerly hills, shot up with flames, and there were rumblings of far-off, but certainly mighty explosions. The whole region must be ready to blow into chaos, and for this reason, if for no other, a man would be a fool to risk himself in it. So the Rock-people had reasoned, and even now, with a tangible and known danger to spur them on, they would have been loath to trust themselves there.

As far as the great plain on this side was concerned, Big-axe and his people had slightly more knowledge. A few times, when hunting, they had pushed out a short way upon it, and had seen nothing strange or particularly dreadful. The powerful and savage terror-bird had once or twice hove in sight, but even a small party of well-armed hunters were not afraid of him, and there did not appear to be anything else that was dangerous. A far more hazardous journey was that across the low ground at the westerly side of the first range of hills. Here were several miles of swamp and fen-land, and here, as their natural haunt, were monsters of all kinds, — spear-back, three-horns, now and then a family of death-beasts, and the phantom-like thing that seemed to be a giant bat. It was in reality, like so many other of the monsters, a lizard. The Rock-people called it the big beast-bird. Besides all these were mighty turtles, with jaws that could snap off a man's leg, great leeches, and now and then a deadly snake. Among the rocks on the lower ground were likewise swarms of huge rats, and they could bite like little tigers, as the skulls that have been found show.

But of course not all the creatures of this region were dangerous; there were many that were harmless, and not a few that were valuable as food. In the little streams were fat eels; some of the smaller birds, though still showing their reptile origin, were not bad eating, especially for a Rock-man; and now and then might be seen, but not easily brought down, a little creature looking somewhat like a tiny horse, but with toes instead of hoofs. These horse-like creatures had not been known to the ancient forefathers of the Rock-people, and as yet they were comparatively rare. They were among the largest haired animals then known, and aside from their value as food, were strange and interesting to the Rock-folks. To them the various forms of lizard life, the giant water-snakes and turtles, and the toothed and hair-coated birds, seemed the common order of creation. They called the curious little horse-creatures " scamperers."

But with a little wondering about the discovery, and some argument from the old people about the other changes that they insisted were slowly taking place — leaning much on tradition and old tales, however, as to this — the Rock-people dropped the subject. Their brains were too small, and too little used to carry along other than the most practical matters to linger on this one.

Big-axe and the others kept a sharp eye out for death-beasts as they went, but, though they saw the tracks of those that had just gone, they caught not so much as a glimpse of the creatures themselves. It seemed from this that even the first poisoned monster had held out long enough to cover at least a few miles.

The company were soon among the short but sturdy trees of the lower hills, and here they felt safer, both from man and beast. It would be easy to find trees that even a death-beast could not pull down, and which had branches beyond his reach, and it would be a small child, indeed, trained and active as these savages were, that could not take care of himself, once among a tree's branches. As soon as all were out of immediate danger the men would ply their darts and spears, and the few death-beasts that were likely to 'appear at any one time must eventually be killed or driven off. As to greater safety here from human foes, it was not on account of present surroundings, but because these woods meant proximity to the higher hills and the cliffs.

By this time the sun, hot at that period in those regions, was fairly well up the sky, and though at this higher level and under the shade of the trees it was not uncomfortable, Big-axe knew that down in the marsh beyond it would tax the endurance even of a trained man. He therefore, after conferring with some of the older men, ordered a halt.

" But we will make sure that we have a safe start," he said. " Wing-foot, do you go back and see whether there are any signs of danger."

Wing-foot, so called because of his speed and staying qualities as a runner, promptly tossed aside his spear and shield, and headed about. His small, wiry figure was soon out of sight among the trees.

" We may as well rest and have something to eat," Big-axe said. " It will strengthen you women and children for the hard pull across the marsh. We shall have to cross before dark."

They accordingly sat down, and the women took from their bundles some small fishes and a supply of snails and wild fruit, and they fell to. Not being used to cooked food, and the luxuries of our modern days, they felt very well satisfied with the little spread, and ate with the relish of healthy animals. After this some of the party sprawled out, and took naps, and in all an hour passed. At the end of that time the bushes on a

near-by ridge crackled, and the half-naked and
hairy little figure of Wing-foot broke through.
He was breathing hard, and even at this first
glimpse it could be seen that his look was
anxious.

"Well?" called out Big-axe, starting up.

"They are coming," puffed Wing-foot. "They
are already over the middle hills. I don't see how
they can help catching us."

There was a wild staring at him for a moment,
and then the wails and terrified cries began.
Even some of the warriors groaned.

But Big-axe, though he was taken completely
by surprise, and instantly saw the terrible peril,
did not for a moment falter. He raised his deep
and strong voice, and with a savage threat
silenced the noise.

"Do you want to help them to find us? All
make ready to go. The men must carry the small
children, and the women can take the spears and
shields. We shall have to risk what is below, for
the heat and the beasts are not so dangerous as
the men. Now all be brave, and don't talk of
giving up. We are not caught yet, and if we
should be, there will be spears and axes to crack
before they suck our bones."

The faint-hearted ones still looked frightened
and ready to drop, but the others brightened and
began to carry out the orders. In another two
minutes the whole company was on a half-run
down the westerly slope of the hill. There was
only one more hill, not a high one, between them
and the marsh level.

Big-axe helped his wife along, and carried one

woman's small child on the other arm. On, at a breath-taking pace, they went. They would, of course, easily gain the marsh, but what then? How could Big-axe expect to profit by that?

Big-axe himself did not at present try to answer this. Possibly it was because he was too busy, or it might be that he had nothing to answer. He continued to urge everybody on, growling at the lagging ones, and cautioning the stragglers, until he got them all at last to the top of the second hill. The marsh level, green, like a shallow sea, and hot and glinting under the fierce sun, lay miles broad before them. Had Big-axe something cheering now to say? Had he caught at some hope? What could he say, and what could be the hope?

He turned to Wing-foot.

"They must be drawing up to us. Do you think we lead them three hundred spears?"

"No," said the runner, gloomily shaking his head; "they must be nearer. They will break upon us soon."

"But as yet we don't hear them, though it is true they strive to come softly, as is their way of false encouragement."

"I think I hear them now!" said Wing-foot, suddenly.

The chief's eyes lighted, and he wheeled about so as to face the rest of the company.

"Listen, all of you. We have still one chance. Notice that clump of trees — I mean the one that rises like a little island out of the marsh. If we can reach it, we shall for the time be safe. I know what it is, for I have visited it, and when

I found we were coming to it I took fresh courage. Do you all take courage. You women and children push on, and the rest of us will delay a little. You have now got your breath, and will be good for such a short dash. It is not over two hundred spears."

There was a stir among the loaded and sweating women and tired children, and in a moment they were in motion again. Some of the old and feeble folks, too, both men and women, braced themselves anew and shuffled on after the others. Luckily for these old people, as well as for the women and children, they were all sturdy barbarians, and had pretty nearly the strength and wind of wild animals.

Big-axe and the other men fell into their wake, and the chief set the example of overhauling his weapons. They were now again fully armed, having taken back their spears and shields.

For a moment there was no fresh sign of the enemy, but as the last of the men started along the boggy green below, a kind of animal howl broke from the wooded rear slope of the hill.

" They are coming," said Big-axe, glancing over his shoulder. He passed his spear to the next man in front, and unslung the great axe from his back. A little lagging made him the last man of the company.

CHAPTER V.

THE howling among the woods grew louder, and in another three minutes Big-axe, who was now walking with his head screwed around over his shoulder, saw a long string of leaping shapes come over the thinly treed part of the higher ridge and drop again into the hollow on the hither side. He wheeled, and stopped short.

"Bull-head, see that they do not fetch in on my right hand. Stone-arm, guard the left. I will look after all who come up in front."

He stood a few paces clear of them, so that the two picked men were merely to protect him from a side or rear attack. Bull-head moved forward without answering, and unslung his war-club. This was a knotted stick four inches thick at the big end, and set all over the head with great, three-cornered points. These points were sharks' teeth that he had taken from a skull dug up on the lake shore. The creature that it had belonged to had doubtless died ages before, when the rising land barred out the ocean with its salt water. Bull-head had won a name with this club, both against human and beast enemies. But as he unslung the club, he did not part with his shield. He knew that this would be needed to protect him from the darts with which the assailants would

begin the fight. The same precaution had also
been taken by the chief himself, and was likewise
observed by Stone-arm.

But as Big-axe stationed his two strong men
and coolly waited for the rushing enemy, Stone-
arm looked at him doubtfully, and after a moment
spoke.

" Big-axe," he said, " is this wise? If you are
killed the men will lose heart, and we can guess
what that will lead to. It will mean the blotting
out of the Rock-people. Let five or six of us that
can fight the best support you. At least, let Bull-
head and me bear the brunt evenly with you."

Big-axe merely turned his face a little that way
and shook his head.

Stone-arm drew down his mouth disappoint-
edly, but without speaking further for the moment, freed a heavy stone sword from some slings
at his back. This sword was his favorite weapon,
and when he was younger he had won fame with
it. Even as it was, with more than sixty years
to weigh him down, he was one of the champions
of the tribe, and it was said that even Bull-head
did not care to cross his purposes. He had been
taller by an inch than Big-axe, but was now
stooped a little, and his great, lank bulk had
shrunk almost to thinness. Yet his eyes were still
keen, and the muscles stood out on his long, hairy
arms. Contrary to the custom of the tribe, he
wore a little tuft of chin-beard, and this was iron-
gray. He was not so keen and far-sighted in
war matters as Big-axe, or he might have been
chief, but he was as brave as a bulldog, and as
tenacious as one in fighting, and he was faithful

both to Big-axe and to what he believed to be the interests of the Rock-people. All his family were dead, and he had lived alone in one of the caves, a kind of well-preserved relic of the older and still more savage days.

All at once the spears of the Fishers flashed amongst the trees on the last hill-side, and with a wild, terrible, beast-like yell, they began to pour down upon the marsh.

Then Stone-arm spoke up once more:

"Think again, Big-axe. Do not risk so much!"

With a kindly smile now the chief turned.

"It is only a wise recklessness. They will be ashamed to push on in a body, for they have made too many boasts of their single-fighting, and particularly of what their chief can do. I shall dare him to fight me, and that will at least gain us a little time. The women and children can be pushing on, and we can go at full speed when we break. I hope to be able to go along with you."

The old man hesitated, and finally mumbled that it might be best. Then he braced forward his shield, for there was no more time left for talk, and stuck his sword in the ground behind him. With his right hand he drew a dart and poised it. Even this little movement made the mighty arm that had won him his name "snake up" with little bunches of muscle.

The yelling savages came on headlong, but they checked themselves just before they were within a spear's reach, and in a twinkling were fanning out and making a long, single line. It could now be seen that there were fully sixty of them, and that their chief, Long-spear, was the leader. They were armed about like the Rock-people, but their shields were small and square.

Big-axe threw one glance behind him, and saw that the children and other helpless ones were making good progress, the stronger of the young women still helping the faltering ones along, and with a look of satisfaction he wheeled back.

Long-spear was taking hurried counsel with two or three of his head fighting men, and was evidently not quite ready to begin. There was a little suggestion of the halting of a pack of seemingly eager hounds when a thinned-out pack of wolves suddenly stops and stands at bay. Yet there was, after all, some reason for this apparent hesitation. Though the green marsh seemed nearly level at this place, it was not really so, for a little ridge here ran out into it, descending on both hands to boggy places, and spots covered with low but stout reeds and scrubby bushes. In some of these boggy places were sudden little deeps, where a man might sink almost over his head, and in others were likely to be water-snakes, and black, shiny snarls of giant leeches. There were enough of these leeches to kill a man in a short time, supposing that he could not stop to rid himself of them. Some of the bushes, too, were sharp and spiky, and would make bad work even on a tough, savage skin. Still farther, in a few places, were outlying pools in which things that looked at first like old gray logs now and then moved, and lazily stuck up what proved to be long, bony snouts. They were beasts of the croc-odile family, and quite as ready as those of to-day to snap out with their spiked jaws, or jerk around their mighty tails.

With these obstacles to hinder a flank attack, and the steadfast and grimly quiet fighters in front, it is not surprising that Long-spear was disposed to hold a brief council of war. It would be a mistake of a different kind from one that a commander might make now if he seriously blundered; defeat did not mean surrender, but death, and very likely the picking of one's bones.

The Rock-people were in no kind of haste. Every minute gave their families just so much more of a start. They stood quiet but ready, and with their half-crouching figures and forking darts suggested so many bristling wild cats.

But the council of war proved to be rather short. It was probable that the rank and file of the savages, like most others of their kind, fought best if led at once to an attack, and that their courage would abate if they had to stop and let their blood cool. At any rate, Long-spear and his chief fighters now finished their clicking and jabbering, and a high-pitched cry gave notice to the others to be ready.

"They must not break our line," said Big-axe as a last cautioning word to his son and Stone-arm. He had hardly spoken when the Fishers brought the wings of their line in, and with one wild screech let fly their darts, breaking headlong upon the little waiting pack of human bodies and forking weapons.

Then was fighting such as few people now on the earth ever saw. These active and beast-tough savages jabbed, and slashed, and pounded,

and when they got a dart through a limb, or an
eye was knocked out, or a gash went in till it
reached a bone, they still fought on. Two or
three of the Fishers missed the first parry with
their shields, and were pierced by the darts, but
none fell. The little spears did not happen to
reach vital spots, and the poison could not taint so
much healthy blood at once. Big-axe crushed the
head of one strong fighter with a smash of the
great axe, and was instantly ready for the next;
and Bull-head and Stone-arm met those who
swung aside to pass him, and broke shields and
heads with their furious blows. Still farther
back, a few of the warriors waded out into the
marsh, and from this freer range let fly a shower
of darts. They had borrowed several quivers of
them from some who were not yet placed so as to
use them. Besides this, such of the Rock-people
behind the chief and the other two as could get
any sort of opportunity also let drive their darts.
The wave of human bodies could not wash away
this barrier, and it was not till several picked men
had rushed out on the flanks, meeting the sharp-
shooters of the Rock-men there, that the general
close fight began.

All the while Long-spear had kept out of the
way of the three champions, fighting well out on
his right flank, and a little beyond the reach of
Stone-arm. The old man had stationed himself
close to the edge of the bit of ridge, and could
not prudently go farther, as that would put too
much of a gap between him and his chief, and,
besides, would require him to stand in a soft and
spongy spot where it would be difficult to find

stable footing.   But still farther on the old man's left there was another bit of firm land, a little oblong mound, and from this patches of tolerably firm footing were dotted along almost to the ridge itself.   That is, these raised spots made a curve that reached from the firm land nearly to the rear of Big-axe's little army.   Long-spear had doubtless noted this outside path, and was planning on its use at the proper moment.   Big-axe had seen it, but it did not seem necessary to set a special guard to watch it, for it ended so close to his own lines that the men there could easily hold the main ridge against it.   Long-spear, followed by a few of his men, darted out a short distance on this side ridge, and from there plied their darts, aiming especially at the warriors close behind Big-axe and his two immediate supporters.   The chief did not know it, but two of his best men were hit by the darts; one was instantly killed, and the other disabled.   In the confusion nobody moved forward to close the little gap, and the brave three kept on with it open behind them.

All in a moment Long-spear gave a shrill yell and rushed along the bit of ridge, followed by six men.   At the end of the continuous hard ground were the little, reedy patches; from one to another of these they leaped, and in a twinkling were breaking furiously upon the rear men of the company.   Upon another yell, the main body of the Fishers drew back, and then made a headlong charge, and in another twenty seconds Big-axe and his two champions were crowded back to the open space behind them, and the Fishers were pushing in upon the head of the ridge, and as far as the broader part of it.

But this was not the whole of the cunning Long-spear's plan. As soon as he had closed on the rear space he shouted to his men, and six followed him, turning off, and plunging into the marsh, and making for that part of the main ridge clear of all the fighters. If they carried their point, they could form up, and as soon as their force was strong enough they could both attack the Rock-people in the rear, and send a few warriors after the fleeing wives and helpless ones. Attacked thus from nearly all sides, and with the fate of their families to distract them from the immediate work, the little defending band must soon go to pieces, and rejoicing and the war-feast would be near. Long-spear began to do his part, fighting like a demon, and his men tried to imitate him.

All this while the boy Sure-dart was standing among the rear men of the company. His friend Hop-foot was not with him, for it had been decided that only Sure-dart and another boy of about his age were old enough and sufficiently cool and steady to stay with the men, and even the two were directed to keep as much as possible out of the hot fighting. The other boy, whose name was Duck-legs, seemed to be perfectly willing to obey this order; in fact, he lost color, and curled lower under his shield, as the strife grew fiercer. Not so Sure-dart. He may have been a trifle pale, but his eyes were boldly wide open, and he merely stooped a bit behind his shield, his muscles in ready play, like a menacing panther's.

He tried to see what was going on in the hurly-
burly ahead of him, and once waded a little way
out on the marsh to find out; at other times he
glanced back to learn how the women and the
others were getting on.

When Long-spear made his final cunning rush,
and the tall, leaping figures flashed up all at once
in the very faces of the rear men, Sure-dart was
the one of the little company that was perfectly
ready.   His shield was instantly quartered that
way, and his dart shot back to poise.   Almost at
the same instant the halting and now confused
Duck-legs was spitted like a Christmas goose, and
fell forward with a dying yell.   Then Long-spear
himself came flying over a little pool, and struck
within four paces of Sure-dart.   After him flew
four of his men.   One had fallen short, and was
for the moment stuck in the cement-like mud, and
the other had jumped into what seemed to be
a harmless, clear pool, and was wading across.

But at this terrible crisis, before even the
active Sure-dart could speed his weapon, something else happened, and it was a something that
belonged with the other wonders of that ancient
day.   The man who had fallen into the mud and
slime was wallowing and floundering out, though
he was slow about it, but the man who had
jumped into the little pool seemed to have found
a pretty good bottom, and was swashing his way
rapidly along.   He stepped upon a large rounded
stone, but slipped off.   He had to stagger to
keep his legs.   Just then the stone canted, the
dark and slimy top was seen to end in a smoothly
rounded edge, and close by the man's legs poked

up a dusky, flat, and snake-like head. The mouth ended in a hooked bill, and the eyes were small and dim. The man yelped with fright, and tried to plunge away; but as he started, the creature raised his head higher, a kind of natural shutter dropped from his dim eyes and they gleamed like a gamecock's; with wonderful quickness he shot out a long neck, thrust his head after the flying, naked legs, and while one was still lifted to step, the billed mouth opened and closed again, taking in the whole ankle. There was a yell, and a terrible pawing and splashing, but as silent as fate, the monster slid along into deeper water, and with a shove went out of sight, carrying the pawing savage with him. When a turtle makes up its mind to hold on, it does; and when a man gets his leg in the mouth of a turtle twelve feet long and of proportional strength, his own endeavors have very little to do with the result.

This was the strange something that happened just as Long-spear was making his rush; it checked him and his followers for an instant, and in that trifle of time the men with Sure-dart pulled themselves together and stood bristling behind their shields.

But others of the Fishers were now coming on by this road, and while the front attack was still kept up, these flankers were stringing out along the small ridge, and sending their darts across at every hand's breadth of exposed body or limb. Long-spear, as cautious as he was bold, here bore back a little, and covered himself with his shield, and the four men that had landed on the ridge with him did the same.

'A moment later another defender dropped, and though the man beside him landed a dart in a Fisher, the exchange of course remained in favor of the stronger force.   It was here that Long-spear went on to complete his plan.   As soon as a few more men had joined him he sent off a band of three to chase the women and other fugitives.

Sure-dart cried out with rage and horror as he saw it, and some of the others joined with him, but for the instant nobody offered to move.   To leave the helpless ones to their fate was not to be borne; and yet, though Long-spear and his gang should be driven away, what would happen if they left them to close in again on the main body's rear?   If Big-axe had all he could do to hold his own now, he must be crushed with so many of his force gone, and fresh enemies behind.

The time while all this was happening was not really long, though it may seem so in the telling, and Big-axe was not so far outgeneralled by Long-spear as he had seemed.   The fact was, he had early noted how things were going, and was at this very instant gathering himself together for a desperate counter-effort.   With a panther-like spring he reached striking distance of a burly Fisher, smashed him out of life with one blow, yelled encouragement to his men, and, with Bull-head and Stone-arm at his side, fairly broke the front rank of the assailants.

There was confusion as the astonished fighters tumbled or scrambled back; and when they finally stopped they were all once more on the sloping end of the hard ground.

Big-axe instantly turned and ran back, his men after him.

"Now is our chance!" he roared. He caught a tall, wiry young man by the arm. "Crumple-ear, take my place, and keep this line good. They have come in behind us, and have sent a party after the women and children. I must go to the rear and stop them. I shall then form there, and as soon as you see me do it you can fall back and join us."

"Let it be so," laconically grunted Crumple-ear.

"Come," was all else that Big-axe said. He spoke to Bull-head and Stone-arm.

The men stood aside, and the chief and the other two, catching such hasty breaths as they could, ran in among them, passed through to the first open space beyond, and with shields down rushed straight at Long-spear and his forming band.

There was no time for strategy and fine figuring now; the scheming chief was where it must be a business of spear and shield, and the heavy decision of axe or sword. To do him justice, though he stared a little, showing that he was taken by surprise, he nevertheless brought his thick lips hard together, put forward his shield, and made ready a dart. His men likewise braced themselves for the shock.

But as the two chiefs' darts flew, and each was caught on the shield, and as both warriors sprang to a close,— the Fisher with shortened spear, and the Rock chief with up-swung axe, — a boy's shrill yell rose above all the other din, and past the very rim of one Fisher's shield, broke a small, half-naked figure, and ran like the wind straight down the narrow way. It was Sure-dart. His eyes were like fire, and his case of darts was in his hand. He was looking at things beyond, and among them at a little party of women and children. In this party were his foster mother and little One-ear, and they were almost eclipsed by the three spear-bristling Fishers.

CHAPTER VI

THE END OF THE FIGHT

BEFORE this there was confusion among the poor women and children and the others of the escaping party. They had seen the three warriors coming fast on in their wake, and they knew what it meant, for there was no such thing as mercy in the work that the men were prepared to do. At the same time, the women and the old men, and even the larger children, did not fall into a complete panic, but like the fighting animals that they might almost be said to be, they growled encouragement to one another, and made ready, when the final moment should come, to make a fierce defence. Nevertheless, it was evident that the three powerful fighters stood fair to work a dreadful slaughter among them, even if they did not finally kill every one.

Sure-dart came on like a running hound. It was wonderful how his bare feet flew. There was yet time to do something, he thought, alone though he was, for he could certainly make a diversion; and if the women and old men, as well as the larger children, did what they could, it might be possible to check the assailants. This would perhaps give time for Big-axe and the others to come up.

The Fishers looked back and saw Sure-dart,

but as he was but one, and a boy at that, they did not pay any serious attention to him. They doubtless could not believe that he was up to anything desperate, however strange and wild his actions were. They were now almost near enough to throw their darts, and each took one from its sheath, and prepared.

But after all, their experience in this kind of warfare, owing to the small number of human beings there were in this little world of theirs, and the long peace between them and the Rock-people, had been too short to be informing, and they were now to find it out. They were to see what sort of stuff a savage mother, defending her children, was made of.

A few seconds more, and they were within easy casting distance, and they halted. The head of the little fleeing company was still strung out in flight, but the rear had stopped. This little group was made up of Scar-face, One-ear, Gentle-hand, two other women, four small children, and Hop-foot.

Sure-dart, never flagging for a moment, was now close at hand. He came on till he was almost within a spear-cast, and then sharply pulled up. The men had not wholly ceased to notice him, and now, after a little clicking back and forth, one of them wheeled about. The others did not stop, but drew back their arms and poised their darts.

Here was where the powerful and fearless mothers suddenly came to the fore. All of them broke out in a savage screech, sprang to one side, to where there was a shivered bowlder, caught up handfuls of the fragments, and hurled them in a shower at the surprised warriors. In the midst of it Hop-foot took a cool step forward, poised a dart, and let it go.

The two Fishers who were facing the party had not guarded themselves very carefully, thinking there was little danger, and the result was that one of them caught a smash from a stone that broke several of his teeth and nearly stunned him; the other was struck on the shin, and it hurt so that he lowered his dart and snarlingly caught the shin in his free hand. The third man was very busy, for he had rushed at Sure-dart; then the boy danced back a little out of range, waited, and as the man came on again, rushed suddenly almost into his face and flung his dart. The man, though powerful, was a little slow, and it seemed that he was not very nimble-witted. At any rate, the dart got in below his shield and struck deep into his thigh. He grunted with pain and fear, and brought up where he stood.

In this little interval the women and Hop-foot, greatly encouraged by their success, recklessly charged, and almost tumbled the two Fishers off their legs. They struck at them with clenched hands, kicked, and bit.

But this time they did not come out so well. One of the men struck his spear through the nearest woman, kicked another off her balance, and with a swinging blow of his fist landed Scar-face on her back. At almost the same instant the man whose teeth had been knocked out rallied, and with a smash of his stone hatchet brained poor Gentle-hand.

There was now a little pause in the fight. The two Fishers at what might be called the front looked around and saw what had happened. It was clear that they were not making much headway, notwithstanding the sudden turn they had given the fight, and that their situation was growing serious. Looking still farther to the rear, to where the general fight was still going on, they saw that Big-axe and his men were crowding back such Fishers as had come in on this side. In fact, as they were looking, the pack was broken. Five or six Fishers staggered back, and three of the Rock warriors broke through. The three were Big-axe, Bull-head, and Stone-arm.

Then the two made a quick decision. Their chief's plan had failed, and they themselves were already as good as between two fires. They clicked something back and forth, and made such a headlong rush that it carried them through the broken ranks in front, and with smashes right and left with their axes they cleared a path through such slow or feeble ones as were in their way, and slapped off at full speed down the ridge path. Apparently without the slightest compunction they left the disabled man to shift for himself.

His fate did not lag. He pluckily braced himself and let go with his longest spear at Sure-dart, but by a close shave missed. The boy had parted with his shield, but for that very reason was on the alert, and with his great quickness he managed to duck below the track of the spear. It raked through the hair on the top of his head, however. This was the last of the really brave

Fisher. Hop-foot ran up from behind and lodged a dart fairly between his shoulders, and at almost the same instant an old man who had run back from the company ahead struck him on the temple with a stone. He was down and finished in a twinkling.

It was clear by this time that Big-axe and his men had made good their break through the encircling lines, and were holding the main body of the Fishers in check. Less than half a minute more, and they were retreating in compact fighting order along the ridge.

The Fishers did not follow. They were still well in the lead as to numbers, but they had lost the advantage of position, and had moreover lost a disheartening number of men. Long-spear, still as shrewd and far-sighted as ever, gave one of his signal yells, and the battle was for the time over. Long-spear himself was bleeding from a cut in the shoulder, and his wind was about gone. That time when he and Big-axe came together he thrust at the Rock chief, but the thrust was met on the shield, and a return blow of the chief's axe all but brought him down. The Fisher's shield was cut asunder, and the slash would probably have gone home even then but that Big-axe slipped. The next moment other Fishers and Rock-people were crowding between, and then Big-axe turned again toward the rear. It was just here that he and his champions broke through, as Sure-dart and the others saw, and then fell back uninterrupted down the ridge and toward their friends.

It was a joyful and yet a sad time when the

chief and the other fighters at last came up. The chief's wife and the woman who had been thrust through with the spear were dead, and the woman who had been kicked, and two old men, were seriously hurt. Scar-face was a little sore where the man's fist had struck her, but beyond that she was merely a trifle confused and shaken. These were not heavy losses, measured in numbers, but to Big-axe and the husband of the woman who had been speared they were severe enough.

For a few moments the two stricken men stood silent, and then, in spite of their training and the stolidity of their natures, the tears started.

But after a little they made an effort and controlled themselves. As soon as a rough, long litter could be put together, the two bodies were hoisted upon it, and the company once more moved on. The injured ones were carried by some of the warriors.

The others of the rescued party, stimulated by the relief from the dreadful suspense and by the presence of the fighting men, seemed to find new strength and energy, and the whole company pushed along at a relatively fast pace.

The two Fishers who had fled along the ridge (this term "ridge" is used in a very restricted sense, as it applies merely to the little, natural causeway above the swamp) were now out of sight, but nobody could say where they had gone. In the general excitement they had been forgotten. It was probable that they had kept on till they came to one of the farther clumps of trees, and where also were some small, diverging mounds and ridges, and had there swung off, intending to make a detour by the way of the more open morass, and so back to their friends. This of course meant a risk, considering the dangerous reptiles and other wild creatures, but it was nothing like the risk of coming nearer their human enemies. That meant instant death as the mildest thing that could be imagined.

Big-axe and his party had now but a short distance farther to go, and in a few minutes they reached the little tree-island.

It was like a stopping-place, or station, along the road formed by the ridge. It was merely a roundish clump of trees, with a few of the whitish bowlders of the region tumbled along its inward border, and rising near the centre. Such soil as there was showed black and swampy, and great roots, uncomfortably suggesting snakes, crowded thickly from its surface. Vines and creepers of many kinds ran everywhere, and in places were so interlaced among the trees that they made a kind of natural hedge. Certainly, unattractive as it was, and not suggesting wholesomeness, it was yet the very place for their purpose. It was a little, natural fort where they could rest and rally, and from which they could conveniently push on to their final and better refuge.

Before this, even in their haste, it had come out who had been killed in the general battle. Eager questions had been answered, and at the end there was renewed sorrowing. Fourteen of the Rock-people were dead, and three-fourths of all who had come back were more or less wounded. These wounds, however, were in few cases disabling, even after they should have stiffened. Not all of those who had been killed died of the first wounds, for several were mercifully despatched by their friends. If left behind they would certainly have been killed in a more painful way, and it was the practical reasoning of their comrades that this must be prevented. Often the wounded men themselves had asked the favor of a friendly blow of the axe. It could be delivered on the temple, or at the base of the brain, and all would be over.

This left the entire fighting party nineteen strong, including the slightly wounded. The Fishers, it was thought — and this was a grain of comfort — had suffered still more; their loss was believed to exceed twenty. This, however, was thought to leave them still over forty strong.

The Fishers had now left the battlefield, or at least, none were in sight. It was thought that they had really gone, for some small, toothed birds of the buzzard family were settling down there, and these creatures were very shy of living human beings.

At this point some of the women and other relatives of the fallen men wanted to go back, desiring to recover their friends' bodies; but to this Big-axe would not consent.

" The Fishers are full of tricks," he said, " and we don't know what they may be up to now. I think they are gone, but perhaps they have merely withdrawn into hiding. They may have gone far enough to satisfy the birds, but yet not so far but that they could rush out and overtake any of us."

There was a little murmuring, and at first it seemed as if a few of the men, moved by the grief of the women, or troubled on their own account, would persist, but finally they thought better of it, and gave in. Like our American Indians, the people of the tribe were in a sense independent of the chief, though supposed to obey him pretty exactly when engaged in war, or when banded to hunt dangerous wild creatures; at other times he rather suggested than commanded, and each family was a little despotism of its own, the father, or oldest fighting man, being the ruler. However, in the absence of exact law, much depended on the force and determination of the chief, and in the present case few if any of the men were disposed to quibble with Big-axe on any fine point of authority.

As soon as this matter was settled Big-axe sent out Sure-dart as a picket guard, and set everybody else who was able to work at strengthening the defences. Rocks were piled up so as to help out the bit of natural wall, and bushes were cut down and made into a kind of wattle breastwork.

When all this was done they were in pretty good general shape. They were not afraid of another attack, at least, not at once, and they were fairly well provided with food and drink. Besides some skins of water that they had brought with them, some of the men knew of a fairly convenient spring. It was in a hollow at the beginning of the higher ground just beyond the swamp. As that was on the side away from the enemy it was decided to take the small risk of sending a few men there. This was done, and enough water was brought to last, with economy, several hours. Of course, under that hot sun, more than an ordinary amount was needed.

At sunset, according to the custom of the tribe, they buried their dead. There was hardly anything of what we should call a ceremony, though the women, as has been customary in our times, among certain European peoples, joined in a kind of wailing dirge. This was done as the corpses were wrapped in their mantles and laid in the graves.

When darkness finally came on the chief stationed the guards, and the rest of the camp picked out such places as were dryest and otherwise most desirable, and lay down. The chief intended to sleep, as the saying is, with one eye open, but he knew that he must have at least a little rest, or he should collapse. The strain upon both mind and body had been tremendous, and he was besides somewhat lame and bruised.

Sure-dart, at his own request, had been appointed one of the videttes. He was certain that he could not sleep, and he preferred to have something definite to do, rather than to be stowed away under the stuffy trees, listening for alarming things, and longing for daylight. As a kind of mark of honor, seeing how well he had fought, and otherwise behaved, and also because he was uncommonly trustworthy, the chief stationed him at the farthest and most exposed point. This was on the little ridge, or causeway, a hundred paces toward the rear.

It was pretty dark, even in the open, when

Sure-dart picked up his weapons and slipped away. It still lacked some hours of moonrise, and out in the marsh a white, steamy fog was beginning to rise. This was confusing the outlines of some things, and hiding others, so that bits of the eye-range lost their naturalness, and took on a touch of disturbing weirdness.

But though all this made anything but a cheerful beginning, the boy kept sturdily on till he thought he had covered the expected distance. Here the little ridge was a bit higher than just at the rear or ahead, and was therefore desirable for his purpose. He could get something of a view around when once the moon should be up.

He put down his shield, for he thought that he could easily pick it up in time if he should need it, and pulled his light cloak over his shoulders. It was far from cold, and, in fact, was stickily and unpleasantly warm; but all kinds of biting and stinging insects were abroad, and they had begun to prick their way even through his tough and seasoned skin. Knowing that the best way to guard against any chance fit of sleepiness was to keep in motion, he picked out a space for a beat, and began to pace slowly up and down.

By this time the fog had thickened to an extent that cut off all but near objects, and for the present he had only the various night noises — the notes of the wild creatures, big and little — for company. Nevertheless, these alone gave him enough to listen to, and at times more than enough, for among the sounds were some that had decidedly unpleasant suggestions. Among the whistling night-birds' screams, droning, humming, and occasional splashing and wallowing, he could catch a sharp hiss, or perhaps a kind of smacking noise, and he knew that the first meant either a snake, or one of the uncanny snake-lizards, and that the other stood for one of the greater lizard-beasts, such as a great stalker, or a thunder-beast. Both of these were vegetable feeders, and were not classed with the savage creatures, yet at times they had been found extremely dangerous. If come upon suddenly, or if their young were with them, and now and then as if moved by some fit of crazy rage, they had been known to make a headlong attack, and to follow it up with the savage pertinacity of the death-beast himself. In that case their great bulk (for the thunder-beast was the greatest of all land creatures known then or since) and accompanying strength left no chance for the poor human creature except a quick dart into some cave or, if there was time, flight up a large and strong tree. It needed to be both large and strong, or else the thunder-beast (this was the name given him by the Rock-people, but we call him the atlantosaurus), if he happened to be the pursuer, would pull it down. And the man needed to perch high, also, for the thunder-beast could stretch up, standing on his hind legs, and put his claws at a mark eighty feet from the ground!

There was still another noise that the boy distinguished from the others, and that he did not fancy. This one was not on the ground, but in the air, though through the obscurity he could not make out a sign of the creature itself. It was a whirring sound, such as might be made by a night hawk, but vastly louder. He knew that it came from the wings of a monstrous bat-like creature, yet not a bat, but a species of lizard, with wings that spanned twenty feet, and a toothed head on a body as large as an ordinary deer hound's. This creature, as he knew by unpleasant experience, sometimes paid a careless night-stroller, and still oftener a sleeper, an unexpected and most unwelcome visit. When urged on by hunger it had been known to flap down on a man, and before it could be fought off, to strike out one of his eyes, and tear a strip of flesh from his face. Ordinarily, however, it would not attack a grown person even in the night, but there was something about its horrible looks, and the though that it might drop upon one, as it were from the skies, that made the whir of its unseen wings disagreeable and disconcerting.

But Sure-dart, in spite of everything, — sounds, the darkness, and all, — did not cower, and he did not retreat so much as a step from his post. Within the limits that he had set for his beat, he doggedly stalked up and down, his trained senses alert, and his sheathed darts ready at his hand.

The lonesome minutes went by, and at last the ghostly mist began to thin, or it seemed to do so, and things around began vaguely to come out. Sure-dart brightened and was glad, for this meant that the moon was rising.

He took a turn or two more, but as he was

wheeling, at the lower end of his beat, something new caught his ear, and he stopped almost in his tracks and listened. He heard it again, and the seriousness and something more came back to his face. There was a reason.

CHAPTER VII

IT was not a very loud noise, but it was distinct from the other sounds, many and riotously blended and strange though some of them were. It was an animal noise, to speak of it with some manner of definiteness, but that does not reach the queerness and almost absurdity of it. At the start it was a kind of bellow, then it toned down to a succession of hog-like grunts, and at last, with a startling and unnerving suddenness, it flattened to a sharp, explosive hiss. It was certainly a noise easily to be remembered if once heard, and it did not need the other sounds of the movements of a great, preponderous body, now also plain enough, to settle finally what sort of thing or shape it was.

Sure-dart knew, though he had heard the strange notes but two or three times before. It was because he knew that he forgot all the cheer of the moonrise, and turned so grave. It was now certain that the unseen monster was heading that way, and was already within three or four spear-casts.

For a moment the boy, trained in the school of desperate emergencies, stood still, and deliberately thought. What he did must be the right thing, for a blunder was likely to be costly. He must bear in mind all the while that there were others as well as himself to think of.

In that brief time the creature had come some paces nearer. It was making rather heavy work of it in the marshiest spots, judging by the squashy noises, and it splashed tremendously when it came to a pool, but nevertheless, it was moving at what was relatively good speed. To judge by the sounds, its great strength and bulk were more than overcoming its disadvantage of weight, and were carrying it unswervingly and unyieldingly along.

But Sure-dart had now finished his thinking, and had come to a decision. He knew enough of the coming monster to understand that it was little likely to attack the camp; for in fact, wild creatures in general will not deliberately begin a fight with any considerable number of grown men. Besides, he knew that this particular monster was not a flesh-eater. It would have no use for human beings as food. No, the trouble lay in another direction. If the creature kept on it would soon be in his immediate neighborhood, and if it saw him, alone as he was, it was more than likely that it would take offence and charge. In that case, as there were no trees close by, and no cave of refuge, it was likely to be all up with him. The only seeming chance would be to make a dash for the camp; but though he could outrun the monster, it would probably be by a small margin, and when he should have gained the shelter the terrible brute would be at his heels. In that event the creature would rush blindly on, after the dogged perseverance of its kind, and before anything could be done it would be trampling about amongst the helpless sleepers. Even if it then took fright and fled — and this Sure-dart was certain it would not do, being then furious and lost to fear — it could hardly get away without doing serious harm. Its weight reached tons, and a single spank of one of its great feet would drive life and shape out of a human body.

And there was still another reason why the boy did not like to flee back to the camp: to do that he must leave his post unguarded, and it might well be that at that very moment those wily wretches, the Fishers, were creeping up to attack.

What, then, was left that could be done? Apparently but one thing,— to alarm the camp. Even then there was likely to be disaster, for in the haste and the unpreparedness for this kind of enemy, some must almost certainly be killed. This again would be one more piece of help and encouragement for the Fishers.

Well, Sure-dart had made up his mind, and, strangely enough, he had been able to think of still another plan. He was determined, before falling back on any of the others, to try it.

Still nearer the invisible monster floundered; but just then the mists and vapors paled still more, and all at once the giant moon — a moon such as we of this day never saw — flashed out yellow and magnificent, and the whole marsh, to the very hills beyond, came out as in a soft and sparkling twilight.

Sure-dart was bending forward a little in his anxiety, and watching for the first glimpse of the great, hulking shape. He knew that it was difficult to be exactly sure of the direction of a sound when heard through a fog, and he was not willing to waste any time; but as the light broke over the great green level it showed him instantly what he was looking for, and he was almost exactly right as to direction.

The creature was still some little way off, but even by a poorer light than this it would have been distinct at twice the distance. It was head-on, and so its length could not be made out, but its shoulders rose in a great dusky mass, and unless the invisible part was all out of proportion, the whole creature was bigger than any elephant.

But it did not look like an elephant. Far more it resembled a rhinoceros, though with such strange and repulsive differences as only that age of monsters could show. These differences would be plainer as it came nearer, but even now they were easily to be made out. In the first place, there was a kind of saw-tooth showing on the crest of the spine, and this looked like one of those astonishing lizard marks that had appeared in some of the other giant creatures. They belonged there, for the monster was in truth but another of those exaggerated reptiles that have seemed to later ages like the ravings of a delirious dream. Its head was snouted uncouthly, it had a short horn like a rhinoceros, but it had a bill like a turtle; it had no visible ears, and behind its head there was a monstrous sort of fleshy frill. This also had points, and the whole almost hid its upper shoulders, as the ruffs of Queen Elizabeth's time did those of the fashionable men and women. This much appeared at a glance, and it needed but another to bring out still more of the monstrous marks. For instance, the eyes walled out a little, and were overhung by great bony plates, and just back of each of these was a long horn. Thus it had the head of a rhinoceros, the snout of a turtle, the horns of a bull, and the frill-mark of a lizard. Had it been still nearer it could have been seen that its body was covered with scales, and not hair, and that its color was a dull green.

Sure-dart did not need to make all this study of the monster, for he had only too clear an idea of its looks; his business just now was of another and decidedly more pressing kind. The instant that he was absolutely certain of the creature's direction and nearness he began to move.

He deliberately turned his back on the camp, and ran lightly a spear-cast up the ridge track. There he stopped, and quietly waited. The giant, already close to the ridge, scrambled out upon it, and raised his hideous head for an investigating look around. The slim, upright shape, clear of other objects and plain in the flooding light, almost instantly caught his notice. Out went his frightful head as he stretched his neck for another look, and then, just as Sure-dart had expected, he gave his snout an irritated toss, and started at a slow trot that way.

Sure-dart threw one more look behind him, making certain that there was no sudden danger from that direction, and began to walk slowly backwards. The monster grunted, evidently growing more irritated at the continued presence of the slim creature, and broke into a heavy gallop. The boy was sure enough now of the first part of his plan, for he had drawn the monster away from the neighborhood of the camp, and it remained to see how the rest of the idea would work. As far as he was concerned, it was all-important just how it worked, for if it went wrong, it would mean to him the end of everything. It was likely that his friends, when they came to look for him, would find enough in the spatters of flesh to make sure that it was he, but that would be about all. He wheeled and ran at his best speed toward the high lands, and the scene of the late battle.

Four-legged creatures, even heavy and clumsy ones, have an advantage in running over two-legged ones. The larger animals, too, always go faster than a person looking on would guess, so that a common domestic cow, for instance, breaking into her clumsy gallop, cannot easily be headed by an ordinary sprinter. Sure-dart, trained in all such work as he was, made no mistake of this kind, but did his best at the start, thinking that the best was none too good. Three-horns, combining a bull's grunt with one of his diabolical hisses, thundered along after.

Sure-dart, though he was going so fast that he could not get a clear look at anything, was nevertheless taking a general account of things a little ahead. It was not many rods to where the first of the small mounds rose like a little islet out of the morass, and it was this that he was noting, guessing the distance as well as conditions would allow.

Three-horns gained a little with every clumsy, but long-reaching stride, and before Sure-dart was quite to the part of the ridge opposite the first of the islets, not more than twenty paces separated them. Now, whatever the risk from the delay, the boy had to check himself and glance around. It was a dreadful strain on his nerves not to have done so before, but he had understood what it might cost. He put on the brakes, as it were, and glanced over his shoulder. It was like a sickening blow to see how near the monster was. It had not seemed possible that he could drive his great bulk along so fast. Sure-dart faltered for one second, but the next his strength had come back, and he shot forward almost as if he had been fired from a gun.

The spurt brought him close to that part of the ridge that lay opposite the mound, or little islet; without a pause he swerved, and in a twinkling was flying out over the soft and oozy green level.

The water gushed and made sucking noises under his feet; he went half-way to his knees once, and the next step trod on something that squirmed, but at the same desperate scramble he kept on. A few more leaps, and he was bounding up the hard slope of the little mound.

Three-horns was certainly outfooted for the time being, for his great weight, in spite of the spread of his feet, and of his vast strength, told tremendously against him, and he could do no more than plunge and wallow. A little farther along he sank to his belly. The footing here was softer than on the other side of the ridge, and the crafty human creature knew it.

" Three-horns' great weight, in spite of the spread of his feet, and of his vast strength, told tremendously against him "

Still, with the dull, unswerving obstinacy of the beast that he resembled, as well as with the fierce pertinacity of the reptile that he really was, Three-horns held on. He, too, could scramble out upon the solid ground, once he could reach it, and surely the slim creature could find no retreat or hiding-place there.

Sure-dart was by no means winded, but he stopped an instant to get a helpful breath, and then sprang down the other side of the mound. To the north the reflection of the strong moonlight seemed to bring out a little sea, but it was really in no way different from the swamp, pools, and little island dry spots that were at hand. Sure-dart, with the exception of the serious underrating of the great lizard's speed, had thus far made no mistake, and that blunder had not as yet brought him to grief. Taking still another good breath, he sprang down the other side of this mound, and splashed and skimmed along to the next. He had not found what he was looking for in the first mound. He distanced the monster to this second mound, also, and on reaching the top found what he wanted. The mound looked like the other, with one exception; but this, to Sure-dart, was all-important: the mound was several feet higher in the middle.

He waited a moment, till Three-horns was again near; then he crossed straight over the top of the mound, and down the other side, and so out of sight.

The instant that he was fully out of view of his pursuer he dropped to hands and knees, and with the sinuous ease of a snake crawled back along the northern, or shadowed side of the mound, and wormed himself chin-deep in the slime and water. He knew the risk he was taking, for he did not forget the giant leeches, and still more, the water-snakes, the great, spiteful crabs,— with claws like a blacksmith's pincers,— and the giant turtles; but he thought little of them as compared with the peril he was trying to dodge.

There was luckily one thing in which these ancient monsters fell behind the warm-blooded animals of our times: they had very poor hearing, and but slight power of smell. Sure-dart took this into account, too, in trying his daring little trick. He managed to work his head back, till it was nearly hidden by a drooping tuft of bushes, and with a little faintness from the excitement waited.

The dull-witted monster, with its pound or two of brains, just sufficient to keep it tenaciously about its purpose, came rushing up the slope of the mound, and, without stopping, plunged and nearly tumbled down the other side.

Sure-dart could almost have laughed, both from the easy success of the trick, and from relief, and he quickly slipped around to the west side of the mound, and made one more short pause. He wanted to be sure that the monster was a safe distance away before he came out upon the ridge. Once he could thus get back to solid ground he could call on what was left of his wind and speed, and make a straight dash for the camp. The sleepers would then have seasonable notice of the possible danger, and without confusion could prepare to meet it. A line of spearsmen showing in the open, should the monster come that way, would doubtless daunt him, and turn him back. At least, the chief would then be responsible as to what should be done. As to his former unwillingness to quit his post, that did not now worry him. If the Fishers were out night-prowling, and if they advanced along the ridge, they would meet something that would give them business of their own to attend to. Sure-dart thought with grim pleasure of what would be likely to happen if the unsuspecting war-party came down from the woods, and ran afoul of the exasperated Three-horns. They would have no time to prepare, and he would be so near that most likely he would fall into a kind of savage craze, and charge straight on.

Thinking of these things helped to pass the little time that Sure-dart thought it was now reasonable to wait, and he stood up and stepped toward the ridge. He was waist-deep in water, and would be shielded from the sight of any creature on the east side of the mound. He kept on toward the ridge till — well, till a certain thing made him very suddenly pull up.

Rising into a great black hump, as it came up from the swamp, but catching the moonlight fully upon it the next instant, and not three spear-lengths off, he again saw — what but the great bulk of his late enemy? No, the foolish illusion passed almost as soon as it came, but not so the creature itself. No, for though it was not the beast that had just chased him, it was another of the same sort, and about as large. It was no doubt the lagging mate of the first monster, now a little uneasy that she could see or hear nothing of her lord. Sure-dart had heard that the male of the species often straggled along ahead of the female, and this particularly at night, when they generally changed from one feeding ground to another. These changes they made rather frequently, he had been told, as in this way they were more likely to avoid the death-beasts, the latter being their only dreaded enemies.

There was no time for elaborate plans, and the only thing that suggested itself to him was to squat down where he was, barely keeping his face out of water, and even ducking that under as the creature came close. There did not seem to be time, without dangerous exposure, to scuttle back to his old hiding-place.

So he squatted down where he had been standing, and tipped back his head, leaving barely his lips and nose clear.

It would be a trying few minutes; for the monster, if she did not leave the ridge, would pass within four or five paces of him. If, however, she should leave the ridge, in some way tracking her mate, then she might come still nearer; in fact, she might pass over that very spot. In that case there would be nothing for it but to spring up just in time, and rush out over the marsh.

He had barely thought this out, doing it quickly, too, as minds sometimes work in emergencies, when a grunt, ending in the steam sound of a sharp hiss, told him that the moment of terrible suspense had come.

CHAPTER VIII

PLUCK AND GOOD LUCK

AS Sure-dart's face was upturned to the sky he could not see the nearing monster, and he dared not take the chance of raising his head for a look. He heard the great beast coming, however, and was sure that she was as yet keeping the high ground of the ridge. In a moment the trampling showed that she was about abreast of him, and out of extra prudence he took a long breath, and ducked his head out of sight.

There seemed to be now but one danger, which was that she might, at this last moment, take the notion to turn aside into the swamp. He did not greatly worry about this, however. In fact, she was already abreast of him. But just here something happened that he had not counted on, though it ought not, of itself, to have been a surprise. Something cold, but alive, touched his foot, and as he instinctively recoiled it flashed, so to speak, up the outside of his leg.

It was not in human nature to stand it. The thing, whatever it was, seemed to be bumping against his dart-sheath, but before it could progress any farther he made a plunging leap, and scrambled out on the islet.

He had more than half expected to feel the sting of the creature's teeth, or the quick whipping of its folds (he had guessed that it was a water-snake) about his leg, but as he almost tumbled up the little slope he found that neither thing had happened.

But something else had. The three-horns, alert, perhaps in trying to find some sign of her mate, had instantly noticed him, and what was more, she had as quickly swung aside, and was wallowing toward him.

Perhaps it may seem strange, but this change of peril from the unknown to the known was a relief. At least, he now had his enemy before him, and could tell the sort of creature he was dealing with. He was becoming a little used, also, to the ways and powers of this big, but rather stupid foe. Still, there was no time to lose, and in a twinkling he was off over the green mush of reeds and mud, and splashing through the pools. He was heading for the next of the little islets, where he hoped to play another trick of doubling. It was high enough above the water for the purpose.

But this time, as he quickly found, the trick would not work. The beast was a little more active than the other, and perhaps not quite so headstrong, for she did not go charging along as if blindfolded, but kept alertly along in his wake, apparently veering from a straight course when he did, and not allowing him to get out of her sight. He did not dare, therefore, to try his doubling trick, for if it failed it would leave him in the tightest possible corner. She would then be the same as within striking distance, and before he could rise and spring away, the plunging horns, or the snapping bill, would have him. There was only to make a straight-away flight of it then, and this, with revived fears, but with the same old desperate resolution, he proceeded to do.

But he was now tiring, and already ran heavily, even where the ground was firm. On the other hand, the great reptile seemed to throw itself along with more rather than with less energy. But it was true that Sure-dart was somewhat worn by his previous exertions, to say nothing of the great tax of the battle, and the later incidents.

Nearer the giant monster came. The boy's breath was coming now with a rasping sound, and his legs seemed like stone. Still he held doggedly on. A moment later something happened in his favor. The monster plunged into an unusually soft and mucky spot, and had some little trouble to get out. Sure-dart, with the coolness of desperation, deliberately took the most of the time to rest and get his breath. When he started on again he was able to put on a bit more speed.

The boy's mind must have tired a little with his body, for after a few minutes he began to lose the keen sense of danger, and seemed to be moving almost mechanically. It was splash and wallow, with the squashing sound of the mud underfoot, and breaths drawn raspingly; and it all seemed to have been going on for a long time, and as if it were always to go on. But there were intervals when he came out of this half-stupor, and consciously drove his tired, heavy legs on again. It was then that he heard once more the grunting and hissing of the giant, but at other times he was not aware that he heard anything but the sounds he himself made.

At last he had the rich reward of his pluck. Before he was well aware of it a broader stretch than one of the mounds held hard under his tread, and he found that he had come upon a bit of the outlying firm ground that pushed itself out from the slope at the foot of the forest. The discovery flashed hot and tingling over him, and gave him new life. His dry lips let out a little hoarse cry of exultation, and he shot with long bounds onward.

Now the low trees lay just before, with bushes and rocks outlying, and a quick, southern widening to the slopes of the battle-ground. He was gaining on the pursuer, for the wine of hope increased his strength, and the better footing was helping. The monster was still plunging and wading through the bog. One swift, almost mad dash, and he was out of the moonlight into the tree-shadows, and clawing at the sipos that wound snake-like around a great, substantial palm. While the grunts and hisses behind him showed that the monster had also fetched the firm land, he was grasping the tough vines, and by their help was lifting and knee-clutching up the trunk. In two minutes more he was out of present danger.

He was in peril now from the reaction. Soon his arms and legs grew weak, and he had some ado to hold on. He could not have done so at all but for the tangle of vines. Meanwhile, something heavy crashed in among the shadows below, and a shock that would have dislodged him but for his new hold, seemed to make the whole tree jar. Three-horns was both expressing her rage and disappointment, and trying the effect of her giant strength.

So far Sure-dart had every reason to be thankful, but it now began to be clear to him that this last-moment refuge could answer merely a temporary purpose, and that he must make a change. The vines and creepers, though so useful for hand-holds and leg-rests, would not answer for permanent supports, say, for several hours. It might easily be that the time would be as long as that, especially if the female should succeed in calling her mate, and the two should take it into their stupid but obstinate heads to carry on a regular siege.

He first peered about and tried to see whether there was another and better tree within reachable distance. Yes, within a few feet was the great, spreading branch of some tree that looked like an oak. The branch was near the top of the tree, which was therefore much shorter than the one he was on, for he was still many feet from the sparse top of that. In that strange forest (as it would seem to us), where trees now found only in tropic lands were next neighbors to those of our temperate zones, this discovery did not surprise him, and he quietly started to make his way to the better quarters. Just then the dusky mass, that he could now look down on and pretty distinctly make out, began to stir and grunt, and as he reached out and drew a small limb to him, meaning to use this to help him to a grip on a larger, the creature broke into one of its loudest, hiss-ending bellows.

Sure-dart paid no attention, but as the swishing of the branches that he was laying hold of grew a little louder, he heard another sound, and as he finally clutched the branch he wanted, and swung himself off, the sound swelled louder, and even as he pulled himself safely to his new perch, the great bulk of the other three-horns came crashing out of a tangle of bushes and undergrowth. What he had feared had come true, and he must expect to stand a siege by both monsters!

And how was this siege to be raised? He could get along for a while without food or drink, or, indeed, it might be possible that he could make his way to a palm that bore cocoanuts and get refreshment from the meat and the milk, but that would not end the situation. When his friends missed him, would they trace him far enough in this direction to guess that he had gone still farther, and so keep on till they had found him? He had become a favorite with all, as he knew; and besides, short as the tribe now was of fighting men, his skilful arm and stout heart could not easily be spared. Yet, on the other hand, to venture as far as this was to take a great chance of again meeting the Fishers, and this was not a risk to be taken lightly. Sure-dart believed that the crafty Long-spear might lurk hereabouts for a while instead of turning back, hoping that the Rock-people might by that time have become careless, and neglect to keep a proper guard. Inasmuch as the attack of the

Fishers had failed, or at least had not been decisive in results, the chief and his principal advisers would be all the more likely to persevere in some plan that would give them better results. It would be mortifying to go back otherwise. All this being true, Sure-dart could see that Big-axe would hesitate before venturing so far back into danger.

Nor was this the end of the trouble. If the Fishers were in the neighborhood, they might hear the noise of the two monsters, and try to learn the cause. If there was not too much danger, they might then turn their force into a hunting party, and endeavor to kill the beasts, by so doing replenishing their stock of provisions. Doubtless they had travelled light, as their business required speed, and therefore light burdens. To be sure, the great lizards did not make prime eating, even for savage tastes, but parts relished well, and it must be remembered that some people of our day eat certain reptiles, such as frogs. We might also remind ourselves that many reptiles of that period had a sort of kinship with modern birds, or, to be more definite, that the birds we know are descended from creatures of a reptile nature.

Looking the ground all over, then, Sure-dart had to acknowledge that he was in a very tight place, and that the scrape he had just got out of by no means meant the end of his troubles. This was pretty hard, considering all he had gone through, and the plucky efforts he had made, but it was nevertheless a cold fact, and must be met as such. Sure-dart was luckily of just the right material to face such an apparent discouragement. He never gave up till he had to — an excellent rule for boys of a later day to follow.

The thing to do at present was to make himself as comfortable as possible, and for this purpose he climbed to a place just above, where two stout limbs started pretty close together from the trunk, and made a roughly good kind of seat. He had the lower of the two limbs, which was broad and flattish, for the bottom of his chair, the other limb served as the back, and he had the trunk to lean sidewise against. There was some danger that he might drop to sleep, and fall off, but to guard against this he meant by and by to climb down a few feet, where a long, stout, creeping plant, or sipo, had worked its snake-like way that far up the tree, and tear off enough for a binding rope. He could tie himself so strongly to a limb that he must awake before his partial weight against it could break it.

All the while the two disappointed monsters below were grunting and fussing, and now and then rooting the ground with their horns. They reared up several times, too, and thrust their hooked bills an unpleasant distance up the trunk; but the whole effected nothing. Sure-dart merely looked down at them, but did not in the least worry. Even the biggest death-beast could not have reached him, and nothing that walked could have pulled down the tree itself.

As he had nothing else to do he began to look about him and try to get a better idea of his surroundings. The tree that he was in was one of a group that partly shut in a small open space, this space being covered with a rush-like grass, the common kind of that day. This grass, in turn, nearly hid the trunks of two or three fallen trees. Otherwise it made a bit of clearing, the woods shutting it in excepting on one narrow side. Here was an opening toward the west, or in the direction of the ridge and the Rock-people's camp. From where he sat, or from any other position in the tree, Sure-dart could not get the range of the whole ridge, but he could see a good stretch of the beginning. To the left of this, or what might be called shorewards, he could see the whole of the first battle-ground, and a considerable stretch of the open slope above. At least, he was placed so as to get a pretty early notice of the coming of friends or foes. The possible exception would be if they came from a strange and unlooked-for direction.

Matters now in a sense quieted down, and remained so for fully half an hour. This gave the boy a rest, which certainly he needed; he leaned back in his place, and in a light way dozed. To be sure, the monsters were still below, and they grunted a good deal, and now and then nosed about the tree, but he was not now minding them. The other noises were merely the ordinary ones of the night,— the croaking and whistling and humming, with sharp or lonesome bird-calls, and the splashing of the larger wandering creatures.

All at once, as it seemed to him, he heard a new sound. It was one that came as a little shock, though he was only half sure that he really heard it, and though it was not a loud sound. He straightened up, and with all his keen senses alert, listened.

It came again. There could be no mistake now, and his ears, like faithful sentinels, had given him a true warning. The sound was familiar enough, though familiarity had not made it commonplace. It was the queer, sputtering hiss of a giant death-beast.

The boy's eyes lighted, and with one of his low, clicking laughs, he squared himself about on the limb. He was in a position now to see everything in the little opening. It was toward this opening that the death-beast seemed to be making his way.

But here the two besiegers below, having evidently caught the sounds, all at once stopped their grunting and fussing, and stood with heads raised. Only their spike-ridged tails switched uneasily. Just then the noise came again, and from the same direction, but nearer. Following it was a distinct crackling amongst the trees and underbrush.

This was enough for the three-horns. They probably had not meant to make a stand, but only to be sure of the direction of their enemy, for now they wheeled, and started at full gallop out into the open.

Sure-dart was never able to explain how the next thing came about. He knew that the death-beasts, like all the great lizards, were stupid, and yet what followed seemed to be the result of a pretty piece of cunning. The three-horns were scarcely out in the open when they stopped short, and in a moment wheeled, and slowly trotted back into the little opening. Not instantly, but quickly, Sure-dart saw what had happened. Coming with long, soft strides along the upper margin of the outside slope, and making but slight noise, was another death-beast. He was almost up to the little opening, as the three-horns started out.

Later, when Sure-dart had time for theories, he made up his mind that this seeming trick of the death-beasts was really an accident. He believed that the pair were roving along, as the three-horns had been, some little way apart, they being in search of something for supper, and that it was a mere chance that one was in the rear of the three-horns, and the other placed so as to cut them off. The only piece of cunning, as Sure-dart thought, was the silence and stealth of the second death-beast, and this was hardly more than a hunting creature's ordinary instinct.

But just at present Sure-dart had something to take his attention besides natural history problems; he was all agog to see what he thought would be the greatest fight of live flesh against live flesh that human eyes ever beheld. In his excitement he slipped down to a lower limb, and from near the bending end of it stooped and peered down.

He had not to wait long for the mighty show to begin.

CHAPTER IX

THE two death-beasts exchanged a sputtering hiss or two, as they came on, and as soon as they were together they ranged up side and side, as if they had been a yoke of giant oxen. The next instant they made headlong into the opening.

Ranged side by side, too, the three-horns received them. The death-beasts rose on their hind legs as they came to close quarters, but the three-horns kept on all-fours, and lowered their spiked heads. For an instant the two rearing giants shot up almost as high as the branch where Sure-dart rode, and he drew up his feet in alarm; but the next moment the monsters were down again, and were completely covering the two defenders. The smaller creatures seemed to give way in the legs, as if they could not stand the weight, and the death-beasts sank a little with them, all the while digging with their fore claws, and crooking their serpent necks, as they tried to fasten with their teeth.

This seemed to be pretty near the end, close as it was to the beginning, for the three-horns looked to be as good as blotted out. It would be strange, indeed, if they could stand such a crushing and tearing. Sure-dart did not see how they

could, as he stood up and looked over an obstructing branch, and tried to get a clearer view of the
tilting and heaving flesh-mountains.

But the first charge is not always the whole
of a battle. The three-horns now proved this.
As Sure-dart was craning his neck so as to see
over the obstructing branch, he noticed that one
of the death-beasts was pushing or crowding
down with her fore feet, and had flung up, with
a snake-like contortion, her long neck. She
seemed to be recoiling from what was under her,
as if something had suddenly gone wrong. In a
moment, as Sure-dart wonderingly stared, she
gave a stronger push, dug her great hind claws
into the ground, and floundered and tumbled off
the body of the creature below.

Sure-dart peered eagerly down to see what had
happened, and was surprised to find that the
three-horned beast, though seemingly bruised and
showing dark in places, which were doubtless
blood-stained, was able to hold up her head, and
was even making motions to rise. She did come
up the next moment, though only after a lurch
and a scramble, and backed away a few paces,
then again defensively lowering her horned
snout.

The death-beast that had just been engaged
with her, on the contrary, lay flattened out, but
raised her head languidly; Sure-dart then saw
that there was a great dusky patch on the side
of her neck, and on bending down, and looking
still more closely, he could see that the patch
extended down to the shoulder; he was sure
then that it was bloody. This looked like the

work of the three-horns's great, turtle-like bill, or perhaps came from a fall upon the terrible spiked frill back of the creature's head. There had been a turning and twisting at the last, and it was impossible to say which supposition was correct.

But as this round, as it might be called, ended, the fight elsewhere grew, if anything, hotter.

The other death-beast had got his great hind feet into action, and it seemed that they were working at the head of the three-horns, which lay flat on its stomach. At the same time, the death-beast was biting furiously at the other extremity, tearing away at the hips and flanks.

Sure-dart had no doubt of the end of this duel, but he watched it closely, both from curiosity, and because he thought the conclusion would be a step toward his own release. It did not take long to work out.

The conquering death-beast rose a little, let the dying three-horns half stagger up, and then fastened again with his teeth, and fore claws, and gave a simultaneous dig with both hind feet. The force would be hard to measure, but it would have ripped an elephant half in two, and it tore the three-horns from his fore shoulders clear through the length of his head. The creature instantly collapsed and came down in a heap, and the death-beast, holding his fearful grip, sank with him. As he reached the ground, the serpent neck twisted, and the head reached back, stopping high up the side, near some of the large blood-vessels. Here it made a dart, and the sharp teeth once more went to work. This time, however, the aim was not to kill, but to feast.

Meanwhile, the other death-beast, thus left to "hoe her own row," began to revive and seem more active. Just then she raised her head, and with a gathering under of her legs, dived forward, and dropped crashingly upon her waiting antagonist.

But the three-horns had backed a little, and that with great quickness, so that only her fore parts were borne down under the gigantic assailant. Wrenching, twisting, and digging with her sturdy fore legs she was quickly up again, immediately drove forward, and gave a fierce dig upward into the broad, crowding breast. At least one of the horns drove into the flesh, and when it was there the desperate beast wormed and bored, and did not cease till the hole was big enough — as Sure-dart believed — to let in a man's head. At least, that wound did the business for the death-beast. She hissed and sputtered furiously, and seemed, reptile-like, very little troubled by the pain, but in not more than half a minute she began to relax her scrambling and clawing, and gradually grew inert and still.

The three-horns tried to clear her head and shoulders, but what with the weight, and the previous wounds, and exhaustion, she could not, and after a few more struggles she too sank down. The two bodies lay in a quiet heap for a moment, but just as Sure-dart concluded that they were both dead, the death-beast lifted her mighty tail and struck out, broke the trunk of a small tree, and with a great heave rose up and drove her teeth into the flank of the pinned-down foe. Then she dropped back and stretched her long neck, which took on a coil, as if it had been a snake. The three-horns did not move,— not even after she had but the weight of the body to deal with, and Sure-dart could not doubt that she also was dead.

The tremendous battle being over,. the boy drew a long breath and got into a more comfortable position. It was time to be thinking again about his own affairs and what he should do.

The first thing, as it seemed evident, was to find out how far the conquering death-beast was taken up with his eating. This might not be easy, for though the creature was not very quick to see or to hear, and though Sure-dart believed its sense of smell was also rather dull, yet there was another difficulty, and that of a most important kind. The creature was not relatively slow in its motions, and it was so huge, and had such a reach, that, if the boy went down to scout and did happen to catch its notice, it would be a hard piece of work to get back to safety. In fact, only the difficulty that the monster would have in working its great body quickly about amongst the trees and undergrowth promised any mentionable chance at all. But something must be done, and Sure-dart thought that it should be done soon, for there was no telling what the monster would do when it was done with its feast. It might go nosing about, and discover the watcher, and then it was very likely to camp down for a siege.

Reasoning in this way, the boy worked cautiously along the branch to the trunk of the tree, and from there, still going slowly and as noiselessly as possible, he slipped into the next, and farther-off tree. The monster's back was all the while toward him, and was now completely hidden by the tree-tops, and Sure-dart thought he would risk the descent.

He made practically no noise in doing this, and at the bottom of the tree stepped off in a tangle of parasite vines and outreaching creepers. Soft-footed, like a cat after mice, the boy crept step by step away, and at last reached the border of trees next the open marsh-line. With one more pause, till he heard the death-beast chewing and craunching into the carcass, he slipped boldly out, and when clear shot away on the run.

It seemed to him, as his speed prevented him from following the noises behind him clearly, that he heard a cracking through the border of small trees and bushes, which would probably mean the rush of the death-beast, but as he slacked a little, turning his head to catch the sound, he could make out nothing. It was very likely his imagination, or else it was the noise of a harmless small creature, or of the wind.

When he was fairly on the ridge he halted and looked back. There was no creature of any kind in sight, and the only noises were the usual ones of the concealed animal life, such as there had been before.

With the strain considerably relieved now, he kept on, and without any sort of hindrance came to the place where he had been keeping guard. Now, in the dusk of the small trees that bordered the ridge beyond, he heard a new kind of noise, and abruptly stopped. It sounded like the careful movement of some large animal.

But as he instinctively crouched, staring in the direction, another and very different sound followed, for a human voice called out:

"It is you, is it, Sure-dart? We could n't tell at first."

And Big-axe and three or four more of the warriors stepped out into sight.

For a moment Sure-dart was so delighted that he could not speak. His legs grew weak with the reaction. But as they came toward him, and Big-axe asked where he had been, and why he had left his post, he made a strong effort, and outwardly was as steady and self-possessed as usual.

"I was forced to leave it," he answered. "I will tell you about it."

He did, and they heard the story with lively, though not demonstrative interest. The experience, nevertheless, was uncommon, even for those hazardous days. While they were listening, some others of the men joined them, and, in fact, the whole camp, which was by this time aroused, was pretty soon gathered around. Sure-dart learned that he had not been at once missed, but that after a while the chief, who was still sleeping with one eye open, awoke fully, and started out to see how things were going. At first he thought that Sure-dart had merely extended his picket work a little, but on pushing along for some distance to see, he found that he was mistaken, and discovered that the boy had disappeared altogether. Shortly afterwards he, in turn, was missed from the camp, and then some others of the fighting men came to look him up. This led to a discussion; and while all were puzzled, it was rather thought that some wild creature had killed and carried off the boy. It was evidently not human beings, or they would have followed up their advantage by attacking the camp. As for any other theory, they could not conceive of a sufficient motive to draw the boy voluntarily from his post, and even if so, to keep him away. They finally decided to station two sentinels in his place, and to send a small scouting party as far as the end of the ridge. They were about to do this when he appeared.

"Well," said Big-axe, when it was at last all clear, "you have been lucky, and so have we as well. A great many bad things had a chance to happen. But now turn in, and get a good rest. We shall not go from here for a while, or till we are sure that the Fishers have really gone back; so you can sleep as long as you like. I will say further, though I do not believe in much open praise, that you have done very well, and that you have earned your place among the fighting men."

Sure-dart had some trouble in hiding his pride and gratification at this praise, but he knew what was expected of a full-ranked warrior, and managed to keep it pretty well hidden. Such a glimmer of it as he could not quite smother did not seem to displease the chief.

Sure-dart, with all present care off his mind, and his body, strong and enduring as it was, thoroughly tired, finished out the night with a sound sleep. Not only that, but he did not awake

at once in the morning when the others began
to stir. The plan of staying where they were till
they felt sure that the Fishers had turned back
was still thought the only wise and prudent one;
accordingly, they continued in their camp that
day and the following night. Even then Big-
axe believed that they should leave a rear guard,
so as to check any crafty late attack, and also to
give the others time to prepare. This was done,
and the rear guard was told off, and left in the
little fort. In case they were attacked by a small
body of the enemy they were to resist, and afterwards were to push on and join the main force;
but if they saw they were to be attacked in force,
they were to hasten on, send word to the chief,
and check the pursuers as much as they could.
By using a little cunning they could pick out
places for a stand that would give them an
advantage.

The rear guard was made up of ten strong
fighters, including the chief's son and Sure-dart.
The boy was chosen partly for his fleetness as a
runner — for it might be necessary to send a
speedy messenger to the main body — and partly
because of his coolness and resourcefulness. Big-
axe saw and fully appreciated these excellent
qualities, little as he had said about them. But
at the last moment Hop-foot put in a plea to join
the company. He wanted to be with his friend
Sure-dart, and also (remember, he was but a
boy) he secretly wanted to get rid of helping
along the small children and carrying a pack.
True, this pack was light, but to carry it was irk-
some, and then with it he could not run about at

will, and make inquisitive dashes after small wild creatures.

At first Big-axe was inclined to refuse the request, but when Hop-foot, with the cunning of some boys of the present day, looked hurt, and said that he did n't want to be treated always as a child, when he was more than half grown, the chief hesitated, and finally gave in. It was time, he thought, that the boy were having a little helpful experience, and this would be a light breaking in. Only one thing slightly troubled him when he was otherwise ready to consent, and that was lest the child should happen to offend Bull-head. The young man was to command the party, and his father knew that he did not like his half-brother,— perhaps in part from jealousy,— and that he was surly and quick-tempered. Moreover, he had, in the past year or so, been impatient of the authority of the chief, and seemed to want a greater measure of independence. Under the simple and primitive rule of the tribe, which made the head of a family the absolute ruler of it,— subject only to the exigencies of great general matters, such as war,— Bullhead was bound to obey his father. The only change would come when the father died, or should happen to lose his reason, or when Bullhead should marry and himself have children. Even then the father would retain a certain amount of authority.

This kind of rule, or law, we call the patriarchal, and it has generally been in force among primitive peoples, and was even, to a certain degree, adopted by the enlightened Romans. But this objection, which the chief kept entirely to himself, he finally concluded to disregard; so he put it aside and told Hop-foot to run along.

The boy did not linger after he heard this, but dashed back to join Sure-dart, who had followed along for a short distance — knowing what Hop-foot was about — and was now waiting for him.

They joined the others of the command in the little islet fort, and Hop-foot, as grave as any warrior, reported to Bull-head.

For a moment the harsh face of the young man darkened to a look more forbidding still; but as Hop-foot bobbed his head, meaning, according to the custom of the tribe, that he was putting himself fully under the leader's authority and would so continue till the purposes of the present undertaking were accomplished — as he did this, the harsh look of Bull-head slightly softened. At least, here was submission to his rule, and evidently with the consent of the chief himself, and the boy really looked obedient. The foolish and unreasonable pride of the fellow was tickled, and as he had time to think about it, he thawed a little more, till finally he told Hop-foot he would accept him, and to consider himself a part of the command. This was a little more than the orders of Big-axe seemed absolutely to require, and so was something of a concession.

As soon as he was dismissed, Hop-foot went skipping off, and again joined Sure-dart.

"Now it seems like old times," he gleefully broke out. "We'll have a little fun, if there's any to be had. Bull-head doesn't seem very cross, and I guess he won't bother us. Father says that we are coming to the part of the country where the scamperers are, and if we don't have to join the others right away, we may bag one. I don't mean, you know, to kill him, but catch him. Some of the men will help. Father saw one caught just by heading him into a pool, where men could wade and catch him as he swam. What do you think? I'd mightily like one for a pet."

"If we could catch one," Sure-dart answered rather sceptically, "he would be all right for a pet; but — well, we can't tell. I never saw but one alive, and that was a little fellow that father brought home. He was hurt, and did n't live long. A terror-bird had got a clip at him. That is, just a touch, but it was enough."

"Oh, I should suppose it would have been. Excuse me from having anything to do with the terror-bird. Hearing about him is enough."

"I never saw one alive," said Sure-dart, "but from what I have heard, a dead one would suit me better. When you think of a bird an axe-length taller than a man, with a bill half as long as the axe-handle and twice as sharp as the edge, and with clawed feet that together spread the bigness of a man's body — when you talk about him — well, the talking is enough."

"But still," said Hop-foot, with a sturdy shake of the head, "I should like to be one of a party to make a try at him. I know you would do your share, too, if you had the chance. Only you always talk about such things as if you were kind of scared."

"I think I am learning wisdom," said Sure-dart, with a smile.

He was beginning to feel that the responsibilities of his new position — his place among the men — were belittling his former boyish thoughts and feelings, and that thus he was growing away from Hop-foot. Yet this was merely in that one thing. He liked the boy as much as ever.

They went on talking till Bull-head called Sure-dart and ordered him to join one of the men in trying to kill or snare something for dinner.

CHAPTER X

THE best that Sure-dart and the man could do in the way of providing dinner for the company was to catch a big eel, and to knock over with a stone what they called a worm-tail. This was a stout little bird about as large as a crow, but with small wings, and a tail that looked like a single long, large feather. It had teeth, and was a flesh-eater, and was pretty tough for food, but this did not trouble the hungry guard. They ate both him and the eel with no preparation except skinning the eel, and cutting off his head, and doing about the same with the bird. As yet these people had never eaten or even seen any sort of cooked food.

The rest of the day and the following night passed, and there was no appearance of danger, and no sign whatever that the Fishers had lingered in the neighborhood. So Bull-head, following the orders of Big-axe, broke camp, and set off on the trail of the main body. It was understood that Big-axe would hasten his party along as fast as possible; but that would not mean anything like the speed of the smaller company, which would probably come up before the general party was settled in its new quarters. Bull-head knew where to find the main body, for he had once before been in these parts, and so knew the general lay of the land; and besides, Big-axe had pointed out the top of a small, oddly shaped mountain that was to serve as a guide. Big-axe meant to pitch camp on a kind of broad shelf of this mountain, where it would be rather easy to make a good defensive fight, and whence it was but a short distance down to a ravine where there was a brook.

The way soon became wilder and rougher, as they began to get among the hills and straggling woods, but they could now get some shade, and here and there a refreshing breeze found an opening and reached them. At this point they found more trees of the oak and beech kind, and fewer of the palm family, and in general the surroundings became less suggestive of the tropics. They had long ago parted with the reeds and canes, and the low, snake-rooted willows, and the only vegetation of the familiar kind that was at all common was the rush-like grass. This, which was much coarser than the grass of to-day, still covered some of the little valley-bottoms and openings among the trees, and also ran in with the few kinds of bushes that were common both among the woods and in the openings. Some of these bushes were bright with berries, but only one kind was considered eatable, and that was tart and slightly bitter. On the way to this higher region, on a dry and stony level, they saw some scrubby bushes bearing a small, unpromising green fruit, and these bushes were covered with little prickly points. The fruit was of no value, and it was to take ages to make it so; but in time this primitive prickly pear was to develop into the pear of our gardens.

Naturally, the live creatures changed with the change of surroundings. Up here were none of the kinds of fish-lizards, great turtles, or even the large dinosaurs ("three-horns" and "death-beasts") that were so common among the marshes, and on the skirts of the surrounding hills. Instead were small quadrupeds (there were as yet no large ones in existence), such as huge conies, gigantic rats,— though these last were also found in the marsh country,— and small lizard-creatures, some of which walked on their hind legs. On the farther slopes of these hills, as Sure-dart had heard, were occasionally seen the little horse-like creatures that the Rock-people called "scamperers," and in fact, these were now and then to be met with as far east as the borders of the marsh region, though they were nowhere numerous. Their day was later, when conditions were more favorable for them, and when they increased in numbers, and developed in size, till at last they could fairly be called horses. But that was some millions of years later. At this time they were little bigger than our foxes, and had but a small show of mane and tail, with toed feet, instead of hoofs. They had four of these toes on their front feet, and three on the hind.

Of snakes there were several kinds, some of them poisonous. There were a few varieties of birds, including the queer little fellows with teeth and long, worm-like tails, and also a bird that had a sort of hair, instead of feathers, and no wings to speak of. Here, as on the lower levels, might be looked for — particularly in the evening — the dreadful bat-creature with toothed nose, or bill, and twenty feet of spread to his skinny wings.

Neither here, nor anywhere else in the world, at that time, was a single deer, antelope, lion, tiger, elephant, or any other haired or furred animal of any size; among the trees were not to be seen darting monkeys, or the flash of bright-feathered birds; and there was not one songster to give a touch of cheerfulness to the sombre recesses of the evergreens, or the more open arches of the oaks and beeches.

There was something almost uncanny, as the Scotch would say, about this strange wilderness. It was not made less so by the fact that the woods proper were not generally very dense; for the kinds of trees now found everywhere in the temperate zone were then new on the earth, and they were particularly sparse in this higher region, so that what there was of forest was made up chiefly of groups of evergreens, yew-like conifers and intervening huge ferns, together with thorny bushes almost as large as small trees.

But neither of the boys paid very much attention to these less striking and exciting matters; they were chiefly on the lookout, particularly Hop-foot, for something new and strange among the animal inhabitants, and both boys constantly had a dart ready for any such. For a time they saw nothing in the least worth bothering with, but soon after leaving the rocks and trees behind them something did appear of a sort to make them pay eager heed.

They were near a kind of long, rather shoal cut, or narrow valley, one which opened almost or quite upon the outside plain, when something scurried out of a thicket, and went bounding down the side of the hill. A single glance showed that it was the rare little scamperer, or horse-creature.

" Oh, there is what I want! " fairly yelled Hop-foot. " Head him off, Sure-dart; run down the bank and turn him back! He can't get across that place."

The scamperer did seem, in fact, to be almost in a trap. At the bottom of the hill was a rocky gully with almost perpendicular sides, and this ran at right angles with the general cut of the valley, and on one side turned back and up into the hill. On the other it stopped abruptly at the end of a practically straight line. The situation will be better understood by comparing the gully to the head of an ordinary hammer, the claws-end standing for the part of the gully that turned back and up, and the pounding end for the straight part. The path that the scamperer was following went toward the gully as the handle of the hammer goes into the head.

Sure-dart glanced at Bull-head, seeking per-mission to go, and got a consenting nod. He was away on the instant, going down the slope with a speed that would astonish a boy of to-day. Hop-foot, rather fast on his legs, in spite of his infirm-ity, hopped and skipped down the other side of the slope, or toward the end of the claws of the hammer. Bull-head, for a wonder, relaxed a little of his gruff strictness, and told two of the men to join the boys. One of these men was Wing-foot, who, as it will be remembered, was the fastest runner in the tribe, and the other was not very much slower. Wing-foot followed the younger boy, and the other man (his name was Long-shanks) took the general direction of Sure-dart, but swung more to the left.

Wing-foot soon passed to the front on his line, and Sure-dart was quickly near the straight end of the gully. The scamperer kept rather hesitatingly along, seeming to falter as he saw the strange creatures after him, but at last was frightened into a spurt, and dashed down to the brink of the gully. There he stopped, seemed to gather his wits and realize what a corner he was in, and the next instant whirled to the right, and made up the slope.

"Stop him, Wing-foot," yelled Hop-foot, as he saw the creature heading straight toward them. He spread out his own legs and arms as he spoke.

But this gave the scamperer a new fright. He stopped once more, wheeled, and then headed again for the gully.

"Don't crowd him!" roared Long-shanks, "or he may jump, and break his neck!"

This seemed likely, and the others checked themselves, and went on more slowly.

The scamperer went this way and that, now in a terrible panic, and at last poked his head over a little break in the edge, and looked down.

In a twinkling he dropped his fore-quarters over, and before the hunters could fairly make a new start he was entirely out of sight.

Hop-foot shouted with vexation and disappointment, and even the older pursuers crossly grunted. They all kept on till they were at the edge of the gully, though not now with any real hope, and successively peered over.

Wing-foot, who was the first, broke out in a barbarian cluck, but did not speak. He waited till Hop-foot had come skipping and limping up. So, too, did Sure-dart and Long-shanks, as they also outstripped the boy and looked over.

"What is it? What are you looking at? Is he killed?" puffed Hop-foot. He looked over himself before anybody could answer the questions.

There was a mere little furrow that led slopingly from the small cut in the bank down perhaps thirty feet. Here there was a shelf, and after that it was a straight drop of forty feet to the bottom of the ravine. On the shelf, which was not much more than big enough to hold him, stood the scamperer.

"Ooo-hoo!" triumphed Hop-foot, in a high cry, "that settled your game!"

"Not quite," said Long-shanks, who, as it appeared, knew something about scamperers. "We can't go down there without a rope," he explained, "and when we do, it will scare him so he will jump off. I know the fellow well enough for that."

According to this the primitive horse was subject to a desperate kind of panic, the same as the modern animal, and under that frenzy would jump unhesitatingly to his death.

" We can make a good enough rope out of some creepers," said Hop-foot, " and as for the rest of it, why can't somebody go around and stand just below him? He would then be as scared to jump as to stand still."

This did seem plausible, and after a little discussion Long-shanks said that he would skirt the gully (going around, of course, by the short end), and stand below the shelf.

He did this, and very soon appeared below. Meanwhile, they had found, at the edge of a neighboring patch of semi-tropical trees, some long, tough creepers which they twisted together to make a sufficiently serviceable rope. It would easily bear the weight of two ordinary men.

" I will go down," said Wing-foot. " I am strong and not very heavy."

The rope was long enough to allow a surplus that could be weighted down; and as stones, big and little, were plenty, it did not take long to put a heavy check-weight on the spare end. Sure-dart and Hop-foot could then easily manage the rest of it, pulling sufficiently hard to bring Wing-foot and the scamperer to the top. The man would, of course, be able to do something for himself, as the little path that the scamperer had used would be immediately before him.

He made sure that the rope was fast under his arms, and stepped to the edge. But there he stopped. So, too, did Sure-dart and Hop-foot.

There was an excellent reason. It was a

reason that suddenly made them bend over the verge, and yell like wild creatures at Long-shanks. As they yelled they pointed, motioning at something behind him. He turned, as the sense of what they meant struck him: with that he understood all.

The other side of the gully was by no means so precipitous as this; and in one place, nearly opposite, it came down in a long shoulder of rocks and loose gravel. There were some trees and thorny bushes at the head of this natural path, and pushing through the tangle was what looked at first like a double row of yellowish palm-leaf fans, all gently waving. There were at least ten or twelve of them, and they were carried at a height, for the first one, of perhaps five feet, rising to ten, and then, at about the same slope, dropping lower, till the last was hidden by the others.

Long-shanks set his lips, turned, and started at a run up the gully.

He had taken no more than three steps when the strange fans gave a quicker wave, the bushes snapped and parted, and a smallish reptile head, bill-snouted, and covered with yellow scales, broke into sight. A broad breast, and short, outward-bowed legs followed, and then came more of the fans, these now showing as great, upright plates along the creature's curved back. But two of these plates were half torn away, blood was trickling down the creature's shoulders, and his bill-mouth was drooping open.

This much of him was scarcely in sight when he put his fore feet down the little slope, slid forward, as some gravel gave way under him, and all in a flash lost his balance, rolling end over end down the slope.

For a moment the watchers saw a sight that seemed hardly real or of the sane world. The monster was not under twenty feet long, and was of a bulk to weigh several tons. This great shape, flashing first a white belly, like a monstrous frog, then an enormous tail, dusky green, covered with scales and banded plates, and spiked near the end, and as often as the back came fairly up flapping the great, living fans — this seemingly impossible thing lurched and floundered its tremendous way down the slope, until it brought up against the tall stump of a broken tree.

With one more lurch, seemingly little hurt, and not at all confused, the giant righted himself, and started at a lumbering waddle down what remained of the slope. Just here he caught sight of the fleeing Long-shanks. With that kind of machine-noise — mostly a hiss like escaping steam — that seemed to be the one loud note of the great lizards, the monster jerked up his huge tail, and lunged forward in pursuit.

"What is it? Can it catch him? What shall we do?"

This, with gasps, from the startled and horrified Hop-foot.

But Sure-dart and Wing-foot had already started at a run up the line of the ravine. Yet Wing-foot, mindful that this was the chief's son, turned his head a little, and shouted, almost from the corner of his mouth:

" It 's an old bull thorn-tail, and he 's hurt and ugly."

The boy understood now. The stegosaurus, as modern men of science have named the creature, was one of the giant dinosaurs which had at this time become rare, and which soon afterwards wholly disappeared. He was huge, and doubtless rather slow, and perhaps usually peaceable, but from his general shape, and his bulk, and his mighty tail (which he was able to use as a kind of huge spiked mace) he must have been dangerous to rouse. A large one stood some ten feet high at the top of his arched back, and was heavier than a good-sized elephant. If one of the survivors of the species, having strayed from his usual haunts near the marshes, or by the great lake itself, had been irritated by fighting with some other monster, and then had caught sight of a smaller, fleeing creature, he would be likely to start in pursuit. Perhaps the strangest thing about the monster, and a strange thing of itself, was that it had what might be called two brains. One very small brain was in the usual place in the head, and the other was on the rump, near the backbone. It would be more exact to say that this brain was a strange enlargement of the spinal cord, but with some functions that the cord does not usually have, and which, in fact, we do not fully understand. It may have helped him, as his other brain was so small, to direct the movements of his spiked tail.

Hop-foot learned this (though of course nothing of the scientific part) at a later time; just now he was thinking of the chance Long-shanks had in the race, and what could be done to help the poor hunter. He knew, of course, that he could not get back to Bull-head in time to accomplish anything, and on the whole, he felt so helpless that he merely squatted down where he was. He had not done any clear thinking, it need hardly be said, but had merely grasped vaguely at the thought that he might do something. Other than this he was staring down, his heart, as the saying is, in his mouth, at the half-naked, swift-speeding hunter, and the arched-backed, lumbering monster, its great fans waving — the two passing, almost like one of our modern moving pictures, rapidly before his eyes.

One thing was already clear: the monster, in spite of his seeming clumsiness, was managing to heave his great body along at what was perilously near a fast gait; at least, it was a gait that was bringing him every moment nearer the man.

CHAPTER XI

LONG–SHANKS ran so well that he turned the corner in the wall of the ravine, where the part of it took its back curve, with the monster still several yards behind him. Then Hop-foot lost the view of them, and could tell what they were doing only by the motions of Sure-dart and Wing-foot, who were now running along that part of the gully-edge. They had left their quivers of darts, as well as their spears, farther up the slope, but they had run to where they were and seized each a spear, and were now again at the edge of the rock. But just here, with their spears still in their hands, they passed behind some trees and bushes, and Hop-foot lost even that vague guide as to what was going on.

He stayed where he was a moment longer, feeling a kind of dread to follow the chase and find out what had happened, but he pulled himself together then, and crossed over to where the gully ended, to the point where his friend and Wing-foot had vanished among the trees.

He did not have to go the whole distance to learn the result. Before he was at the borders of the trees he heard a smothered yell, followed by a shout from the bank, and on the heels of that an angry howl,— it was the animal-like note of a Rock-man, and he thought it was the voice of Wing-foot. After that an instant of silence.

"He's dead," said Hop-foot to himself.

He slowed down to a walk, dreading more than ever to go on, and almost faltered when Sure-dart came running out of the woods. Sure-dart had parted with his spear, and was empty-handed, and his look was very grave.

"You'd better not go over there," he said, nodding in the direction of the trees. "It's a bad sight. I am going down to stay with him — with the body — till Bull-head comes. We shall probably bury him there."

Hop-foot, in spite of his savage blood and training, and notwithstanding what he had seen and known of violent deaths, was deeply shocked.

"And I almost feel that it was my fault," he followed a first exclamation by saying. "If I hadn't started to chase the scamperer it wouldn't have happened."

"Oh, you needn't feel like that," said Sure-dart, comfortingly; "nobody could lay any blame on you."

Nevertheless, Hop-foot looked troubled, and drew a long breath. But as Sure-dart, who had begun to move on, was saying something else, Hop-foot rather startled him by throwing back his head, and breaking out in a fierce barbarian snarl.

"Where is the beast, Sure-dart? What became of him? Is he out of our reach? Didn't you at least plant a spear in him?"

"Yes," said Sure-dart, his own usually pleasant face darkening, "we both did that, but he got away.   After he killed Long-shanks — it took him only a moment — he shook out the spears we had planted in him, and made off.   He went up a sloping place in the other bank."

"Well, and is he to get away?"   Hop-foot stood straight, his eyes full of rage, and the cords showing along his strong little jaws.

Sure-dart, who had less of this revengeful spirit, and who did not forget that Thorn-tail was a mere beast and with almost no intelligence, shook his head.   "I don't know.   It will be as Bull-head says.   I should like to pay him for what he has done, but still, it is n't as if a man had done it.   I don't suppose he knew any better. But I am losing time, and I must go."

He started on, and Hop-foot, still full of wrath, turned in the direction of the higher land, where he had left Bull-head and the others.   The boy had gone only a few steps, however, when something flashed upon him, and he stopped and turned.   Sure-dart, to his surprise, had done the same thing.

"The scamperer," said Sure-dart, "what are we going to do with him?"

"That was what I was going to speak of. Do you suppose he is there still?"

"Most likely, but at least, we can quickly tell. Do you still want him?"

"I don't know," said Hop-foot, with a sigh. "This dreadful thing happening on account of him almost — Oh, there he comes!   Catch him! Stop him!"

The impulse of the hunter and pet-lover combined was a little too much for the sadness of the occasion, and Hop-foot for the moment forgot his regret and anger, and thought only of the escaping scamperer. The little creature had come up the steep bit of path again, and was showing his head above the bank. At the moment he was looking timidly and inquiringly around.

Sure-dart caught just a bit of the fever also, and started toward him. When pretty close he stopped, picked up the abandoned rope, and turned one end into a noose. This done, he started along, moving now slowly and glidingly, and at the moment when the scamperer, at last taking fright, was wheeling to go back to his shelf, he gave the lasso a skilful fling. He had done something in that line before, and his aim now was so true that the noose dropped squarely over the scamperer's head and slipped down upon his neck.

" Hold him! " shouted Hop-foot, skipping to Sure-dart's side, and catching hold of the rope.

" The anchor-stones will do a good deal of the holding," answered Sure-dart, " and if you will just keep your grip I can fix things all right."

Hop-foot accordingly got a good brace, and with the stones was able to hold the creature, though the little fellow, jumping about like a deer, and now and then throwing himself almost on his haunches, made a surprisingly good fight. Sure-dart was quickly at his side, and in a very few moments had whipped a spare end of the rope (one he had cut off) about the strong little legs, and with slight further trouble he brought

" ' Hold him ! ' shouted Hop-foot, skipping to Sure-dart's side "

the legs into a bunch, and rolled the prisoner upon his side.

"Now stay with him, and see that he does n't get up," said Sure-dart. "Some of the others will be here soon. I must n't lose any more time. I ought to be down there now, to protect the body from wild creatures."

"Look out for Thorn-tail," cautioned Hop-foot, as he was leaving; "he might take the notion to come back."

"Not much danger," answered Sure-dart, "for he must be pretty sore, with one hurt and another; and now that his fit of ugliness has spent itself he will want to be quiet. That is the way with about all his kind. The regular flesh-eaters are different."

He hastened along, taking a piece of the rope with him, and by securing it about a rock near the shelf was able to slide down the rest of the way into the ravine.

It will not take long to tell the few other things that were done before the party again took up its march. Long-shanks was buried, an unsuccessful search was made for the thorn-tail, and shortly afterwards Bull-head gave the order to start. Sure-dart had made a sort of head-halter for the scamperer, and untied its legs, and it was thus able to walk, but it proved to be about all both boys could do to lead it. In fact, it was not all the time a business of leading, but part of the time of following, and of lively following at that. Once it caught Hop-foot off his guard, and gave such a jump that it landed him on his stomach, Sure-dart nearly tripping over him. However, there were some signs that the little fellow was becoming resigned to his fate, and in time might be tamed.

Once started, the party covered the ground at a good rate, and long before dark, Bull-head keeping his landmarks carefully ranged, the peculiar hill, or low mountain, with its deep shelf, came in view.

The mountain might perhaps have been called merely a high hill, though the top was several hundred feet above the level of the plain, and fully two hundred above the comparative level at its foot. The shelf was about fifty feet above the ground below, and something like a hundred feet long. It was reached by a natural path that ran up steeply from a flat of open ground, and ended gradually at the western swell of the hill itself, this final point being a great face of bald but slightly seamed rock. Above the path the rock, in places mixed with earth and a few bushes and creepers, went up almost perpendicularly to the crest of the mountain itself. Back of this crest the rocks and earth sloped down to the general level below, and were broken here and there by ridges and hollows. It would therefore be easy to climb up from that side. From the point where the little natural path started the mountainside rose sharply almost to the summit, and this face was composed mainly of great slabs of granite-like rock, though with some outcroppings, near the top, of the bluish and cream-colored chalks that were so common in that region.

The path was narrower at the top than at the

bottom; and it required only a glance to show that it had been formed by the giving way of a great upper section of the rock-face, followed, perhaps for hundreds, or even thousands of years, by the action of rains and floods, and very likely, also, of earth disturbances. At that time the Rocky Mountains, which were the great blue heights to be seen across the plain, were but newly pushed out of the earth; and the tremendous up-heaving and down-tumbling of that region were not, even then, fully over. There were still occasional earthquakes, and volcanic spoutings; some of these the older people could remember, and declared that they were frightful and terrifying beyond what they could put into words.

The shelf, then, was a natural fort of great strength, and especially so for the character of the simple warfare of that day. The spring where the defenders could get water was among the rocks in the level stretch on the southern face of the mountain, and scarcely two hundred paces from the foot of the path; therefore this prime necessity was convenient in case of only a short warning of an attack.

But with all these great and even singular advantages, the place had yet one weakness. This was the openness of the shelf, which was not shielded from one dangerous kind of attack. An enemy on the crest above could shower down stones or darts, or could even carry up great rocks and roll them down. Besides, in the power-ful heat that at times must beat upon the place, any sort of food would quickly spoil. To be sure, the barbarian stomachs of the garrison would not rebel at a moderate taint, but even that limit would soon be passed. Then, too, the weak and infirm of the company would wilt and give way, and even the strong warriors would be more or less affected. It was clear, then, that a change in the present natural conditions must be made before the place would be wholly what they wanted.

Of course all this was not at once apparent to Bull-head and his company, as they came up; but it will be easier and more convenient to state it here, giving it in some order of connection. At the moment Bull-head noted merely the general features, and some of his men gave no close heed at all. They saw, just here, the others of the chief's band appear on the shelf and signal a welcome, and this took their whole present attention.

There were the usual clicking and chattering when the two bands were at last together, but they were suspended when it was seen that Long-shanks was missing, and when Bull-head, at the command of Big-axe, made his explanations. This primitive military report was very brief and to the point, and was not bolstered up with any excuses. Bull-head, with no show of emotion, merely said:

"Long-shanks was killed by a thorn-tail. He was trying to catch a scamperer — the one over there. Hop-foot wanted the scamperer, and I let Long-shanks and some of the others help him. We hunted for a little while for the thorn-tail, but could n't find him. We saw no signs of the Fishers, though we waited in the old camp over night."

Big-axe knit his brows, and it was easy to see

that he was disturbed and displeased. Still, he did not at once speak, and when he did, it was with seeming calmness.

" I am sorry to lose so good a warrior as Long-shanks, and wish that there was more to reconcile us to his death. Had you reported him killed by the Fishers, I should have been content. Yet that cannot now be helped, and so I can merely speak of him, as I do now, as a good man, and promise that his family shall be cared for. As for the Fishers, though they seem to have turned back, I think they have done so only for the time. I believe they will by and by follow us, and that we shall again have to fight them."

He said no more for the moment, and turned soberly away. The company about him broke up, and Bull-head and his party mingled with the others.

That evening Sure-dart, happening to be near Big-axe and Bull-head as they were talking together, found out what the chief meant to do to strengthen the defences of the camp. It was to be made more of a fort by digging into the face of the mountain just above the path, and making a long, shoal, covered way there, so that the party could hide from a missile attack from above, and also get out of the fierce sunlight. It would likewise then be possible to keep food longer fresh, and to care better for the supply of water. Should an attacking force, on the other hand, dare to slide down the face of the rock, or to come up by the path, the besieged could dash out at them, and with no enemy to trouble them by an attack from behind, could doubtless sweep the shelf clear.

The outward end of this covered way, it seemed, was to be close to the head of the path, and a breastwork of stones was to defend the path itself.

The next day the chief set about executing this very plan, and every man, woman, and child who could do anything to help was put to work. Big-axe himself, while directing the others, also labored vigorously.

Poorly as these savages were off for tools, they still were able to accomplish what we must regard as rather surprising results. With their strong arms, tough hands, and good wind, they worked steadily and energetically, and the comparatively soft chalks of the lower rocks broke rapidly away. There were also, as has been noted, some patches of earth and bushes, and of course these were quickly disposed of. When the men struck a mass of the granite, they gave up at that point and resumed at the first workable place. To be sure, this plan made it impossible to keep an open communication throughout, but these cut-offs of hard rock were never more than a few feet in extent, and there would be no great risk, even with an enemy on the crest above, in dodging from one point to another. As for any danger from below, the distance was too great for the ordinary cast of a spear. Besides all this, the chief had a further plan by which they were to cut down some trees, and in places make a cover or sloping roof to the shelf. In addition, it would serve to enlarge their living quarters. As a mere matter of comfort, too, they could lay a stone wall at any point along the shelf they liked, carrying it close to the margin, and then make a roof of logs. These would make what were in effect square huts, with rock and earth backs.

But at present not so much was thought of comfort as of defence, and all that was attempted was to dig out the covered way, and make the breastwork at the head of the path. This last was only a small matter, but they were unable, before nightfall, to make more than a beginning on the other.

The next day all were hard at it again, though now a few were directed to go after some game and to bring water. They had various kinds of hides and skins to hold the water, and convenient places under the covered way, in the chalk formations, could be dug out to hold more, but a safe and reliable supply of food was a more troublesome question. Now they missed the lake, with its boundless supply of fish, and the marsh country, with its turtles and many kinds of small lizards. It was at this time that some of the workers, both men and women, began to grumble, saying that they thought so much hard work unnecessary, for they did not believe the Fishers would trouble them again. For their part, they said, they were for staying here only a short time, and then, as the Fishers would be pretty surely out of the way, they would go back to their old home. To this company of grumblers, it should be said, did not belong Sure-dart, the veteran Iron-arm, or even Bull-head.

At first Big-axe paid no attention to the talk, but by afternoon it had become louder and more open, and when it was taken up by a few of the warriors it seemed time to notice it. Big-axe therefore passed the word along to stop work, and called the whole company about him. He stepped upon a large stone, that all might easily hear him, and without any preamble began.

"Some of you are grumbling at this work," he said, "and think it is useless. These same grumblers would also like to go back to the lake. Well, what do they know about the Fishers, and their ways? I say, after fighting them, and knowing them, that they are not the kind to hold so lightly, and that I believe we shall hear from them again. Remember, they would get much good eating out of us, and would make slaves of those they did not want to eat at once. Then, too, they would have our caves, and would have all the fishing of that part of the lake to themselves. With so many things to tempt them, and with a chief as cunning and persevering as Long-spear, think you they will give up, and let us alone? I tell you no, and I am going to plan according to that belief. If you are not satisfied, find out what others agree with you, and if more than half finally take your side, I will, of course, following the custom, abandon the plan. But in that case I will no longer be your chief. I shall leave you and, with those that choose to follow me, shall cross the plain to the great mountains. I had rather risk the unknown flashes from the ground [so the Rock-people, knowing little of fire, spoke of the flames from the fire-holes and craters of the still unsettled and disturbed mountains], and whatever other dangers may be there, than stay here, and perhaps fall into the hands of the Fishers. Make your choice forthwith, and let me know it."

This speech, very long for a Rock-man, and spoken with decision, had an immediate and decisive effect. The grumblers looked blank and did not open their mouths, and the others joined in a shout of indorsement and approval. It was all settled, and in less than a minute every back was bending again to the work.

It was now that Sure-dart, who had himself been inclined to think rather lightly of the danger from the Fishers, changed his mind, and was ready to believe that the shrewd and experienced chief knew what he was about, and was taking no precaution that wise care did not warrant. Thus stimulated anew, and rested by the little delay, he went to work with fresh energy. He noticed that the others about him did the same.

About dark the hunters came in, and though they brought little game they had a good excuse, and a strange story it was. Sure-dart and the rest for the time forgot even the Fishers in listening to it.

CHAPTER XII

THERE is no need to give the hunters' story in their own words. At best it would have to be interpreted out of what we should call a monkey-like chattering, broken with queer clicking, and set off with many gestures. In substance the account was this: The hunters, having found nothing worth killing in the edge of the woods or along the farther borders of the hills, had pushed straight out into the plain. Here, besides dry, almost bare ground, cut up in places with little ravines, or thrown into volcanic knobs and mounds, were small fertile spots, and these made irregular groups of the nature of oases. There were groups of palms as the principal trees, but also a few other kinds, and strong undergrowth, and the usual rush-like grasses.

The hunters pushed out to the nearest of these small land-bound islands, and stopped to eat a few of the nuts that some of the palms bore — a sort of scrubby variety of cocoanut, and almost tasteless, yet containing a little milk. They were stretched under the trees, in the welcome shade, and were paying no particular attention to things out of their immediate sight, when they heard a little distressed sort of squealing, and in from the open plain beyond rushed a scamperer. He was bleeding from a gash in one of his flanks, and was so wildly frightened that at first he did not seem to notice the hunters. They all scrambled up, not knowing what next to expect, or what kind of pursuer they should have to deal with, and for the instant paid no further attention to the scamperer. He swerved a little, and plunged into the tangle of border trees and bushes.

The four men drew cautiously back to the foot of a large palm, and made ready their weapons. They thought that the unknown beast could hardly be one of the great lizards, for those creatures rarely strayed so far from the low marsh country. Possibly it might be a terror-bird, and if so the four should easily be able to dispose of him. In fact, they thought they could vanquish a pair, supposing that they had the rather hard luck to meet them. They were aware that the feathered giants often hunted in pairs, a male being accompanied by his mate. This idea of the fighting-powers of the birds, it is well to say, was based on second-hand knowledge; it so happened that none of the party had even seen one of the creatures. They were all young men who had never been in this region before.

But rather to their surprise no pursuer appeared. They waited several minutes, meanwhile peering through the openings among the trees and bushes, but not a creature above an insect came in sight. They now began to think that the scamperer had come a longer distance than they had at first supposed, and that its panic had continued even after it was out of danger.

Finally satisfied as to this, they lowered their

weapons, and went back to the bit of clear space, where they had been at first. Here they picked up the nuts they had left, and then started for a little exploration of the neighborhood. In particular, they meant to search a bit of spur of this oasis that lay farther out toward the plain, and while they were about it to scan the plain itself.

They carried out this plan, but at first made no discovery. There was no dangerous creature in the spur-oasis, and none in sight in the open immediately around. But after this they took a longer range, and especially they scanned the tree-border of a large oasis directly to the west. Here, after a little uncertainty, their keen eyes made out some moving objects. They stood still and watched them, and by and by first one and then another came out clear of the trees, and in the strong light it was then certain what they were.

Their general look was that of gigantic herons, though herons, as we know them, had not yet appeared on the stage. It was difficult, at this distance, and with no other creatures near as a gauge, to say how big they were, but they were certainly taller than ordinary men, and they were more bulky than our modern ostriches. They had tufts of feathers on their heads, and seemed to have stout beaks. By the way they moved they seemed to trust mainly to their legs, and not to be much good at flying. Their color was not easy to be sure of, but it was sober, and inclined to brown, and at least the feathers were nowhere showy. There could be no further doubt; these great creatures were terror-birds.

The hunters talked a little, and decided to stay where they were, keeping in sight, and giving the birds a chance to make war if they were so inclined. If they were peaceful and stayed where they were, then the hunters would let them alone. It would be too great a risk to go out and attack them in the open. Still their great bodies, tough though the flesh might be, would be a valuable addition to the scanty meat supply of the camp, and the hunters were willing to take somewhat more than an ordinary chance.

This plan decided on, the four moved out a bit farther into the plain, and there stood, and finally walked about, of course watching the birds keenly meanwhile. It was soon evident that the feathered giants saw them, for first one great head was raised, and then the other, and for at least half a minute the two stood almost rigid, and gazed. This, the hunters said, was both exciting and a little trying.

But at last the heads went slowly down again, the two shot out their long necks this way and that, as if undecided, and finally both stalked slowly off. They kept on in the same direction that they had originally been going, which was nearly north.

This gave the hunters new confidence in themselves, and a measure of contempt for the birds. They agreed that the stories about them had been colored, and that the creatures were not half so savage or anxious to dine on human flesh as had been made out.

Paying little further heed to them, the men also turned north, keeping along parallel to the birds' course, and crossed to the next oasis. Here they found more nuts, some edible berries, and, to their surprise and pleasure, the dead body of the wounded scamperer. The deep gashes in its sides and flanks had drawn so much blood that it had been unable to get any farther.

For convenience the hunters cut him up, and divided the pieces among them, the whole giving them, with the nuts and other things, a fair load each. Here, as they owned, they should have considered their work done, and have turned back to the fort. Instead of doing so, they deliberately pushed out into the plain and headed for the oasis that the birds had quitted. They had a little hope of finding some of the monsters' huge eggs, and if they did they would have both a trophy and something additional to eat.

They reached the oasis without mishap, and the birds did not turn back, or at least they did not at the time. In fact, they were not observed to look around. The place was very much like the others, and the hunters found only a few valuable nuts, and no eggs. They were soon ready to leave; and now they felt that they had wasted some of their time, for they were a pretty good distance from home, the sun beat down in waves of heat in the open places, and they had little to show for their extra work. They were about to start when one of them suggested that they stop long enough to get a look from the western side of the place, toward the mountains, and as this would not take long, the others were willing. They crossed to the outside fringe of trees, therefore, and looked forth, and at once they made a little discovery.   At a spot not far out in the plain there were some low, rocky ridges, from the midst of which rose a faint, white, steamy cloud.   It looked like the clouds that they had seen rise from the great mountains themselves, only whiter, and of course infinitely smaller.

It was in reality a smoke, but they did not know it.   None of them had ever before seen one near at hand, and they had never been within long miles of a fire.   It was known that there were fire-holes in the skirts of one spur of the mountains, and one wandering hunter had been burned by going too near.   Beyond that the nearest that any of the party had seen a flame was when a mighty sheet, perhaps when the earth was rocking, had shot skyward, quickly dying out again, or had trembled waveringly for a longer time along the torn crest of some rent and sinking ridge.   They had also seen fire springing up from trees struck by lightning, but again not near at hand.   They looked at this near-at-hand wonder now, and immediately resolved to have a still closer look at it.   They started on the instant, and made quick work of crossing the short distance to the ridges.

The first ridge was like a low wall, its sides yellowed as with some powerful stain, and entirely bare of vegetation.   There was a deal of fine, powdered stone, dark in color, on the top and farther slope of the ridge, and this drift, as it might be called (it lay in a manner like drifted sand on the seashore), continued to the next ridge.   They kept on, crossed the next ridge also, and then came abruptly upon the mystery.

From the middle of a small basin, and shut in by the ridges, was rising the strange white cloud, and it drove up from a rocky hole as big as a modern cart-wheel. All about the powdered stone was yellow and reddish, and they saw that a fine spray was falling on it from the cloud. Down in the hole itself, at but a short distance, was what appeared to be water, but it was in motion, as if somebody was stirring it, rolling, and popping, and now and then flying in a little jet upwards.

They had already begun to notice a slight, queer smell, and this, as they came nearer the mysterious hole, grew stronger and more insistent. It was not a pleasant smell, and they stopped before they were quite at the hole, feeling a little doubtful about the effect of it. Finally, they skirted the hole and looked over the next little ridge. Here, to their surprise, were very few of the stained rocks, and powdered stones, but there was another mysterious hole near the middle of a small basin or hollow. This, too, was bubbling, and otherwise in a bit of turmoil, but it did not throw up much of a spray. As there was this time no strange odor, they went boldly up to the hole, and one of them stooped and thrust his finger into the water.

He drew it out with a yell, and jumped back. In his pain he relaxed his hold of his piece of the scamperer's flesh, and it dropped into the hole.

The others were of course amazed and startled, and asked the dancing experimenter what had happened. He held up his finger, which was very red, and looked as if it might have been sun-baked, and snarled that the water was hot. He looked around for something to relieve the pain, but finding nothing, he left them, and made off over the nearest ridge, to the plain. They understood that he had gone to dig up a little cool earth, in which to wrap the finger. This was one of their ordinary remedies for such mild burns as they had needed to deal with. Pieces of falling stone, picked up thoughtlessly by hunters, when the mountains had been spitting them out, was the limit of a burning substance that they were familiar with.

They thought they would get the piece of meat out of the hole, and follow; one of them, after a little prodding with his spear, found it, and started to lift it out. Just then the fellow who had so suddenly left them, popped as suddenly into sight again. In fact, he was moving faster than before, and his face showed trouble considerably greater. It was not now pain, but fright.

" They are coming," he shouted — " the terror-birds!"

This very nearly threw the others into a panic. They looked at one another, and made no move either to fight or to run. But then, as the other man came up, and pluckily seized his spear, they pulled themselves together, and as he was hastily saying that the birds were already nigh, they spread out in line, and with him fell back to the slope of the nearest ridge. They stooped, gripped their spears firmly, and were now as ready for the strange battle as they could be.

The enemy was very quickly at hand. Up over the crest of the farther little westerly ridge shot

a great, flat-topped head, with wide-apart eyes
and a huge, curved bill. After the head came
a long neck, feathered, and as big around as a
strong man's arm. Next there shot up a broad-
chested body, feathered also, and supported by
two sturdy legs. These legs were as big as
little saplings, and looked about as rough and
strong. The feet were made up of long, strong
toes, ending in sharp claws. These claws curved
upward a little, and their points did not press
hard upon the ground. Consequently, they were
but little blunted. They might be said to match
the great, curved bill, which looked somewhat
like an eagle's, but was far larger. It was as big,
indeed, as the end of a modern ice-pick, and was
fully as sharp. The creature must have weighed
more than a large man, and was nearly all bones
and great muscles. It towered above the tallest
of the hunters a good two feet.

It was barely up in full view, when its terrible
mate shot up beside it. The two stopped for a
moment, one of them gave a little harsh cry, and
the next instant they both thrust their dreadful
heads straight out, and in this goose-fashion, and
flapping their stubs of wings, they almost sailed
down the slope, and shot like living engines up
the other rise, and upon the waiting men.

Not one of the men could tell exactly what
happened then. As one of them said, the air
seemed full of great gaping red mouths and
giant bills and claws. Though the two men that
mainly received the shock had each held his spear
steadily, and at a good angle, and though each
had seemed to get the weight of a bird's body on

his point, yet each had been upset and knocked upon his back, and both birds had been able to whirl and plunge at the others. Luckily the other two had stood in flanking fashion, looking a bit inward, and so had found a chance, as the birds broke past them, to put in each a vigorous thrust. Now, placed separately on their defence, they had drawn their spears back, and each drove home a stiff and powerful thrust.

They also were bowled over, though not quite so completely as the first two had been, and with a scramble were up again. One had a deep groove of a wound in his arm, where a claw or one of the great beaks had driven along, but the other was unhurt. Desperate now, and furious almost as the birds themselves, they caught their stone axes from their girdles, and rushed in, smashing blow on blow.

It was all confusion and wild desperation. The other two men, already on their feet, joined in. Hitherto none of them had dared to uncover the defence of his spear to throw a dart, but now the headmost fellow pulled one from the case, and drove it with his hand into the exposed side of the nearer bird. He had not time to drop the shaft of the dart before a side-kick sent him heels over head and ripped a strip of flesh from his shoulder.

Here the case seemed desperate enough, and it looked as if the men would soon be mere mangled flesh. But this was not to be, for as the last man was twirled from his legs, his nearest companion smashed so hard a blow down upon the thrust-out head of the second bird, that the creature pulled up short, and then settled slowly to the ground. It was in the other bird's way for an instant, and in that brief time three of the hunters were in a rough line again, two with ready axes, and one with his spear. The man last kicked over was so dazed and shaken that he still lay on the ground.

The little break in the fight proved also to be near the end of it. The bird that was still on its feet saw that its mate was down, and looked that way, seeming to be surprised, and perhaps daunted. It was at this precise moment that the youngest and quickest-motioned of the hunters let fly a dart, and caught the standing bird in the middle of its long neck. The skin and flesh were so tough and hard that the dart went in but a little way, and then dropped out, and the bird merely drew back a step, and gave itself a shake. Nevertheless, some harm was done, and the result was strangely important.

The bird stopped where it was, and began to stretch its neck, and then to draw it in, as if it had been taken with a severe cramp. While it was still at this the other bird showed signs of coming to, and a moment later gave a lurch, and with the aid of its wings got upon its legs. The hunters were getting their breath, and preparing for more hot work, but at this crisis they discovered that there was to be none. With wings hanging down, and moving feebly, the bird that had just risen began to walk slowly away. Its mate, still in trouble on its own account, saw it, and after a hesitating moment slowly followed. There was not the slightest disposition to stop them, and quickly they were over the westerly ridge and out of sight.

Relieved, and glad to get off so, the hunters waited a full minute or two. Feeling then that they were safe, and that the terrible creatures were not coming back, they lowered their spears, and turned to go. All four were more or less hurt, but none was crippled, and they were anxious to put as much good ground between themselves and the feathered giants as possible. Considering how seriously wounded the birds had appeared to be, this was speaking well for their fighting qualities. The hunters, in fact, were sure that their victory was in part due to luck and to the heedless and rather stupid way in which the birds had charged. Had they known enough to separate as they came on, and attack the flankers instead of the centre, they would have bothered the defenders, and would themselves have escaped the flankers' side-thrusts.

The party had proceeded but a few steps, when one of them thought of the lost piece of meat. It was still in the hot water, where the man who had started to spear it out had left it. They thought it was probably spoiled, yet might be worth saving, and one man ran back, and with his spear forked it out. He had to let it lie on the ground for a few moments to cool, but as soon as he could handle it he dumped it into a piece of lizard hide, made a bundle of it, and slung it over his shoulder. A little later, at the last oasis, they stopped and bound up their wounds; after that they made no halt.

Nothing else had happened, and so here at last

they were, their cuts and bruises witnessing their story. The scamperer's flesh, too, which they had dropped at the top of the path, was further evidence.

One thing they were prompt to say — they would never again speak lightly of a terror-bird!

CHAPTER XIII

A DUBIOUS PROSPECT

THE curiosity of the camp was now turned toward the piece of cooked scamperer. It must be remembered that eating and drinking, to an uncivilized people, is a matter of the first interest, and it is so the more that the getting of food of any kind is often a business of great labor and trouble.

They crowded around the whitened and (to them) strange-looking piece of flesh, and begged the chief for some trial morsels. He gave each a small piece, and tried one himself.

"I like it," immediately declared one young man.

"I call it rather flat," said an older one.

The veteran Stone-arm ate his piece in silence.

"What do you think of it?" the chief asked him.

"Not very bad as to the taste, but I am not so sure about it on some other accounts," he answered. "If we were to eat it right along we might grow delicate, and perhaps lose our strength and vigor. I think it would be safer to go on in the old way, and not risk experiments."

This opinion was indorsed by several others, all, however, middle-aged or oldish people. Some of the younger ones thought the cooking an improvement, and were for treating more meat in the same way. They had meanwhile put a little salt on one piece, and those who tried it declared that it tasted much better than the raw meat. They also told Stone-arm that he was prejudiced, and had no reason to give for his fears.

This was pretty evidently true; even if he were right he could not at this time know that he was, for he had not yet had the experience. Nevertheless, the old man would not take back anything, or say that he might not be right, but instead (there was a little of our common human nature here) he maintained his idea with the more positiveness. In fact, he had not been really positive at first, but now he seemed to be. His main argument was that cooked meat was not natural meat, and that any departure from nature was dangerous. To this, again, the others answered that they already bruised and water-soaked some of the roots they ate, and that some had also found it agreeable and resulting in no harm to bury a piece of very bloody meat for a while in hot sand.

Finding himself worsted, the old man began to lose his temper, and was starting to retort with true savage bluntness and directness, when the chief broke in.

" We have got more important things to do," he said, " than to wrangle. We should be planning the work for the morrow. Stone-arm, I want your advice about extending the covered way."

This broke up the discussion which, indeed, might have led to something unpleasant, if not serious, and the principal warriors went aside with Big-axe, and joined in considering the plans for the future work.

But it was soon clear that even some of the older fighting men were beginning to think that perhaps the chief was overcautious. As time went by it looked less and less likely that the Fishers would trouble them, and it really did seem as if they might dispense with a part of the hard labor. They were already in a good state of defence, they thought.

Big-axe soon discovered the feeling, and this time he determined to answer them with something more than mere belief and opinion. He decided to send out a scouting party. " Yes, to the very neighborhood of the Fisher village, if that should be necessary," he wound up by saying.

There was no " red tape," like that of modern times, to bother him, and it took not over twenty minutes to complete the arrangement, and pick out the men. The party was to start at daylight next morning.

As there might be discovery and pursuit, only the fastest runners were chosen. Wing-foot was the speediest of them all, the others being three of the younger warriors. Wing-foot, who was cunning and prudent, as well as fleet, was to command. At first Sure-dart thought he was to be one, but for some reason — certainly not one that was uncomplimentary to him — he was passed over.

It was between sixty and seventy miles to the village, and if the scouts went as far as that they could not be expected to return before the noon of the second day. In fact, it might easily take them well into the day after that. But of course this was on the theory that the party might be obliged to go the whole distance. It was likely — or so, at least, Big-axe thought — that they would not need to go so far. He reasoned that the Fishers, if they meant to strike at all, would be at it soon, before the Rock-people could thoroughly entrench themselves, and so they might have a war-party already on the way.

As in many cases before, his judgment proved sound. The scouts got away at daybreak, but it was hardly an hour past noon when they broke out of the woods again, significantly waving their arms. Their story was short. The Fishers were not two hours behind them.

Then was commotion, and a swift turning to Big-axe as the one man for the hour. Those who had fussed and fretted, and some who had thought him overcautious, joined now with the most timid in ignoring all but him, and crowding up for orders.

He, in turn, was ready. He found no fault, and reproached nobody, and he set every man, woman, and large child to work. Some brought up water, and put it in the hollowed stones; others distributed food at convenient places along the covered way; and still others worked like giants in finishing the blocking up of the path. Some of the largest stones, for convenience, had not been pushed quite into their places. These were now handled, and shoved squarely across the path. The farther side was made as steep as possible, but on the inside they left places where they could climb up and use their darts and spears. The whole barricade was now fully ten feet high.

The plan of widening the covered way by building along the outside edge of the path a low wall, and then roofing it with trees, they had not been able to carry out. There had not been time. However, Big-axe and a few others had personally lugged up several small trees, and started one stretch of the outside wall; this extra bit of covered way the chief and his son, putting out their great strength, were now able to finish. It was not more than ten feet long, by about six feet wide, but it was likely to prove of great use. The tops of the trees were set in little notches in the cliff, and the big ends were jammed into spaces in the wall. The trees, being green, and of tough kinds of wood, must present a considerable resistance, even to large falling stones, and they would do so the more that they were untrimmed. The branches on some of them were half as big as the trees themselves.

After an hour or so the men on the wall began to look for the enemy, for of course there was no knowing just when they would come. They might be going faster or slower than when the scouts saw them, according to whether they were planning a swift and headlong attack, or a crafty delay. It might easily be, for that matter, that they would put off the assault till dark. Big-axe was rather of the opinion that the cautious and crafty Long-spear would do so, not knowing, as it might be supposed, that the little garrison was using the time to such good advantage.

It turned out somewhat in this way, but not exactly. There was no alarm for nearly four hours, but then some bushes on an easterly knoll seemed to sway more than the wind would account for, and a second later a shaggy human head poked out. It was drawn rather leisurely back again, but only to be followed, an instant later, by a half-naked body, and Long-spear himself straightened up and looked that way.

While he was still doing this, and by his slow and deliberate manner seeming to mock and sneer at them, other bushes swayed and gave way, and a whole long line of the wolfish figures spread out in the open.

Big-axe was standing on one of the highest rocks of the path barricade, and carefully counted the bounding figures, as one after another broke into sight and joined the line. Anxious as he was, he seemed every whit as cool as Long-spear himself.

There were now forty men in the straggling line, and it seemed that this must be just about the whole possible number. Behind Big-axe, as he stood on the rock, were drawn up just twenty-nine men and boys. Only seventeen were really full-grown warriors, and of the boys several were not yet in their teens. Of these was Hop-foot, who was at last, in this extremity, permitted to fight. Moreover, three or four of the men were a little stiff and sore with old wounds, though perhaps they would forget this as the stress of battle came on. Finally, some of the women could be counted on for a kind of weak reserve. If it came to a close fight at the barricade, for instance, they might be of use. Their desperate hands could fling down a heavy stone, or thrust with a spear at a reckless climber.

About this time Long-spear seemed to recognize Big-axe, for he stepped a little forward, and in a mock salute flourished his spear. Big-axe only set his lips a little tighter, and did not seem to heed him. He would not give back insult for insult, but when the time came Long-spear would find him ready with another and more practical answer. Meanwhile, Big-axe looked in other directions, trying to make sure that this was the whole force of the enemy. There were certainly no others in sight, and he was confirmed in his previous belief that Long-spear had few or no more. Even this number seemed to account for about the whole of the chief's fighting force. The village would appear to have been left to the protection of the old men, women, and children.

Big-axe now left the rock and went about giving a few final orders, by his steadiness and a cheerful word or two also trying to hearten his little army.

But for some reason or other the storm did not immediately break. After a few minutes Long-spear turned, and evidently jabbered something, for the whole wolf pack broke from the line, and scattered in a random way about, some straggling off among the trees, and several sprawling out in the first convenient shade. The sun was still warm, notwithstanding the late time of day.

" What do you think they mean? " Bull-head

in perplexity asked his father. Several others were also ready with the same question.

"Perhaps waiting for darkness," answered Big-axe, speaking, however, with a little hesitation. "They may have heard that we were getting ready for them," he went on as with a bit more certainty, "and thought they would do what they could to check it. By showing themselves, they would cut us off from fetching more food or water."

This did seem, on the whole, rather a likely explanation, and Bull-head and the others let it go as the right one. At least, nobody could think of a better.

Dusk soon began to come on; the figures under the trees and sprawled about elsewhere lost distinctness, and where the shade was deep were not easy to make out at all. Still they kept their lazy and unhurried air, and had every appearance of men comfortably and confidently waiting. To a degree this was more wearing and harder mentally to brace up against than an immediate and headlong assault. That would at least stir the blood, and take the whole attention, whereas this eventless delay fretted, and seemed by degrees to wear down the courage.

Suddenly the men placed as sentries at the barricade jumped up, and broke out in dismayed exclamations.

There was a rush that way, eager questions, and Big-axe and the other leaders looked for themselves from the top of the barricade.

It was all grimly plain and simple enough. Without fuss or noise, at least forty more fighting men had come down a little hill-slope just to the north, and had joined Long-spear's band.

There was no puzzle as to the mere fact of this; to the question that naturally followed — Where did the new men come from? — nobody in the fort had at first any sort of answer. One looked at another, and the steadiest seemed for the moment dazed.

Big-axe was the first to rouse himself, and to try both to understand and to face the situation. Without at the moment speaking, he stooped and jumped lightly off the wall, walked a few steps to where the range around was wider, and took a long and careful look.

The swarm on the barricade and at the foot of it meanwhile broke out in talk and apprehensive mumblings, the shock of the surprise having passed to that extent, and a few of the women groaned, and in a restrained fashion wailed.

But in the midst of these noises Big-axe appeared again on the barricade. He had finished his observations, and Bull-head and Stone-arm had flung him down a rope and steadied him up.

The sight of his great massive figure, and still more of his seemingly calm face, checked the noise, and when he jumped down among them and began to speak there was well nigh dead silence.

" These new men are from the far islands," he said. " I can tell by their skewered hair, which they fasten on top of their heads. I have never seen any of them before, but I have heard of them, and I am sure I am right. Other than this they are hardly to be told from the Fishers, though their shields seem to be shorter and broader."

He stopped, and with care tightened his belt.

"But the danger? What shall we do?" cried several in a breath. Again some wailed and groaned.

"Why," he said without change of countenance, "I take it there is only one thing to do. It is what we have been making ready for, and of course it is to fight. I am sure nobody desires to be roasted and eaten."

He waved one drop-jawed fellow aside, and went to where his spear stood.

"What we have before us," he said as he picked it up, "is in one way very simple: we have only to fight till we are all dead, or till the Fishers and their friends have had enough of it. If we all do the best we can, I think they will have a fit of homesickness."

"I, for one, will try to bring that about," with a cold, fighting grin spoke up Stone-arm.

Bull-head, though slower to speak, proved equally ready, and after he had spoken several more joined in. Sure-dart and little Hop-foot were among these, the lame boy adding a thump of his spear against his shield. The tide of despair now seemed to have turned, and though more than one, looking through the growing obscurity at the swarm of dusky shapes, fetched a sharp breath, or mumbled to himself, still, there was a general brightening, and those who were to fight stood up straighter, and moved their weapons about with steadier hands.

And yet, Big-axe himself, being for a moment

alone, set his lips together till they made only a thin line, and the light went out of his face, leaving it like the face of a sick man.

He knew what the end was altogether likely to be!

CHAPTER XIV

BUT this giving way was only for a few minutes; after that, by a mighty effort, the chief pulled himself together, and was again his sturdy and composed self. When he went back among the others he seemed as grimly cool as before. It is possible that the moment of partial collapse had been in reality a bit of saving relaxation from the dreadful strain, and that he afterwards kept up the better on account of it.

By this time the figures on the hill-slopes were so dim and vague that there was no longer any use in trying to make sure of them; the watchers at the barricade gave it up, and merely sat about glumly, keeping their attention only on the open stretch at the foot of the hill. It now began to be decidedly uncertain whether the besiegers would attack that night or not. In fact, on some further consideration, Big-axe began to think that there was to be no immediate assault, and probably none till the next day. Then the assailants would be fresh, and would have all their plans fully settled, and they would also gain something by seeing clearly what they were about. As missile weapons of any mentionable range had not then been invented, the objection of a greater exposure by a daylight attack was of slight importance.

The more Big-axe and his experienced fighters discussed the matter, the more inclined they were to believe that this guess was the right one, and that they should see and hear nothing more of Long-spear and his swarm till the next day.

Yet as this was merely a guess, the chief would not depend on it, and made the same preparations for a night attack as he had arranged before. He sent two active men down to the foot of the rock, where they were ordered to scout around, and report the first sign of danger; and he kept five men at the barricade. A rope made of the creeper stuff was dropped down, so that the scouts, if they had to make a dash of it home, could climb quickly up. A point about half-way along the path, where the rising face of the cliff was not quite so steep as in some other places, and where desperate and active men might slide down, was specially watched and guarded, and the old people and others who were not expected to fight were ordered to get under a part of the cut-out rock. This was not merely to give these helpless ones better protection, but also to leave more fighting-room for the warriors.

There was now another time of suspense, perhaps as trying as any thus far. The moon was not due for a considerable while, and then it might be clouded over; meanwhile, it would be almost absolutely dark. The chief had ordered all talk to cease, and this made the time seem to pass more slowly, and added to the nervous tension. Everybody was listening for boding sounds, and it is not surprising that a good many thought they heard them. This went on till the moon at last rose, and it became possible to make sure of something, and see rather than guess.

Still nothing that turned out to mean danger appeared, and off where the enemy were supposed to be could be heard at intervals minor noises, as if there had been no significant change or stir.

So the night at last wore through, and the gray of daylight came. As the eastern hill-slopes brightened out of the vapors, and the light struck under the trees, lumps that were not stones and stumps came out, and some began to move. The Fishers and the Islanders were still there.

Big-axe immediately took a look about the fort, and then ordered breakfast; there was no knowing what time there would be for it later. After the sun climbed higher, what were left of the night mists were burned up. Still later, and not very long, either, the tingle of the heat began to reach the rocky shelf.

The two scouts at the foot of the hill had been recalled, and everything was again in the old readiness.

" I wish they would begin, if they are going to," said Hop-foot with a long breath. He spoke to Sure-dart. " This waiting is growing harder all the time," he fretfully added.

" I think pretty soon we shall have the enjoyment of the change," Sure-dart grimly answered.

He had never made a surer prophecy, nor one speedier of fulfilment. Hop-foot sniffed a little, and looked at his darts, but he had no more than done it when a little noise came from the barricade; and as the boys glanced that way they saw that the guard and everybody else there had jumped up, and that all were gazing across the open flat.

"Come on!" almost screamed Hop-foot. He began to skip toward the barricade.

But before he was half-way there, though the distance was short, the men on the top of the wall had wheeled and were bellowing down:

"They are coming! they are coming!"

Everybody was at once on the stir; the fighters took their places, and the others crept out of the way into the shelters. A few of the more sturdy of the women, and some of the old men and larger children, fell in behind the warriors, ready to give what help they could. Big-axe had delayed a moment, while he made sure of the disposition of the guard at the rear of the shelf, but now he walked quickly to the barricade, and climbed up. He seemed as cool as ever, and moved without any sign of hurry. He was closely followed by Bull-head. Old Stone-arm had been left to command what should perhaps be called the rear guard.

If Long-spear and his confederates had taken things leisurely before, they made up for it in speed and impetuosity now. As Sure-dart sprang upon the wall, and got the full range of the open below, he found that the whole savage swarm was spread out over it, and were coming on at a run. Just then they broke out in their wild, wolfish howls and unearthly yells.

Though they were not running at top speed, thus saving their wind for the assault itself, yet they came on so fast that it seemed hardly a moment before they were across the open and tearing up the path. They seemed to think that they must surely carry everything before them, and that this one dash would settle the whole matter. At least, it might be inferred so, for Sure-dart saw that they had massed in one long column, and had not sent any men around and to the top of the hill. Even the crafty Long-spear appeared to share the general, almost contemptuous, confidence, and was shouting and tearing along with the rest.

Up the path the head of the wave surged, and now four or five half-naked wild creatures — they could fairly be called that — were trying to spring up the face of the wall itself, using their spears like vaulting poles to help, and yelping like wolves. Those next behind shot up darts and stones, thus in a crude way covering the assault, and still others tried to make a defence of shields.

Big-axe had cautioned every one of the defenders to be careful, for they had not a single man to spare, and therefore they now threw forward their shields, and protected themselves from the first pelting of the darts and stones. As the shower subsided, they coolly lowered their shields, and bent down and thrust hard with their spears. Three of the climbers collapsed and tumbled backward, and a fourth would have gone, only he was supported by the arms of those behind. His head had lopped to one side, and the spear had fallen from his hand. Another jab from above sprawled him out; then those supporting him let him go, and he sank out of sight among them, probably landing on the bodies that had gone down before. For the moment the wall was cleared.

Bull-head began to laugh. "Oh, you disappoint us!" he roared down at them mockingly. "We are waiting for you, and you don't come. Where is the brave Long-spear? Is he tired from the march, that he does not come forward? I should like to take his hand, seeing that he has come so far to visit us!"

This was in true savage style, and proved to hit the mark. Some of the crowd answered with furious howls, and several managed to clear room enough to shoot up their long spears. One of these grazed the ear of Bull-head, but the others kept on harmlessly in the air, and doubtless went off into space. The path curved rather sharply at this point.

"And you can't throw your spears any better than you can climb!" broke out the taunting Bull-head again. "If you will wait, perhaps we will send down some of our little boys, who will teach you!"

But the last words were almost drowned in a fresh din of yelps and howls, and in the midst of them the headmost of the gang made a wild forward rush. The others pressed closely after, as if they meant to thrust the leaders by main force up the wall.

This time the defenders had to do their best, and the best seemed hardly likely to answer. Four of the desperate crew, helped by many hands, got a footing on the wall, and before they were fairly at balance shoved out fiercely with their spears. One Rock-man staggered, and went backward off the wall, and spears from below at the same time reached and pricked the legs of the other defenders. As the first assailants got their full balance, they dropped their spears, and whipped their stone axes from their belts, turning a little then so as to hold that end of the wall.

It was now that Big-axe did that which sent his name down the years in the legends of his people. Dropping shield and spear, and grasping his great axe with both hands, he plunged, as it almost seemed, headlong upon the triumphant four. The axe fell as if it had the force of modern machinery behind it! The man who faced the shock was smashed off his feet, and crushed in, as if he had been a cardboard toy! Then, before the others seemed able to stir, the great mass rose again, swept down, and a second man — this time struck a little at a slant — was swept to one side, and with crushed skull went headlong, as if he had been a clumsy diver, into the jam below.

The rest followed like the quick finish of some game. The great axe went with a *clack* to the stones, as the chief dropped it, and before the two men who were still left could tell what to expect, or how to put themselves on a better defence, the great bulk of the chief was almost in their faces, and one man found his half-raised arm gripped, and himself held like a shield before his mate. One instant so, and then a tremendous shove sent him against the other man, and both staggered, and toppled over backwards,

"It was now that Big-axe did that which sent his name down
the years in the legends of his people"

going with flying, pawing arms down upon the heads beneath.

It was all done so quickly that a few seconds would actually have covered the time. Friends and foes alike fairly gasped, and could not move till it was all over. Then Big-axe was picking up his great weapon, and again quietly covering himself with his shield, and Bull-head and the other defenders were getting the sense of what had happened, and beginning to roar and yell.

It will be guessed that this exploit and sudden turn in the tide of affairs sent the Fishers and their allies nearly wild with fury. They howled and fairly screamed, and as Big-axe stepped back to his place they broke forward once more in a wild and up-boiling human wave.

Sure-dart was standing a little back of the main line of the wall guard, and had not thus far had a chance to put in any work. As this new torrent crashed in, and sent its advance wave flying high, he saw his opportunity. He balanced one of the darts that had given him his name in one hand, and with the other drew his shield closer. Hardly a second later his work was ready for him.

The Rock-man immediately before him staggered back, thrust through the thigh with a spear, and as Sure-dart stepped to one side, the man stumbled and fell. His fall uncovered a short, monkey-built savage, with his reeking spear already drawn back for another thrust. This man, painted dull yellow across his hideous face, had his mop of hair piled on the top of his head, and skewered there by four or five little reed darts. He was one of the strangers from the unknown region, and of the people said to call themselves the Islanders.

The fellow saw Sure-dart just before him, and bent a little for another thrust.

He was quick, but Sure-dart was distinctly quicker. Like a tiny flash of lightning, the little ready dart flew, and though the man threw up his left arm (he had dropped his shield when he made his dash up the wall), the dart scratched across the wrist, and drove straight into one of his gleaming, wicked black eyes. A screech and two hands went to the spot, while the spear clattered down on the stones. It was followed by a shove from an eager savage behind him, and the man dropped helplessly forward on his knees. He was kicked this way and that for the next few seconds, as the fighters rushed past him, or fell back again, and at last dropped, or was knocked back over the wall.

Sure-dart was before this ready with another of his little deadly stings, and it took the next man — who had likewise left his shield behind him — in the right arm, and the pain of it made the arm fall. The ready axe of Bull-head finished this piece of work.

Sure-dart now glanced to the right, to see how things were going there, and was just in time to see the chief parry a spear-thrust with his shield and drive what seemed a death-blow down at a climbing savage.

Sure-dart had no more time for looking around; he stepped in with Bull-head to drive back three or four more scrambling and up-pushing fellows, and for the next few seconds was very busy.

But it had before this become evident that the fire of the rush was dying out, and that the pushing, jabbing, and scrambling up the wall was, in comparison with what it had been, almost languid. The tremendous fight of the defenders, together with the advantage of the wall, and the disadvantage to the assailants of the crowding together in the narrow path, was beginning to make itself felt. All at once there was a jabbering, and some directing cries, and not only the wall, but the space immediately below it, was clear.

Bull-head set up a roaring yell of triumph, and so nearly battle-mad was he that if his father had not just then clutched his arm he would have jumped down and rushed on the retreating throng. He stopped, however, as he felt the powerful grip, and in a moment seemed to get back his senses. The others, except Big-axe, were now also making a triumphant din, which was joined in by the anxious little company behind them. Big-axe merely smiled in a grim and satisfied way, and turned again to watch the further movements of the retreating swarm.

They had taken their dead and wounded with them, dragging the dead by the feet, with their heads trailing along the ground, and were falling back slowly down the path.

CHAPTER XV

THE SECOND ASSAULT

SURE–DART was still on the wall, and here he was now joined by Hop-foot, who was yelping and snorting like some wild animal, which, in fact, we might almost say he was. As he saw the retreating company he set up so high and piercing a screech of triumph that it sounded above every other noise, and made the rear men of the retreating crowd look around. Sure-dart laughed, and slapped the little fellow on the shoulder. There was a shiver of joyful excitement in the laugh that seemed almost like a suggestion of nervous tears.

And now the question was,— What would the sullen and disappointed pack do next? On the face of it they had got such a rebuff that there was no encouragement to try again, but this was merely a first hasty impression. Cool and far-sighted men like Big-axe were of another opinion, and were not ready for any pleasant and rose-colored prophecies. It seemed to the chief that more was to come, though, to be sure, it might come in a different way, but one that might well be more dangerous to the little garrison than the other. There was still to be tried a siege, with all its dangers, and the horrors of hunger and thirst, the thirst intensified by the terrible downpour of the sun on the naked face of the cliff.

It was perhaps from thinking of this that Big-axe, as at last he went down among the company, met the exclamations of joy and relief, and the clamorous boasting of some, with hardly a smile, while his face darkened again, when nobody was looking, with something of the old shadow.

However, the camp in general did not appear to notice, and three out of four seemed to believe that the worst was over, and that Long-spear and his allies would never be able to muster spirit enough even for one more really earnest assault. But Sure-dart, always quick to observe, — he had learned to study the chief's face, — was one of the few who could not bring themselves to such a happy conclusion; his rejoicings were therefore tempered by the thought of what might yet be in store. Nevertheless, following the example of Big-axe, and with a manliness beyond his years, but which his harsh training had helped to bring out, he kept his suspicions to himself, and managed to put on a look as hopeful as he had worn at first.

The retreating party crossed the open again to the shelter of the trees, and Sure-dart and the others could see them lay some of their wounded down, and drag the dead back out of sight. There was a gathering together of the leaders soon afterwards, including Long-spear, but of course the watchers could not tell what they said. The man who seemed to be the chief of the Islanders, and who was a short, squat, oldish savage, apparently of great strength, was seen to flourish his arms about a good deal; several times he stooped, and seemed to illustrate what he said by drawing something on the ground, but this, too, was all "Greek" to the observers. Not long after this the little council broke up, and the leaders, like the others, withdrew into the shade.

As nearly as the Rock-people could tell, this first battle left the respective forces without any great relative change. Only two men of the garrison had been killed, but two had been severely wounded, one, however,— the man thrust through the leg,— being still able to perform some kinds of service. It appeared that there was no poison in the wound, and it had not bled very much, so that he could hobble about, and manage to use a spear, or darts. The other man was entirely disabled. Several others had slight hurts, including the chief, but nothing, for such hardy barbarians, worth mentioning. There were, therefore, fifteen men still in good condition, the warrior with the wounded leg, and half a score of boys. To these could be added, on a pinch, the little band of picked women.

As for the enemy, Big-axe and the others at the barricade thought the total loss, in killed and disabled, must reach ten or twelve. However, this was guesswork, since not even a dead body had been left on the field. In thus taking pains to carry off their dead and wounded, the Fishers and their allies had acted as our modern American savages usually did, though perhaps not wholly from the same motives.

The sun was now getting a good sweep at the

little fort, and everybody, save only a small guard, got as far as possible under cover. Even the guard managed to put up a little awning of lizard skin. There would be no further attack for a while, as even Big-axe felt sure.

The afternoon slowly ran its course, and the light began to fall at a noticeable slant, the heat at the same time losing a little of its disagreeable power. Luckily, the shelf where the garrison was did not face the west, but nearly the south, so that the sky battery of heat did not play upon them broadside on, so to speak. Yet it did reach them in a way to make them decidedly uncomfortable, and cause them to creep under their penthouses of overhanging rock, and the bit of covered way. Everybody was thirsty, and Big-axe was obliged to put a guard over the water supply, for it must be economized, there being no certainty how long the siege would last. At the same time, he did not forget that he must keep up the strength of his fighting men, and that this called for a fair supply of water.

At last, as the west was reddening, and the blue of the distant mountains was darkening almost to black, the human tigers on the hill-slopes began again to show themselves. A few minutes later nearly the whole of both companies were in groups in the open.

" Now," said Big-axe, speaking to those about him, " we have a chance to make a really hopeful fight. I was afraid that they might content themselves with a long siege, and not make another general assault, and that would have been very bad for us. Our food and water could not last beyond a limited time, and after that we should have had to go out, which would of course have meant the end. As it is, they seem to be on the point of making the kind of fight we want. We can do better against spears and axes than against hunger and thirst."

It is likely that Big-axe put fully as much encouragement into his speech as he felt, but it did really seem as if the assailants were meaning to repeat their assault, which Big-axe was sincere in saying was less dangerous to his little force than a long siege. That Long-spear and his allies could not see this was apparently a little strange, but it was not wholly so to Big-axe, and will not be to us, if we consider a few important facts. One is that savages, the world over, lack the patience and self-restraint of civilized peoples, and if they cannot win their fights in a few dashes they become discouraged, and refuse to try further. Or, if the chiefs are more resolute, and wish to keep on, they usually cannot hold their men; the weaker go, and this leads to the breaking up of the whole force. There are no restraints of discipline and penalties, as with us. In the present case there was an added difficulty, for the assailants were not all of one tribe and under one head, but were alien one to the other, and under divided commands, each chief thinking only of gaining all he could for himself and his band, and entirely indifferent to the ultimate fate of the others.

The shrewd Big-axe, then, understanding the situation, was ready to believe that another assault, with all its risks to the storming party, was really meant, and that perhaps it was virtually forced on the two chiefs by the circumstances. It might, to be sure, merely precede a regular siege, but even if so there was a little hope in it, for another repulse — which Big-axe believed his desperate and now hopeful little band was equal to — must be a most discouraging set-back, and at least would make any spirited after-movement less probable. The great danger, and the one he had all along mainly dreaded, was the effect of the double attack he had spoken of, — one up the path, as before, and one from the top of the hill. Yet he had gradually come to believe that he and his little band could meet even this, and he thought so the more from the look on the men's faces now. Instead of a kind of sullen desperation, were confidence and an eagerness to be at work. Such a change takes the wooden feeling out of legs and arms, puts power into blows, and makes wounds seem trifles.

It was very soon clear that Long-spear and the other chief were intending to make at least what military men now call a demonstration in force. Nearly, if not quite, all the men had come out, and were standing as if ready to start, and the two chiefs were a little way in the fore, by their gestures giving some last orders. Big-axe believed that they were in earnest and meant serious work, and not merely a little harrying affair, intended to worry and take the spirit and strength out of the garrison. Not only that, but he looked to see his other surmise verified, and the assault made from two points at the same time.

The truth as to this was not left long in doubt. The two chiefs quickly finished the little they had to say, and the whole pack began to move. They did not come on quite so fast as before, but there was no halting, and they trotted down the hill-slopes, across the open, and to the little flat at the foot of the path itself. Here Long-spear and the Fishers halted, but the Islanders, with their squat chief at their head, pushed on around the foot of the hill, toward the easy northerly ascent. There was no need of further guessing, for it was plain enough what was going on. The double assault was on!

It did not take the Islanders very long to reach their position, for it was only a few minutes later that Sure-dart looked up and saw five or six mop-crested heads peeping over the edge of the rock.

" Are you ready, Stone-arm? " asked Big-axe, just then coming up. " Remember, no darts are to be thrown, or anything else done, till those fellows are within sure range. Even then trust rather to your spears and axes. They will be more certain, and we have no darts to spare."

" I have it all clear in my mind," said Stone-arm, promptly and confidently.

Big-axe then turned to Sure-dart.

" Stay here with him. You can be of more use, for you will have a better chance to use your darts. At the wall it will be mainly heavy work."

The chief then climbed the barricade and took his old station. He could do no more at present for the little band he had left behind him. They must depend on themselves, feeling what that meant,— very likely the safety, or the ruin, of every man, woman, and child on the rock.

It was but a few minutes after this that the mop-headed fellows at the top of the cliff waved their hands at the Fishers below, and this proved to be a signal. Long-spear stood to one side, gave one of his unearthly screeches, and in a twinkling his part of the pack was swarming up the path.

Sure-dart heard somebody say:

" They are not crowding one another so much this time, so they will have a better chance to use their darts "; but this was all he knew about that part of the work at the time.

The topknots above were showing higher, for the fellows were now standing and were evidently about to try their daring slide down; and back of the first men were gathering others. Several of these were bending over, as if they were lugging heavy loads. They were evidently doing the artillery work, and getting ready to prepare the way for the assault by a storm of rocks. This was somewhat in the nature of our modern warfare, where artillery often paves the way for an infantry or cavalry charge.

But Stone-arm and his little band merely waited till the men with the rocks had tugged them to the verge, and began to tumble them down, and then quietly slipped under the covered way cut in the face of the rock. The women, children, and other non-combatants had already taken refuge there, except a few women who formed what might be called the reserve. These now sought shelter with the fighting force. As for the defenders on the wall, they were not greatly exposed, owing to the fact that the cliff at that point receded a little, so that great stones could not be cast far enough out to reach them, and small ones, for the present, could pretty well be guarded against by the shields. As soon as the assault became close, it would be impracticable to continue even the light discharge, as the assaulting party would then be nearly blended with the defenders.

Stone-arm and the others had waited till the last moment, but all got under cover in safety. Another storm, probably as a scare, followed, and then some small stones and gravel rattled down; and Stone-arm and the rest heard some rapping noises, as if made by poles or staves, against the face of the rock. The defenders of course knew what this meant: the storming party was coming down, and some were steadying themselves by their spears.

But the orders were to lie close till the last moment. Otherwise the men left above would doubtless throw stones over the heads of their friends down upon those on the shelf. Sure-dart, who was next to Stone-arm, heard the old fighter fetch an impatient sniff, but still hold back, and with hardly less difficulty he controlled himself, and waited for the right moment.

It came when a lanky, mop-haired fellow dropped with a slap of bare feet down into the path, jumping from what must have been a considerable height. He almost lurched off over the edge, with the effort he made to keep his balance.

" Now!" roared Stone-arm, and with a scramble he was out, and his whole party after him.

The fellow who came first never got his face around to the cliff again. While he still staggered, a Rock-man drove a foot into the hollow of his back, and with a scream and a useless flinging out of arms, he kept on as he had started, and went off over the cliff.

That was easy enough, but not so what followed. As Sure-dart looked up, the whole face of the cliff seemed to be covered with sliding and hopping men! They lay flat, and boldly slid down long rock-faces, trusting to digs of their spears to keep them from going too far, or daringly jumped short distances, where there were bigger breaks in the ledge, or turned back about, and climbed cautiously down where the rock was almost perpendicular, yet where there were small chinks, and hand or toe holds.

Sure-dart drew back his arm, marking one active fellow who was sliding down directly toward him. The man was trying to check his speed with the butt-end of his spear, and was lying as flat as he could on his back while doing it. By the rather wild look in his face, when he raised his head to see where he was going, he was thinking more about the peril of the passage than of the danger when he should land. It seemed almost cowardly to take advantage of his helplessness; but on the other hand, it would not do to let him land, and give him an even fighting chance. It was not a business of chivalry, but of life or death, and a terrible death at that. Moreover, some such advantage was needed, even as

a matter of nice chivalry, to balance the terrible
disadvantage in numbers. Sure-dart did not
hesitate, then, but, as the fellow was shoving
down with his spear to get a final steadying point,
he stepped forward, and with the man's raised
head for a target let drive a dart.

His aim, as usual, was true, and the dart
seemed to go in at the fellow's half-open mouth.
There was a wild flinging up of arms, the spear
came clattering down, and the man's body followed, striking like a weighted sack across the
little outer wall or parapet.

Meanwhile, there was a bustling time at the
other points, and out of the corner of his eye, so
to speak, Sure-dart saw others of the company
trying to do what he had just done. Some, however, including Stone-arm himself, were coolly
waiting till the slider or jumper was within reach
of a striking weapon. As well as Sure-dart was
able to tell, not an Islander had thus far effected
lodgement on the shelf. There was no time to see
what was going on at the barricade, but there
was no lack of noise there, including human yells
and shouts, and the clattering and thudding of
spears and axes on shields. One thing was cheering amid the uncertainties, and that was the great
roaring shout of Bull-head. It was peculiar as well
as loud, and carried with it a note of fury mingled
with taunting and derision, such as no other man
in the camp was capable of. Sure-dart heard it
now, in the little gap of time following the tumble
of the Islander.

But as the boy whipped out another dart, and
looked up to meet the next slider, he was checked

and — it may seem absurd to say it, but it is true — he was almost made to laugh at what he beheld. A somewhat portly but powerful Islander was working his way cautiously down a long rock-face, and in doing so had turned about, so that he was on his stomach, and was clawing and scrambling along, getting the best hold he could with his hands and bare feet. He had thrown away his spear, but his axe was slung over his back. Just as Sure-dart looked, the man got to a small projection of rock, where he checked himself, and cautiously turned to look down. Sure-dart was not within reach, but little Hop-foot, who had evidently concluded that the pace was hot enough to require his help, was near, and he proceeded with promptness and great energy to act. He caught up the spear that the Islander had dropped, and began to use it with great vigor on the only target that was at the moment within reach. He jabbed with such vigor and effectiveness that the man yelled, for the moment forgetting about the need of keeping his balance. Down he came, with a wild flop and a jump, and landed on the shelf. There Hop-foot fell upon him, this time with shortened spear, and another thrust settled the whole matter.

" I 'll never be a dinner for you, anyhow," triumphantly snarled the boy, as he drew the spear back.

It was perhaps five minutes since the first Islander came down the rocks, but in that little time a great deal had been done. So helpless had the sliders and hoppers proved, after they had once launched themselves to come down, that not a single one had yet landed in safety on the shelf. Nor had any of the defenders been hurt; the only harm that the little band had suffered was from a few stones thrown almost at random from above. By them one Rock-man was knocked down and stunned, and another had been gashed across the back, but not so as to disable him. Sure-dart, turning to look after the next convenient slider, saw how it was, and though he was usually quiet, like Big-axe, he gave a really savage whoop of triumph.

It had a much louder echo, which came from Stone-arm and the rest, for at this moment the other fellows on the faces of the rocks and ledges drove in their spear-butts, braced with their feet, and came to a full stop. They plainly had had enough, and were not coming any farther.

A moment more of the delay, and some began to jabber at the others; this was followed by a shouting up at those above, and then by a general facing about, and a desperate scrambling upward.

Again the defenders whooped and yelled, and several wildly danced.

But by this time they were reminded of the stress there might be elsewhere, and Stone-arm hastily ordered Sure-dart and Hop-foot to watch the climbers, and report instantly if any started to come back; then, with the rest of the company, he rushed off to the barricade.

Sure-dart looking upward at the climbers saw that several had edged together, leaving some openings down the face of the rocks.

" Quick, under cover! " he cried to Hop-foot; " they are going to roll down more stones! "

His watchfulness probably saved Hop-foot's life, for just then the men left at the top dislodged several great stones, and sent them thundering down. But the two boys were safe under the firm penthouses of the rock. One great stone struck the middle part of the roof of trees and brush that the chief and his son had built across the path, and in spite of the strength of the wood, and the sloping way in which the roof had been laid, it broke it in. One old woman had taken the notion to shelter herself inside, and as the wood cracked she sent up a wild shriek; but, after all, she was not harmed; the roof had rather slowly yielded, and at the last moment she had wriggled to another place.

Stone-arm and his company were none too quick in getting to the barricade. The assailants, fighting even more desperately than the day before, and using better judgment — not crowding, this time, but giving room for dart and spear throwing — had twice placed several men on the wall, and now, after a furious assault, were maintaining five men there. The others were crowding fast after.

Big-axe, in this emergency again throwing aside everything but his axe, called to Bull-head, who dropped all but his club, and the two rushed like furious bulls on the five Fishers, smashing down two, and terrifying the others into jumping off.

But this supreme effort, following the other tremendous exertions, had almost exhausted the two champions, and they were near to staggering as they turned to pick up their shields. Both, too, were wounded, and though the wounds were not disabling, they were letting out a considerable quantity of blood. It was possible, also, that the missiles that had made them were poisoned.

"Give us room!" thundered the gallant old Stone-arm, as like a boy he leaped from rock to rock till he stood on the top of the wall. His followers were close behind. "You two back and rest," he went on. "We are the same as fresh."

As if to prove this he made an agile jump, and with his ponderous stone weapon split the shield of a climbing Fisher, and shivered as if it were of glass the arm that held it.

All alone though he was, the Fishers nearest him shrank back, and two that had been climbing up, and already had their knees on the top, turned and jumped down. Even a small reinforcement at a critical time in a battle often turns the scale, and it was so now. For a few moments the pack below raged and blustered, and some made motions as for another assault, but not a man finally raised himself on the wall.

"Come on! Come on!" panted Bull-head, using the first good breath he could get for one of his taunts. "It seems as if we should never have you with us as our guests!"

But again the heart was out of the pack. They had already seen their allies, well nigh in a panic, scrambling back up the cliff, and now the desperate fellows on the wall were strengthened by this veritable old fighting machine and his nearly fresh men. It was too much, and slowly and sullenly, as on the previous day, they drew back, wheeled, and marched off toward the woods. They did not seem to pay any attention to their allies, and it could not be seen that a man turned his head to look back.

Again the little garrison gave itself up to the greatest noise it could make. This meant something where there were so many strong lungs, and sound and seasoned throats. Sure-dart was shouting with the rest, when Big-axe, coming from the wall, stopped beside him. The chief was smiling, but it was easy to see that he still had his worriments, and that they were not light ones.

"Sure-dart," the chief said, "we must take advantage of this little breathing-spell. Do you and some of the other young and active men go down and get water. Take the largest skins, and fetch all you can. Wait, of course, till the gang is down from the hill, and the whole pack is beyond the open, but be ready."

It made Sure-dart feel a bit large thus to be spoken of as a "man," and he was besides proud that he should be one of those chosen for what was really a dangerous bit of work. He answered with alacrity that he was ready, and asked whether he was to pick out those who were to go with him.

"Yes," answered the chief; "I leave that to you."

"You think, then," Sure-dart said, his look growing more serious, "that we are not done with these fellows? I thought they had had enough of it."

"I don't want to do or say anything to

dampen the good feeling," answered the chief, and he dropped his voice, " but I will say to you — and you have more sense than most grown-up men — that I certainly think we are not done with them. But they will not, I believe, try any more assaults. What I think they will try is a siege. If we can stand that " — his look grew very grave — " but never mind now. Be ready to start after the water."

Sure-dart sighed, but with an effort such as he had already learned to make, he hid his feelings, and with a brisk air, and what seemed a cheerful face, went about preparing for his little excursion.

CHAPTER XVI

SOME SHREWD AND PLUCKY WORK

SURE-DART waited till the retiring gang had reached the hill-slopes, and some had gone among the trees, and then he started. He took four young fellows and five of the more active women with him. These could carry all the water that the skins they had with them would hold. Big-axe would have had the party wait till dark, but for two things: one was the chief feared that then a guard would be put at the foot of the rock, as the first step toward a siege; the other was that there might be some prowlers out, and the darkness would help these, if they happened that way, to surprise the water-party.

They all rushed at full speed to the spring and plunged in their clumsy vessels. In their haste, notwithstanding the nervous strain, they did not once stop to look toward the dangerous quarter. Sure-dart himself, knowing that he could run faster than any one else in the company, and noting that all could not get at the water at once, held back a little, and finally dipped in his water-sack over the shoulders of one of the slowest of the boys.

As the boy tried to get out of the way, and did pull his loaded skin out of the water, a high, long cry came from overhead, sending a little shock through the party, and causing every head to come up, and every face to be turned about.

All understood the cry, which was a warning, and so they were not surprised at what they saw. Seven or eight men were coming at a run down the slope of the opposite hill! Then were cries and mutterings, and scramblings with the bags, and a rush of the first ones loaded out of the hollow where the spring was.

The others followed as fast as they could; but some were clumsy with nervousness, and a woman who was the last of all spilled her whole precious load, her eyes being toward the coming men, instead of about her, so that she made a bad stumble.

"Never mind," said Sure-dart, who was near her, as the woman, with an exclamation of dismay, stopped and hesitated. "Push along," he added, "and help Short-legs."

Short-legs was a wiry, short-legged boy, who was active and a fast runner, but who, with more ambition than judgment, had taken with him one of the large skins, instead of one of the smaller. He was now trying hard to go fast, but his great load reduced his pace to a mere scrambling walk that was almost a stagger. Still, he was pluckily doing his best, not asking help from any of the others, though some, bigger and stronger than he, carried lighter sacks. The woman rushed to this boy's help, and lifted the heavy end of the skin. In a moment, seeing a better way, they swung the skin down between them, and were thus able to handle it to advantage.

But the best they could do the runners from the forest came along several feet to their one. Evidently the two chiefs had been taken by surprise, and had not expected such a bold and prompt little dash; but when they had discovered it they had been swift to act, seeing how important the matter was. These men, all fast runners, were now only a few spear-casts away, and matters for the little company began to look dubious.

Sure-dart glanced toward the barricade, and saw a stir among the guard there. He felt certain that Big-axe would not leave him in the crisis, and that the stir doubtless meant a relief party, but it did seem as if it were slow in coming.

Nearer still came the swift-footed fellows from the forest, and still nobody from the wall had shown signs of leaving it. Even the coming runners themselves appeared a little surprised at this, and Sure-dart saw them look more than once toward the barricade. They seemed to think it strange that they were to have such an easy job of it.

Yet a little nearer, but now the runners wavered and slackened their pace. It had apparently come into their minds that they must, if they reached the water-party, come pretty close to the enemy's lines. Sure-dart saw the hesitation, and shouted to the toiling little company to make one good spurt.

But though the coming runners saw that they had somewhat miscalculated the distance, or else their own speed, or that the chiefs had done it for them, they could not bear to turn back now and lose the tempting prize. With a little clicking and jabbering back and forth, they shot on again at their former speed.

Sure-dart halted.

"Diver," he called to the largest and strongest of the young fellows, who was noted for his skill as a swimmer, and also for his courage, "stay here with me, and help me to check these fellows. The rest of you push on."

Diver unhesitatingly dropped his water-bag, and rushed to where Sure-dart stood. At another word he moved a few feet away, so that both had plenty of room, yet where each could, so far as the circumstances would allow, support the other. It looked desperate enough, but of course there was still a chance that help would come, and in any case the two brave boys — Diver was only two years older than Sure-dart — were doggedly resolute to check the runners, and save the precious water. Possibly their very boldness, with friends so near, would bring the pursuers for a moment to a stand, and who could say what that might do? Besides, they thought they could not reach the fort unless they dropped their loads and left the slower ones of the party to their fate.

It is said that fortune favors the brave. It proved so, surely, in this case. The runners, when the gallant boys stopped and faced about, their deadly little darts coming out of the quivers, slackened up, and began to jabber again to one another. In so small a fighting force as the Rock-people had the deeds of every prominent fighter were likely to be noticed, and the Fishers and their allies had already noted the quiet deadliness of Sure-dart's work. From the looks of him now, to say nothing of what his companion might be equal to, there was an excellent chance for somebody to test the pain of death by a strong poison.

Sure-dart and Diver, with lips set, poised their darts. They had no shields, but neither had the runners any, and the runners had no poisoned weapons at all, but merely the safer arms for a runner, — light spears, axes, and stone knives. The fellows came a bit nearer, still clicking away to one another, and then began to spread out, as if to turn the flank, so to speak, of the defenders.

But at this most critical instant Sure-dart saw another look come into the face of the man nearest him, and the man came to a sudden stop. It was doubt, if not fear, the man was showing. Almost at the same moment the next runner, looking past Sure-dart, yelped out something, and like a flash whirled in his tracks. Sure-dart understood a little of the Fisher dialect, and thought the man said, " We are in a trap."

Explanations did not need to follow. There was a shout from behind the two boys, and Sure-dart instantly read in the faces of the runners what had happened. It was the rescue party at last!

The runners turned, and the rescuers, plunging by Sure-dart and Diver, tore after them. The runners were a bit out of breath, and the pursuers were substantially fresh. Moreover, Big-axe himself, Wing-foot, and the four other warriors with them, were as fleet if not fleeter than the fastest of the cutting-out party.

Away flew the once-pursuers, and fiercely rushing after them Big-axe and his fleet fighters. Then Sure-dart and Diver got the sense of it all, and, with a yell on their own account, sprang away after.

It was clear that whatever was done must be done quickly, or the tide would again set the other way. In fact, the nest by the trees was already buzzing, and men were catching up their weapons and starting down the hill. Therefore Big-axe and the others did their best, and this best quickly brought them up with the slowest of the runners. One was struck down by Wing-foot, who was in the lead; but at that all the others stopped, and before the chief and the rest of the company could get nigh there was a spread-out line of ready and desperate men. Wing-foot halted, whirled about, and duckingly ran back on his support. He just missed an angry javelin in so doing.

The two forces, as to numbers, were about equal, but otherwise there was a great difference. Big-axe alone was more than a match for three ordinary Fishers, or Islanders, and there was not a man among them that could cast a missile weapon like Sure-dart. Besides, the other men with Big-axe were strong, and handy with their weapons. Bull-head and Stone-arm not being fleet runners, had not come along. In a twinkling battle was joined.

A minute saw the beginning of the end of it. Big-axe crushed the man before him, Sure-dart planted one of his little deadly stings in another, and a powerful Rock-man got his spear into the vitals of the fellow opposed to him. On the other hand, a tall Fisher turned the thrust of the Rockman assailing him, and jabbed his own spear into a fatal spot.

The result was too one-sided. The defending line wavered, two fiercely tried to keep up the fight, but the next instant the others threw down their spears and started in fresh flight. Of those who would have stayed, one was instantly knocked down, and the other sprang away after his mates.

"Stop!" roared Big-axe. "We have done enough. Back, while we can."

They almost spun around on their heels, for to be sure there was no time to lose. Already more men were running down the hill. But the daring little party could afford to stop, as the chief had said, for they had lost but one man, and had left behind them three dead enemies, and one at least desperately hurt. Their own loss of one killed did not appear to be equal relatively to the loss of the enemy. Besides, they had saved the precious water.

CHAPTER XVII

NATURE COMES INTO THE FIGHT

IT was a big party that now came racing and yelling down the hill-side. Nevertheless, it effected nothing, for Big-axe and the rest had too good a start, and were too fast even for the scattered fast men who were in the advance. All got safely back to the wall, and were leisurely helped up. The pursuit had already stopped. The water was by this time safely put away, and there was general rejoicing, as indeed there well might be. Things seemed to be going better than any but the most sanguine could have dared to hope.

There were now fresh preparations for an attack, should any be ventured, which, however, was unlikely. Big-axe said that he believed there would be none. He had already gone over his muster roll — to use the modern military term, — and found that he had left just ten grown men, twelve large boys, including Sure-dart, and the small contingent of women. There had been two men killed at the barricade at this last assault, one being the man who had previously been wounded in the thigh, and one totally disabled. He thought the allies now had left under fifty serviceable men. As the boys in the garrison, other than Sure-dart, could not be considered as nearly equalling the same number of grown warriors, it was apparent that the allies still had a strong advantage in efficient fighters.

While these new preparations were going on, Sure-dart had been spoken to by Big-axe and complimented on his pluck and coolness.

"You did just what I wanted you to," said the chief, "which was to hold on as long as possible, and tempt their party to come close. I had to let you take some risk, but it was for the good of all. I thought we had a chance to thin them out, and lose few if any ourselves, and that we must take the chance. We came out of it well, for they could not afford to lose four to one."

To this Sure-dart answered that he was glad the matter had come out so well, for at one time he had thought the rescue would come too late, and his party be lost, with nothing to offset it; and he added that Diver ought to have a part of whatever credit there was for the stand the two had made.

"I have already told him so," said the chief. "As for you, I like the way you are doing things, and I think if you keep on you will some day be chief. That is, if we manage to get out of this trouble."

He passed on, leaving Sure-dart very well pleased, and inwardly a bit proud and elated.

It was now dark, and the usual preparations for the night were made, with one exception: no scouts were sent outside, as on the previous night. That was because there was something of a stir from the direction of the woods, and Big-axe guessed that the enemy was meaning to come nearer. In fact, it was not likely to be otherwise, considering what had just passed. While straight-out assaults were relied on, the condition of the defenders as to food and water was of no particular consequence, but now that a siege was to be tried, it was of great consequence. Therefore, the little fort must be invested so closely that other dashes like the recent one would be impossible. It did not take long to prove this theory true, for a few minutes later the watch on the barricade were able to make out dusky shapes flitting about in the obscurity, and shortly afterwards some drew closer, and formed a tolerably large guard.

A little later still voices were heard above, and a spiteful rock came crashing down the slope, and bounced off the path. Nobody was hurt, but the warning was regarded, and all but the guard on the wall crept under the protection of the rock penthouses. The guard, as previously explained, was placed so that large rocks could not be sent down upon them, and they curled up, with their own shields and some spare ones to cover them, and were in little danger. But this final disposition of the two bands made it pretty certain that the nature of the attack had indeed changed, and that a siege was meant.

The breeze had gone down with the sun, and though there was a slight fog or mist, it seemed merely to make the air closer and more uncomfortable. There had been no rain for several days, and of course the rocks and ground had been drying and storing warmth, and in all the open places there was nothing moist or cool, and no spot that was really comfortable. To make things vastly worse, swarms of flies and various other insect pests were a-wing, or most active on their legs, and these now began to get in their work. As the defenders could not now safely move about, they were the more plagued and tormented, and that in spite of some little tricks of protection that their experience had taught them. They had found that certain kinds of earth, rubbed on the exposed parts of their bodies, would keep off some insects, and that another earth, especially if mixed with the juice of certain acrid plants, would keep off still others. Yet other kinds of tormentors disliked earth impregnated with salt, such as the Rock-people sometimes rubbed on their meat. There was plenty of this earth on hand, and a little search brought to light a few of the other things; but in the main the supply was short, and much wriggling and twisting and complaining were heard in consequence.

The besiegers were somewhat better off. They could move about, and could get at plenty of earth, with which to make suits of mud armor. Besides, many of them were already plastered over with earth paint, and this greatly helped. After a while, too, some cut switches and then they took turns in fanning away the tormentors. The guard on the wall could hear the swishing of the branches, and could also now and then catch impatient grunts, and what probably passed in that primitive day for oaths.

But the allies had another most important thing in their favor: they had no fear of an attack from the fort, and so, with a guard posted, could sleep as well as the other conditions would permit. The little garrison, on the other hand, not sure of their foes' real intentions, hardly dared to sleep, and were constantly listening for suspicious sounds. They were in a way to wear out pretty fast, therefore, which was doubtless one of the things that Long-spear and the squat chief had counted on.

Sure-dart, though young, was cool and sensible; he made a determined effort to ignore both flying and creeping things, and nervous fears, and to get at least a nap. He finally succeeded, but did not then sleep soundly, and often woke up. Still, the time was going, and it must sometime be light. Then foes, big and little, could at least be seen, and so be the more satisfactorily reckoned with.

The moon now rose late, but at last Sure-dart awoke from another nap, and found that it had grown light enough to see near things. He was lying on some rushes, under a shelf of the rock, and with nothing to cut off his view of a wide sweep of sky, especially to the south. He had a fair easterly range, too, and so could take in the growing light there, even down to the red edge of the moon itself. Thinking that he could sleep no more just then, he sat up and threw a general glance around.

There was nothing except the growing moon that was new. The shelf, to the cut-off of the wall, was still bare and open, though with the sticking out, here and there, of restless hands or feet, or the projection of some weapon. In the other direction, the broken-in hut was succeeded by the deserted remainder of the open part of the shelf. On the barricade he could make out the huddled-up figures of two of the three sentinels. They were sitting on one of the top stones. The third was a stone lower, and was just now leaning on his spear.

The moon rose higher, and the light grew stronger, but it was not a clear light. The haze gave it a red, sombre cast, and took from it the little illusive romance that makes other moonlights beautiful. The size of the moon itself was also exaggerated, and as it redly climbed above the wooded hills, and seemed broadening across that whole quarter of the sky, it was almost terrifying. Showing at all times greater than the moon of to-day, it was enlarged also to the eye, as our moon sometimes is, and seemed like a red-hot world drifting down through space upon this one.

The night itself, like the most of those primitive nights, could not be said to be quiet. Besides the mutterings of the restless sleepers — or those trying to sleep — and the grunting and grumbling of some who were fighting off insects, were the noises faintly coming up from the enemy's camp below, and a little stirring about on the rocks above. And still besides these were the ordinary natural sounds, — the drumming, whistling, and croaking of reptiles, — such reptiles as this modern earth never saw, — the booming and squawking of strange night-birds, and the humming, buzzing, and knocking of small flying things against everything animate and inanimate. Most were invisible, and so there was uncertainty in their coming and going and a little vagueness about their presence, and this added to the help-less irritation of trying to fight them off. Many, however, were merely a little too curious and sociable, and did no harm, a few being great beetles that knocked into one's face, and then fell down with a tremendous buzzing, and others turning out to be huge moths, that fluttered around, and if caught clung to one's skin with obstinate, scratching feet.

There was of course nothing new and surpris-ing to Sure-dart in this mere stir and swarming confusion of the night life of the place, and this alone would not have kept him awake. He swung his feet out into the path, and arranged the rushes more comfortably under him. If he de-cided to try for more sleep he could succeed bet-ter after a restful change of position.

The thing that he looked at the oftenest was the giant red moon. He thought he had never seen it quite so monstrous and sinister. It was clearing the horizon now, and giving more light, but not ordinary moonlight. Things under it came dimly out, and with hard, black outlines and deep shadows, where usually would have been silvery shimmerings and blue bits of duski-ness. There was a sombreness and suggestion of something almost unnatural about it all, and a feeling as if new and strange things might hap-pen, and the effect on the mind was one of uneasiness, and a longing for good wholesome daylight once more.

Nevertheless, as with a kind of fascination, Sure-dart continued to look, and watched the giant red ball push itself up, as it were, from the rim of hills and woods, and float clear into the dusky open above. He must be growing a bit nervous, for just then a whirring noise, as of a bird's wings, made him start, and he looked around to see where the sound came from. There was nothing at the moment in sight. He waited, glancing this way and that, and listening, beginning to guess now what had made the noise.

Only another few seconds, and then he had a chance to know, and what mystery there had been was at an end. As he was looking skywards, and away from the moon, something that could be likened to an army tent dropped down from a high place, fell flapping past, a noise like a magnified squeak, and ending in a sort of sputter, coming from it.

Strange and disconcerting as such a vision would be now it was almost cheering to Suredart. He knew what it was, and though there might have been circumstances when he would have looked serious at the sight of the creature he was not troubled now. It was that giant, bat-like monster of the lizard family that we have named pterodactyl, but which the Rock-people called beast-bird. This one had a body as big as a fair-sized dog's, with a bird-like head, ending in a long, toothed bill.

Had the creature caught him asleep, or disabled, or even alone, provided that he did not at once start up, and show that he was able to fight, it might have been a different story. That sharp saw of a bill, with a lean but strong neck behind it, could get in very quick and serious work, and the claws on the hind feet were adapted to back it up. The creature was bold, too, and doggedly stubborn when once it had begun to fight.

But it had some cunning, as well, or instincts that served the same purpose, and was not likely to be dangerous at this time. Sure-dart thought afterwards that it had smelt or seen the scamperer, and was looking for a chance to make one of its sudden, fierce dashes at it. If so it was disappointed, for the scamperer was cuddled down close to Hop-foot, and this was in the row of the armed men.

The creature rose from its dip into sight again, and took a short turn overhead. Then it went higher, sticking its long neck down, as Sure-dart could see, as if looking the situation finally over. Just now it was a strange and almost unearthly sight, with its monstrous cloak-like wings, cut out black against the sky, its poked-down head, with the great bill and the awkward, dangling legs. It would have given our forefathers cold shivers, for they would surely have taken it for the Evil One.

A little uneasy, notwithstanding his belief that the thing would not risk a dash, Sure-dart crept out of his nest, taking his spear with him. At sight of him, or perhaps discouraged already, the monster lifted its unsightly head, and flapped heavily off. Sure-dart watched it till it made a black dot against the blood-red moon, and finally seemed to be swallowed up in it.

Sure-dart now thought of what he was doing, and that he was in a little danger, for the light

" Sure-dart crept out of his nest, taking his spear with him "

would show him to any watching enemies above. He therefore turned to crawl back into his nest. As he faced that way, he saw that Hop-foot was looking out of the next space.

" Gone, has n't he? " the boy said softly.

" Oh, then you were awake? Yes, he seemed to fly into the moon."

" I am coming out, too," the boy said again, after a little pause. " I am half roasted, and I want to stretch my legs. I guess there 's no danger."

He did not wait for Sure-dart's answer, but crept out.

" It seems as if the air were all used up, and nothing left to breathe," Sure-dart sniffed and said. " It is kind of strange, too, up on this high land."

" Maybe it means a noise-storm " (thunderstorm), Hop-foot suggested. " And say," he went on, " if it does rain hard it will be a good thing for us. It will cool off things, and we can catch some of the water."

" Yes," Sure-dart began to answer, " and so I hope — What was that? "

He stopped abruptly to ask the question, and certainly he had reason.

From far — there was no saying where — came a low, dull roar, that was like, and yet not like, a tremendous wind. It deepened, died away, began to rise again — all in an instant it was lost in a mighty, deep-down thunder and crash that might well have split open the foundations of the earth!

As it died out the ground under them jarred,

and they heard from far another but lower wind-like roar.

They gasped. They knew something about earthquakes, but this, with its terrible ripping up of what seemed the earth's very foundations, was different, and they were shaken and bewildered.

Now began to be heard frightened cries, and confused questions, and out into the path rolled and scrambled men, women, and children. There was no thought of any other danger, and, in fact, little clear sense of anything, or of what had happened.

A light breeze stirred, and they smelled strange, rank odors. They turned to the west, from which the puff of wind had come, and found that the sky there was lighter. As still they gazed, they saw what was like another moon swiftly reddening the peaks of the now visible mountains.

There was no more talking. The strange light shone on pale, staring faces, and shaking limbs and bodies.

A long minute more. In that time the red had grown redder, and the mock moon had pushed up into sight. Still a little later, and up higher yet the great red ball had pushed. Now, in spite of the distance, they could make out fiery sparks flying in jets from it. They flew faster, but at the same time the mighty uplift began to lose its roundness, and grow lean and pointed.

Now it had stopped rising, and was standing still. It threw off no more sparks, and even the glow was fading. It suddenly faded out, but that was because of a quick and deep blackness that was spreading over that part of the sky.

A little boy screamed out. Something had dropped on him that was like a feather, but that seemed to have the point of a knife. His mother, forgetting her own fright for the moment, stooped to soothe him, and to find out what had hurt him. Something hard, like a small nut falling from a tree, struck her between the shoulders. At the same moment a man near the other end of the path snarled with pain.

His face was in sight one moment, but the next the man six paces from him could not see it; the darkness had reached them, and with it the cause of it. The air was full of the little falling substances, and of the black, soft particles, some as big as small feathers, and a rain of what seemed fine dust. They shouted in the blackness to one another, and families tried to feel their way together, and some snarled or shrieked, as a hot patch of the feathery stuff fell on a spot of bare flesh.

After scrambles and some falls and bumps against the rocks, all managed to get back into their stone nests. Faster still the dreadful stuff came down, and now they found that there was something besides a smother to it; they began to feel pains in the chest, and some were dizzy. One old man, crazed and muttering, staggered out, and after pawing about a moment, fell off the rock.

It was small comfort that, as this was going on, they could hear frightened roars and yells from overhead, and from the valley below. The most of them heard as with the outer senses only, and dully. Even Bull-head forgot his roar. Rage and hate were going, as life drew near to death.

CHAPTER XVIII

JUST what was said and thought, and just how the next few minutes passed, it would be impossible with any definiteness to say. At a time like this things big and little are generally recalled in a confused way, and like the broken and disjointed parts of an oppressive dream. The poor creatures lying in what seemed to be their tombs were in a way stupefied by what was happening; the most of them soon ceased to speak or move, and awaited death in the way stricken animals do.

Whatever the time may have been — and it is impossible that it could have been very long — a change, though at first a small one, began to be noticed. Sure-dart, who perhaps was less dazed and confused than the most of the others, was one of the first to notice it. He thought that he could breathe a bit more easily, and that the wall of darkness, with its twinkling of little fire-flashes, seemed less dense and compact.

He was, as has been seen, of a hopeful nature, and was tough, and full of barbarian vitality. He roused, and with a little thrill of hope turned more fully about and again looked.

Yes, he was almost at once certain that there was really a change. Some of the smothering, breath-sapping feeling had gone, and the dreadful pack of blackness around had certainly thinned and lightened.

He called to Hop-foot:

"It's growing better. I am sure of it. Can't you get an easier breath?"

"I don't know," answered Hop-foot, weakly. "I have n't tried."

"Try, then. Come, get yourself together. Don't give up. We are not dead yet."

This breaking out of the voices from what had come to be a stillness roused others, and in a moment Big-axe spoke.

"It is a little better," he said. "Yes, and there comes a breeze. As soon as it drives more of this stuff away we will turn out. It's safer here just now."

He had put his own head out while he was speaking, and had felt the breeze on his face. But he was for keeping where they were for a few moments longer, as he had already noticed that when thus near the ground, and sheltered by the overhang of the rock, they breathed more easily, and escaped the smothering and sometimes burning feathery stuff, and the ashes.

There could be no mistake about it now; the dreadful cloud was fast thinning, and it was already light enough to see a little way around. Big-axe scrambled out, and, like cliff swallows popping out of their nests, the others followed. Nobody remembered any danger from a human source.

The blessed breeze came with a bit of real strength now, and what was left of the vapors and powdery stuff sluggishly drifted off before it. The moon, though still red and dim, cut out its shape vaguely, and the whole east, though now catching the driven murkiness and blended vapors, was distinctly lighter.

There was a glad mumbling, and some broke out in laughter, and a few of the older or more excitable ones whimpered. Big-axe and the most of his fighting men said nothing, but even the dim moon-rays brought out the new light on their faces. All drew in long breaths of the changed air, and some walked up and down, threshing their arms about, and trying to throw off what was left of the torpor and heaviness.

But before this several of them, coming to their full senses, had found that not all their friends and companions were with them. Then there was a quick rush back, and a looking into the spaces. The truth was instantly clear; several of the old people, three children, and one wounded warrior were dead. Besides these, two or three others, also old and feeble persons, were in a collapsed state. As quickly as possible all but the dead were taken out, and placed where the air would come to them, and a little of the precious water was sprinkled in their faces. Barbarians though the Rock-people were, and not up to our pitch of thought and feeling, they were by no means wholly brutal or without kindness of heart; in fact, they compared favorably with many uncivilized peoples of our day.

While this was still going on, the chief and a few others were trying to find out what the enemy were doing, and how the terrible bombardment had left them. Out in the open, as they were, they must have received a sharp peppering from the fire particles, and though the party on the hill would early catch the relieving breeze, those below, being behind the hill, must have got the benefit considerably later. In fact, the open below was still foul and murky with the dreadful cloud. On going to the barricade, little could be made out, though here and there a dim shape seemed to be moving about; but there was a blending of grunts and groans, and snarls of savage impatience. Above there was hardly a sound, and though the space about the verge of the rock was much lighter than any part of the ground below, no shape of a human being could be seen.

On the whole, this was rather encouraging, and they could afford to wait patiently till more could be learned. It was reasonable to suppose that this very disturbing experience, even if it had not brought serious results, had severely tried the besiegers' nerves, and had tended to reduce what was left of their stubbornness and resolution.

At this point there was a further change in the conditions, for the breeze stiffened and became a moderate but steady wind, and as it further drove off the murkiness and vapors, it carried with it the heat. In another half-hour it was almost cool.

And now Nature seemed like herself again. The hot blasts, the odors, the dun clouds, and the gigantic, fiery moon had given place to pure, cool air, harmless white clouds in the far-off sky, and a natural-sized, golden-bright globe that was like the old-time moon. The dusk of the woods and the outlines of the hills were once more distinct, and last, but to the watchers by no means least, every winged torment had been gathered into the net of the breeze and whirled away.

Yet this, in a measure, seemed to bring back some of the other original conditions. The human wolves outside must be refreshed and encouraged too, and who could say that they would not now be heartened for new efforts. So that, after all, the position of things had not so materially changed.

To find out all that could be learned with regard to this, Big-axe and the others took advantage of the growing light, and again went to the barricade. From there they scrutinized everything that was in sight below, and tried to find out what was going on above.

They soon made one discovery. Either from sheer fright, or because the pelting of the fire-flakes was there peculiarly tormenting, the Islanders had left the top of the rock, and were camped close by their allies on the open below. Beyond this all that the anxious chief and the others could make out was that the entire gang below seemed listless and sullenly sluggish. Few were stirring about, and none appeared to pay any attention to what was going on above. Whatever else might be true, they had tamed down wonderfully from their first restless eagerness.

It was not so very long from this to morning; and as soon as it was fairly light the anxious spying from above was again taken up.

There was now more stir below, but still without any particular appearance of zest, or energy, though it was true that this time a little attention was paid to the fort. Some of the fellows looked up at it, and for a time watched those on the barricade, but even then it was with an air more of curiosity than of apparent rage and hostility. It seemed as if they were wondering how much better or worse than themselves the garrison had come out of the terrible experience.

As the light grew stronger, so that things hitherto vague and dim came out, the watchers on the wall made another discovery. They had already found that on the path and everywhere on the open rock a gray, stony dust had fallen, and with it patches of stuff like light cinders, feathery, and in some cases black; they now found that this strange shower had extended at least over the whole eastward eye-range, for it had powdered the trees on the near hills, dulling their green to a forbidding and unnatural gray. The whole view was as of some place struck with a blight, or like one of our northern landscapes in the late fall, when the frost has struck the green from the grass and the trees. Or it might have been likened to a patch of scorched and sand-blown desert.

This was what they saw immediately around them, and to the limit of their view toward the south and east. Remembering then the direction the terrible cloud had come from, they looked that way, getting a range now to the west, and off to the distant pile of mountains.

At first they saw nothing new, and the mighty

blue tumble seemed to stretch unchanged from the point where west became north, to a far point where west ran in with south. There was apparently nothing whatever to show for what had seemed the ripping up of the whole under world, and the blowing· down on them of the dust and burned bits of some uplifted region of it. This was as they took it in at first, half thinking to see such a ruin as would lie broad to the eye, and mark a change from what had been. Some, indeed, stopped here and turned to other things, but a few were not satisfied, and looked yet again, noting this time the range peak by peak, and ridge by ridge. They had become tiresomely familiar with every one of these peaks and ridges, for there had been little else to see, as they crouched in the rock shelter through the long wearing hours.

And now they found what they were looking for. A young woman first saw it, picking it out as something new in the familiar picture. One careful look from the others showed that she was right, and that all they had heard and seen was at least in part accounted for.

Between two great peaks that ran up clear against the sky-line, with nothing between, there had shouldered up another peak, and this had spread and overflowed till the three points were left as mere saw-teeth above the great general mass. It was nothing less, then, than the birth of a new mountain — one belated when the others yielded to the ancient mighty crumpling and upward crowding as the earth was cooling.

But those ancient observers, knowing nothing

of all this, merely gaped and wondered, and were satisfied with their little discovery. They thought that a mountain driven up out of the earth was enough to throw to an incoming wind a shower of ashes and cinders.

Meanwhile, the more practical of the company had been carefully going over the nearer field of view. They had found that the spring below was half full of the flakes and ashes, and that all the trees and bushes in sight were plastered over with them. Certainly this meant something, and possibly a good deal, for now it was going to be difficult for the enemy to get easily at either food or drink. It was not to be supposed that the fruit would be eatable, or that the water in the spring, with its load of rank mineral stuff, would be fit to drink.

The thought now was: What effect would this have on the besiegers, coming as it did on the heels of so many other failures and disappointments? It was easy to ask the question, and it had the help of a little hope in it; but the answer must come later.

The morning and then the rest of the day passed, the only change in the besiegers' camp being that several men took their weapons and went off over the hills, doubtless in search of food and water. They came back toward night, three of them bringing some small game, including a scamperer and two marsh-hoppers,— creatures of the lizard family about the size of our common domestic hens; the others carried bundles of roots, and a lizard-skin partly full of some kind of berries. This seemed to be the best they had been able to do, though by the time they had been gone and the heavy way they walked, they had covered more than a few miles. Whether they had found any near supply of water, of course the watchers could not tell, but from something that shortly afterwards followed, they thought not. This something was that several men, before it was quite dark, went to the little hollow where the spring was, and began prodding about with their spears. It looked as if the prospects of a water supply from other directions were pretty poor. After some minutes of trial, one of the men seemed to have found a spot that was hopeful, for the others joined him, and all went sharply to work. They dug with their spears, and used also their knives and hands, and after a while they had dug a pretty deep hole. Then they waited, but after fully half an hour they got only water enough for a good drink each. Apparently discouraged and disgusted, they went back to the company.

A later effort to get water was made that evening, when a large party went to work on the spring itself. They delved and pawed, and threw out dirt and filth, and when they appeared to think they had done all they could, sat down, and waited for the result. This time, they had a measure of success, for when they finally tried the water, they managed, though evidently with an effort, to get some of it down. Then they also went back to camp.

"That helps them," said Big-axe, with a troubled scowl. "I was in hopes they couldn't make it work."

Ten minutes later, while he was standing on the barricade, Wing-foot walked up to him.

"Chief," the young man said quietly, "I think I can spoil those fellows' new plan. Let me have one man that I want, and I will go down and undo their work. We will throw the stuff back into the spring. Yes, and we will bring up some of the water, if it is good for anything."

Big-axe, though he did not often, or on light occasions, show surprise, showed some now, and seemed a bit moved, besides.

"How would you do it?"

"With a rope, and a little care. We have enough skins and other things to make a rope that will reach from the cliff to the ground. We two will go down, and tumble as much as we can of the bad stuff back into the spring. It won't take much to spoil the water again."

The chief smiled, showing his strong white teeth.

"It sounds well, and perhaps I will let you do it. It would be worth something to see their faces when they found it out. Who is the other man you would want?"

"He isn't exactly a man, but he can do the work of one, and for a job like this he is my choice of the whole company. It is Sure-dart."

The chief thought for a moment.

"You may try it," he said then. "You would start, of course, before the moon got up?"

"Yes. It would need to be dark."

"They have no guard there," the chief then said reflectively, "for they didn't think of anything like this. Well, I didn't either." He smiled again. " I think you had better not try to fetch any water," he went on then, " for what you could handle would not amount to much, and it would bother and incumber you. We are not pressed for it, either, as we have a fair supply left. No, you must leave that part out."

" Well, perhaps it would be better."

" You may go about your plans, then."

It was between eleven of our time and midnight when Wing-foot and Sure-dart, their rope in shape, and dangling down from the rock, told Big-axe that they were ready.

The chief first looked carefully down, and all around, and satisfied himself that no strollers from the camp were near. Without speaking, but with a grave look that showed how anxious he felt, he nodded, and himself took a guiding hold of the rope. It was not a very strong affair, and as far as possible it must swing free, and not chafe against the rocks.

The two adventurers had laid aside all their weapons save their stone knives, and were very nearly naked. Wing-foot took the rope in his hand, and slipped over the rock. He was to give a little tug, when he should be at the bottom, and then Sure-dart was to go. The rope itself had several great knots, besides some little ones, so that it was the better adapted to the purpose. Wing-foot made the signal, and instantly Sure-dart started. The chief, bending over the verge, kept the rope clear, and saw the dark, swaying spot that Sure-dart made bring up in the shadows below. The strain on the rope ceased. Big-axe could barely make out the two shapes, as they slipped away from the foot of the rock and went soft-footedly off in the darkness.

With a look more anxious than most of his people had seen on his face before, he drew his great axe up to him and sat down to wait.

CHAPTER XIX

TO BE MADE INTO FRESH MEAT

WING–FOOT and Sure-dart were meanwhile slipping softly but quickly toward the spring. As it was so near they were speedily there, and without losing a moment began their work. Things immediately around were quiet, and more so than usual; for the night creatures seemed displeased with the new weather, and the most of them were silent, and the breeze had fined down, so that it made little stir among the trees. From the enemies' camp came now and then some minor noise, such as a small momentary outbreak of talk, or the groaning and fussing of somebody in pain from wounds; but that was at present all.

It was a longer job to put even a moderate amount of the cinders and other stuff back into the water than they had thought. In the first place, it was not heaped up in one spot, but thrown about, and in the darkness they could not always find it; besides, they had no proper tools to work with, and, in fact, had to depend mainly on their hands.

After a little of this kind of work they grew impatient and a bit nervous, and began to claw about energetically, and to handle the stuff, as they lighted on it, with small regard to the noise.

It did not make very much, anyway, and they took the chance.

At last they thought they had done enough, and after a whisper between them knocked off. They slipped their knives back into the loops in their girdles, and began to run. They could tell, even in the obscurity, where the hill rose against the sky.

They did not look around, and so did not see four creeping shapes come out of the bushes beyond the hollow, and dart softly but swiftly along in their wake. Yet these shapes, coming down from the camp, had passed within half a spear's cast of them, and then had wormed unheard into the bushes. These bushes clumped out hard by the spring itself, and from there it would be convenient to make a rush. But just then the two finished and started off, and instead of the rush the hiders waited a moment, and then came sneaking after.

At first, on account of the rough ground, the two runners held back, and did not go much faster than a dog-trot; now, on the more even space above, they let out a notch.

Now they were near the rock, and its great face loomed black, and cut off what light there was. There was a small noise behind them, and they both slackened, and turned their heads. It was suspiciously like the slapping of bare feet on the hard ground. And it was that, for while their heads were still screwed around, the noise sharpened, and four black human shapes took outline against the darkness.

There was no lack of plain-enough noises now.

The four yelled, and other men creeping down the slopes answered them, and at the camp broke out a clatter of spears and axes on shields. From the rock above came down shouts and encouraging cries.

Wing-foot and Sure-dart were not looking over their shoulders now, but were running as only two of the fleetest human beings then on the earth could run. The looming figures behind began to grow dim again.

Wing-foot, pelting to it wonderfully, and going almost as fast as a hunting dog, was now in the lead. Sure-dart, however, was not many paces behind.

The rock was nigh. Wing-foot stopped, and began pawing and plucking at the rope. He had it now, and was off the ground.

Sure-dart stopped, breathing hard. It was not so much lack of breath as something else, for the rope would hold but one at a time. Death, in the shape of the looming-up figures, seemed at hand.

He had not lost his knife. He drew it, and turned. Nothing else came into his mind to do, for here could be no surrender. That would be merely a shorter road to a smashed skull, and an unknown number of hungry stomachs. Better to fight it out, then, and go down in hot blood, perhaps hardly knowing when the ending blow came. Besides, that was the way a Rock-man and a warrior was expected to do.

Out of the " tail of his eye " he saw Wing-foot hoisting and hitching his way to safety. That was right in him, for he could do nothing by staying, and it was properly a case of " first come, first served."

He stood up straight, but a little sidewise, his knife drawn back.

Now the gang was upon him. There were yells, and — something or other was wrong. He could not exactly see, and he thought his knees were sagging under him. The yells seemed farther off — he did not hear them at all.

It was merely that a stone had struck him on the side of the head: It did no more than stun him. One man bent over him, knife drawn back, but the warrior who had thrown the stone, a tall, strong fellow, pushed him aside.

" No! he is mine. We will take him to the camp and eat him."

It was a short speech, but very much to the point. Besides, the speaker was Long-spear, and the man, like all the others who had come up, was a Fisher. He mumbled something, but stood back, and obeyed his chief. One of the late comers had a spear, and the chief took it, and lashed the boy to it with belts. Then two men took up the load, and with a little care, on account of the darkness, the whole gang swarmed off across the flat.

Wing-foot was safe. He had pulled and hitched so fast that he was two spears' lengths clear of the ground when Sure-dart went down. Some of the gang had thrown stones at him, but in the obscurity they had missed, and a few who seized the rope and shook it did not break his desperate grip. Probably they would soon have thought of taking hold together and snapping the rope, risking a heavy thump from the falling climber, or else they might have whipped him, so to speak, against the rock; but before they were ready to do either they found that they had lost their chance to do anything. The shrewd and cool fellow had stopped, and, with a turn of his leg around the rope to sustain him, had jerked up the end of it, and made it fast. Then he went on steadily and uninterruptedly to the top. There were no spears or darts seasonably on hand to throw at him.

Sure-dart, lashed, like a captured bear, to the spear-shaft, was meanwhile carried to the camping ground and dumped down. By this time he had come to himself. He got a sharp thump on his wounded head, as he brought up, but it did not stun him, and he did not mind it. He had more serious things to think of.

Long-spear and the others seemed decidedly pleased at their capture, and Sure-dart could not blame them for it, as it was really the first successful piece of work that they had so far carried out. Even one prisoner, and a boy at that, was something, especially as he was an uncommonly smart boy, and as the ranks of the defenders were now so thin. But Sure-dart was not only almost sick with horror at what lay before him, but he was mortified as well. But for the haste and carelessness with which he and his companion had worked, he would probably have escaped trouble, as it was undoubtedly the noise, slight as it was, that had attracted the attention of some of the keen-eared rascals.

It was only a few minutes after he had been

dumped down that a Fisher came along, and with some pieces of lizard-skin lashed first his wrists together, and then his ankles. He did this without untying the belts that still held him to the spear. They seemed to be determined to lose nothing by any carelessness on their part. When this fellow was through with him, the man previously on guard came a little nearer and sat down by him.

But wild creatures, whether men or animals, early pick up various shrewd and cunning ways of getting out of scrapes, and perhaps are helped besides by what we call instinct (though it is hard to say how far this term properly applies); and so Sure-dart, a superior little animal, had already started to do something toward getting out of his scrape. When they tied his wrists together he thought of an old trick that Big-axe had told him about, and swelled out the muscles of his wrists as much as he could, and slightly pushed his wrists apart. He managed this slyly, so that it was not noticed. Though there seemed to be a very poor chance to get away, even if he could get rid of his bonds, yet that offered the only chance that there seemed to be at all, and he quickly caught at it. He now began to test his bit of work.

His joints and muscles were supple, and he had gained a little space by his swelling-out trick, and he soon found that he could get rid of the wrist fastenings. This he did, and then started at the leg bonds. Here he would, of course, have had an easy time, since he had the use of his fingers, but that he would have to change his position a bit in order to work, and this might attract the notice of his guard. In fact, he now had to wait several minutes, till the guard was looking another way, and then, very cautiously, made a little crawl. The guard looked back, but did not seem to notice anything new, and Sure-dart once more lay still.

But even if he should get rid of the thongs about his wrists and ankles, there would still be left the bands about his body, which lashed him to the spear-shaft. They were secured in such a way that it would be very difficult to get rid of them undetected, and yet he could not stir a foot with them on. As the spear projected both above his head and below his feet, he could not rise, and even if he managed to shove the spear up, so that his feet projected, he would still be unable to go faster than a walk. Besides, any movement so pronounced as thus altering the position of the spear must quickly be noticed.

Yet all this, though it must be thought of, could not be allowed to weigh anything against the need of doing something; and something, accordingly, he soon tried to do. Reaching down as far as he could, and at the same time trying not to change noticeably the position of his body, he finally got the leg thongs off. He did not, of course, throw them aside, but kept them across his legs, so that a casual glance, in the poor light, would make them appear still in place. In this way, also, he had managed the wrist fastenings.

All this took a number of minutes, perhaps a half-hour. Meanwhile, he was left to himself, except for the guard, though the nearest of the others were hardly more than a spear's length off. He found that there was a talk of some moment going on, and that seemed considerably to excite the talkers, especially the leaders and older warriors, and this was helping him greatly by taking their attention from him. From what he could understand of the talk (both dialects were considerably like the speech of the Rock-men, seeming to indicate that the three peoples came from the same original stock) he found that the leading men among the Fishers, including Long-spear, were for continuing the siege, while the Islanders seemed to be for making one more assault, and if that failed, to give up and go home. There was only one thing on which they seemed fully to agree, and that was that Sure-dart should be kept till morning, and then taken out, and in full view of his friends should be tortured, killed, and eaten.

The whole matter interested Sure-dart greatly, especially the last part, and though this was only what he was looking for, yet, when he came to hear it put so fully into words, it gave him a new and most unpleasant thrill, and nerved him afresh to go on with what he was doing.

By this time he had made one discovery, which was that several warriors of both of the tribes were sore and rather stiff from wounds, and that two had died of poison from the defenders' darts. Not only that, but several had been made sick by the change of food and water, and by the fumes of the terrible shower from the thrown-up mountain. In this connection it is to be thought of that savages, though they may be strong and hardy, are often unable to stand a small change of food and climate, and that many kinds of powerful wild animals cannot stand them at all. The Rock-people had already felt some ill effects from the change, especially the older and weaker ones; and yet, high up on the rock and away from the ground damps and the settling fumes of the bad vapors, they were better off than the besiegers. Sure-dart was therefore the more encouraged, as far as the result for his people was concerned, than he had been at any time before, though for himself personally he had only a kind of desperate hope.

After a while the Islander chief (Sure-dart had found that his name was Strong-back) came along and looked at Sure-dart, and pleasantly gave him a few light jabs with his spear.

Sure-dart could hardly help wincing, but he had time to think that it would not be the thing for a warrior of the Rock-people to do, and managed to hold himself steady. He had the satisfaction of thinking that the long weapons of the Islanders, like those of the Fishers and of his own people, were not usually poisoned. These pricks were not very deep, either, and not at all crippling.

Strong-back grunted, but whether with satisfaction at the pleasure he got from the pricking, or out of respect for the boy's pluck, it was hard to say. He turned away, and went about his business again, to Sure-dart's great relief.

Then the desperate little fellow went at the thongs that bound him to the spear, and by dogged perseverance found and untied the knots.

The next thing was to wait for the right moment. It really began to look like a possible

chance, and Sure-dart felt some of his old confidence and steadiness coming back. He got everything ready for a fling and a jump, and even
rubbed his somewhat numbed legs, that they
might not work too slowly.

And then came, almost as if it had been a stun-
ning blow, something new and totally unexpected. The most of the warriors lay down to
sleep, and when the guards were posted another
Fisher came along, and sat down beside him. The
fellow had a hound-like air of alertness and
watchfulness, and even put his spear down in
a handy position beside him. Sure-dart could
not help a little sigh, but was able to hide his
disappointment otherwise. Inwardly he felt, as
he might have expressed it, as if somebody had
hit him in the stomach. His very fingers turned
cold.

Soon it came to him what this extra watchfulness probably meant. His captors thought that
the lion-hearted Big-axe might lead out a desperate rescue party, it being perhaps in his mind,
too, to do what damage generally he could, and
in that case the guard would see to it that they
got no boy, unless it was a dead one.

It is merely painful to dwell further on the poor
fellow's disappointment. He was watched so
closely all night that he could hardly stir without
the notice of his guards. Once, when he was
tired of lying in one position, and turned a little,
the second guard punched him with the butt of
his spear, and told him to lie still. After that, till
sunrise, he moved as little as possible.

As soon as it was fairly light the camp began

to stir, and first all hands had breakfast. This, light as was their supply of provisions, did not take long. Then they got together and started to settle the great question of their future policy. Now, as Sure-dart saw, a number of the Fishers sided with the Islanders, and wanted to make one more assault, and if that failed, to give up the whole affair. Here there was some friction between Long-spear and Strong-back, and the Islander who had, it seemed, a little irritating wound, and was not well besides, growled out some rather sharp things; among them he hinted that Long-spear was pretty careful of his own safety, as had been proved by his conduct in the former assaults. It was a fact that Long-spear had not appeared to be very eager in the hottest part of the fighting, and had not been wounded, and that Strong-back had been nearer the barricade, and had got a long-distance jab from a spear. Long-spear, though he was more crafty than eager in battle, and had a good command of his temper, fired up at this, and for a moment it looked as if there would be a lively little war in the camp itself. However, after some sharp jabbering and gesticulating and the interference of some of the older warriors, the trouble was patched up, and the original talk was resumed.

It was wound up pretty soon this time, and ended with rather a queer compromise. There would neither be an assault nor a prolonged siege, but they would first torture Sure-dart, making believe, as they did it, to be off their guard, and hoping thus to draw out a relief party, and if this failed they would give up the whole affair.

This settled, they picked up poor Sure-dart, and carried him farther out in the open, where he would be plainly in sight from the fort, and in a leisurely way, meaning to give the garrison time to plan and attempt a dash, made ready to begin the torture.

CHAPTER XX

THE LAST CHANCE

IT was pretty nearly "now or never" with Sure-dart. He had no serious hope that Big-axe would do anything in the way of a rescue. How, as things stood, could he? Once out in the open, and surrounded, the end was certain. Sure-dart did not believe that the chief was so blindly brave, and had so little thought for the safety of the rest of his people, that he could be tempted out. He would doubtless see that the seeming carelessness of the two bands was assumed. No, whatever was done the boy felt he must himself do. At least, he must do the first and essential part of it. Could he break away, and get near safety, then he had no doubt Big-axe would take a chance, and try to help him.

Though he was in sight from the fort, yet he himself could not get a good look in that direction, for there was a small bush just in front of his face. Too desperate now to mind whether his captors saw him or not, he gave a strong wriggle, and then could see the whole side of the hill, including the barricade.

Ah! Big-axe was on the top of the wall, and so were Bull-head and Stone-arm. He recognized others, too. All were looking that way, and he had no doubt they had already seen him.

It added a sharp pang to his situation to see home and friends so near, and yet separated from him, as it seemed, by the gulf of death itself. A kind of desperate feeling, that perhaps touched madness, came over him. He was ready to do something.

He twisted his head around, and looked at his captors. The nearest were five or six paces away, and they and nearly all the others were looking towards the two chiefs. This, it struck the boy, was a part of the plan. The chiefs were pretending to be discussing something, and the others listening, and none were apparently expecting an enemy. In fact, a few had gone down to the spring, and still others were moving in the direction of the woods.

"But you never can catch Big-axe in that trap," Sure-dart muttered to himself. "He is n't the hot-headed fool you seem to think him."

Even at that moment, when hot-headedness, or almost anything else, would have been welcome, the boy was cool enough and fair enough to see the other side of the case, and could justify the chief.

But there could be no better time to make his start than now. He had drawn the thongs more closely around his waist, wrists, and ankles, so that his work on them would not be noticed, but here he shook them all loose again, and gathered his legs partly under him.

His face was still turned away from the hill, but just then his ears caught something new, and it surprised him into a pause. Big-axe, his powerful voice raised to a shout, was speaking.

Cheered a little, though he hardly knew why,

Sure-dart lifted his head and listened. He could hear the words plainly now.

The chief was challenging Long-spear and Strong-back to single combat, and he said he would fight them one at a time, but with no resting spell between; and if he won, Sure-dart was to be released. If he lost and was killed, of course they would get rid of their most dangerous enemy; if he was disabled, the conqueror could of course kill or take him. For weapons they could have axes, swords, or spears; he would have his axe alone. No shields were to be used. The fighting ground was to be a few spears' lengths in front of the barricade, the allies to retire, during the fight, to a distance equal to that from the wall to the fighting spot.

" It is all he can do for me," thought Sure-dart, " and he takes a great risk at that. Only they won't accept it, for they don't dare, and so I must still rely on myself."

But it did not at once appear whether he was right or not. The two chiefs affected to be ready to accept, but wished to think it over a little, especially as the interests of their men, as well as their own, were involved. The two turned back, and another one of their jabbering times began.

Nearly every man was now back to the prisoner, and they were now in truth, what they had pretended to be before, for the moment unmindful of him.

" If I let this chance go by," Sure-dart said to himself once more, " I sha'n't get such another. I won't wait. Here's for it! "

A quick shuffling with the thongs, another

drawing up of the legs, a shooting up to his feet, and down the slope he was rushing. For the space of time it would take one of our old-fashioned clocks to tick twice, there was hardly a sign of stir from behind, and not a loud cry. Clearly the surprise was so complete as to be almost bewildering.

Then — and it was well-nigh a relief to the strained senses of the flying boy — the din broke out, and the low bushes crackled, and the hard ground gave back the slapping of naked feet.

Sure-dart put out almost a savage effort, but the long bundling up and inaction had stiffened his legs, and, in spite of his roused and tingling nerves, he could not limber up, and strike his usual gait. He was going heavily, and as it seemed to him, no faster than an ordinary runner.

A dart hissed close by his head. One pursuer, at least, was probably out of the race. The dart must have been thrown from a standstill, and the thrower could hardly hope to make up the lost ground.

The faces on the wall grew plainer. He could see that some were almost puckered with scowls of suspense, and that some, like Big-axe's, were set, and yet, in a grim way, smiling. Big-axe himself stood quietly in his place, but the most of those nearest him were flinging up arms or hands, or even jumping up and down. It was a race to appeal even to a stoical savage!

Not very many paces more! The most of the gang must have stopped, for the slapping of the feet sounded lighter. It was time to expect Big-axe to take a hand in the game, and Sure-dart, slackening the merest trifle, looked up at him.

Yes, the chief was already putting his foot down on a rock in the outside of the wall, and was preparing to jump. Bull-head and four or five others were stooping at other places, and were making ready to follow. But here came a little jar against his right leg, and a stinging pain. He gave a kind of hop and skip, and started anew, but now the leg was almost numb. Must he fail, and only this to gain? Staggering now, and going from that to a limp, he forced himself over a few more yards.

He saw, yet hardly knew that he saw, Big-axe wildly swing his arms. The chief was yelling something, too, but close as he was it sounded far off. Bits of blackness, followed by flashes of light, passed before his eyes. But somehow, some way, there wormed itself into his darkening consciousness that the chief wanted him to drop — to lie down. It was at least an easy thing to do. He did it. He stooped a little, put out his hands, and let himself go.

After all, even a slow thought is quicker than a swift arm. Little whizzing things flew over him, as he went down, and knocked harmlessly against the wall. The boy did not know it. He did not know, either, that the throwers, turning, as they saw what had happened, ran back, and did not stop till they were up with the slower runners.

And still more, he did not know when Big-axe, Bull-head, and three or four others, springing down from the wall, rushed him up to the top of it, and from there carried him gently down to the path, and put him on a lizard skin. The long strain, following days of other strain, and that both mental and physical, the hot sun, the shock and pain of the wound — these were enough to strike down, for the moment, even this hardy young fighter.

The little that the old men and women, who were now left in charge of him, knew how to do was done, and it was not long before he was sufficiently himself to open his eyes, and move his lips. He did not talk, however, and soon dropped off in a heavy sleep. It was over an hour before he came out of this.

Meanwhile, the chief and the other principal fighters were on the wall, waiting for what looked like another attack. It did not come, and instead, the besiegers, sullen and silent, went slowly back to their camping place. Bull-head, sure not to let such an opportunity slip, sent his roar of derision after them, and called them some decidedly uncivil names.

Sure-dart, when he opened his eyes again, was much better, but weak and dull-headed. He asked whether the enemy had gone back to camp again, and whether there had been any more fighting; and when these questions had been answered, he was content to lie still and close his eyes. His wound, which was more disabling than serious, had been dressed, and was not as yet very painful. There were no signs of poison, and nothing more than time, and a little further home doctoring, seemed to be needed to make him as good as new.

In an hour or so more his head felt much better, and he roused, and wanted to talk. He said he had first something to say to Big-axe. The chief was sent for, and Sure-dart told him what he had picked up in the camp — the allies' plans and what they had finally decided on.

This was by far the most important as well as the most cheering news yet, and Big-axe, usually so self-contained, now broke out in a mighty grunt of joy and relief. Yet, as cautious and far-seeing as ever, he then restrained himself, and whispered to Sure-dart that for the present they had better keep the news to themselves. They would wait, the chief said, till the thing itself had happened, for then there would be no chance of a disappointment. He should fear the effect of so great a one on his tired and almost worn-out men.

A few more things were said, and after that they spoke of the chief's proposal and challenge, and of the very sudden way the matter had ended.

" I would n't risk waiting," said Sure-dart, with a little grin, " for I was pretty sure that if I did I should soon be turned to a dinner. They would n't have agreed to anything. Yes, I am sure the two were glad when they saw me cut for it, and so get them out of the hole. You say that Long-spear, who is one of the fastest runners in the gang, did n't get a good start after me, and soon turned back. I am guessing he had all the start he wanted."

" Whether he did or not," said the chief, with a drawing together of his heavy black brows, " I think it was well for him that he did not come on. I should have risked something, as things stood, to get to close quarters with him."

At this point some of the other fighting men

came up, and Sure-dart told the substance of his story over again.

" If I had n't been careless," he wound up, " I should n't have had all the trouble."

A little later they moved him to a shadier place, and finally into his old nest, or rock-bunk. Later in the day his wound pained him, and he was somewhat feverish, but the chief did not spare the water, and before morning he was better. Soon after light he heard a commotion on the path, and in a minute or two one of the women ran up.

" They 've gone! they 've gone! " she almost screamed. " Yes, the men-beasts have gone! They stole away in the night. They were ashamed to let us see them go! "

And this good news was soon confirmed by some of the men. There was not a Fisher nor an Islander in sight.

CHAPTER XXI

BUT the cautious chief would not at first take anything for granted. He sent out Wingfoot and another swift runner as scouts, and it was not till they had come back and reported that there was not a Fisher nor an Islander to be found this side of the middle hills, that he finally called the news true, and safe to go by. Then was a rush down into the open ground, which was almost like getting out of prison, and a poking about among the trees and bushes, with a little dash by some eager ones after small game, and wild fruits and berries. Even the old people seemed roused by the change, and smiled contentedly as they took little walks about, or sat in the shade of the trees. The children, who were much like children some millions of years later, screamed, and ran, and tumbled over everything and into everything. As for the warriors, they had some little dignity to sustain, but just now they did not try to sustain a great deal, and some of them were not above hooting and breaking out in what we now call pigeon-wings and double-shuffles.

But then, it is something to have a narrow shave from death, and to escape, for one's friends and oneself, an enemy's dinner pot.

As misfortunes never come singly, so it sometimes appears to be true that bits of good luck
do not. That very afternoon it rained, and this
not only cooled the air, but filled the spring, and
washed the stony dust and other unpleasant volcanic stuff from the trees and bushes. One party
had previously cleaned out the spring, so that it
was in shape for whatever addition of water it
might now get; and as soon as the storm was
over, a hunting and berrying party went out into
the refreshed and cleansed woods. In all, notwithstanding the scouring of the hungry enemy,
they found, besides some berries, small game,
including lizards, rats, snails, and tortoises. The
last two they ran across in a swampy place in the
low ground to the south.

We should hardly call the whole a very tempting bill of fare, but the Rock-people were not so
particular. Besides, they were very hungry, and
even some of our latter-day folks have found
hunger a wonderful remover of scruples. Once,
during our Revolutionary War, two hungry fellows, escaping from the enemy, were glad to make
a rattlesnake into rations; and others have eaten
rats and mice; and still others — half-crazed,
one would like to think — have turned cannibals.

After this first great rest and refreshing, the
talk began to turn on a grand hunt, to bring in
sufficient food to last a while; this Big-axe ap-
proved of. Out of prudence, the hunting party
was not to be large, and the others were to stay in
the fort.

As all were still pretty tired and worn, however, to say nothing of some who were sore from

wounds, it was decided to put off the hunt for a week or so, meaning, of course, the time we call a week.

And now were several days of real rest, and what for the active savages was a time of laziness. They still went on short hunts, and for fruit and root gathering, and one small party went as far as a stream some miles to the south. Here they caught several fish, but other than this everybody idled and rested.

Sure-dart was fast getting well of his wound, but was still lame, and did not think it prudent to go on any of the longer hunts, or to stand long at a time on the injured leg. But he hobbled out short distances, Hop-foot and often little One-ear going with him, and managed to bring in some small game. With the boys' help, he also gathered fruits and berries, and dug edible roots.

One day he and the boys were out like this when Hop-foot saw a small animal run out of a thicket, and make for a piece of swamp. As the creature crossed a bit of higher ground Hop-foot had a fair look at it, and saw that it was one of the huge rats that had now become rather common, and as it was not bad eating, he skipped and hopped along in chase. The creature could easily have outrun him, but Sure-dart was in the bushes near where the swamp began, and Hop-foot relied on him to turn the animal into the open again. He shouted, and Sure-dart, followed by One-ear, came out. Sure-dart instantly saw what was wanted, and ran toward the creature, dart in hand.

Rats such as we know will turn, when cornered, and show fight; and there is no reason to suppose that those primitive ones would not do the same; and so, as Sure-dart made his rush, cutting off the rat from the swamp, he was looking for a sudden change in the animal's movements. He was thus on his guard, because a creature as big as a smallish dog, with teeth almost like a young tiger's, and the power to jump several feet from the ground, was not a pleasant close acquaintance. But in this case the rat, perhaps not feeling that he was yet called upon to fight, turned again, and this time made a run for a patch of bushes. Sure-dart let fly his little shaft and ran forward, drawing his stone knife as he went.

His aim, usually so good, was just a thought at fault, and the dart, missing the rat by an inch, struck a small, outreaching branch of a bush, and glanced off. The rat scuttled into the brush, and when Sure-dart ran up, it darted into a tangle of bushes, creepers, and dead undergrowth, and from there, easily beating the slow progress that the hunter could now make, shot out again, and whipped over into a spur of the main woods.

Sure-dart saw that the hunt was up, and with a disappointed mumble went to look for his dart.

He thought he knew where it had gone, but when he went there he could not find it; and when Hop-foot and One-ear came up he was still poking about in the bush after it.

" Too bad you missed him," said Hop-foot, beginning to look also after the dart, " but it was a close shot. Oh, I see it."

He meant the dart, and started toward it.   It was fully as near Sure-dart, though a branch had cut it off from his view before; but as Hop-foot spoke, he took another step, and saw it, and then reached out to take it.

Rather oddly, it had driven in between the twisted branches of a slender wild vine, and was held lightly and almost level there.   As Sure-dart reached out his hand for it he pressed against the upgrowing branch of a tall bush; and this, seeming to have been caught and held back by another branch, flew free, and switched against the butt of the dart.   The consequence was that the dart shot out from the vine, and flew five or six paces, striking then the trunk of a small sapling.   It hit with so much force that it did not fall down, but stood straight out.

"Well, what next?" growled Sure-dart.   He had been vexed at his miss, and this new little bother decidedly irritated him.

He kept on, however, and pulled the dart out of the tree.   In doing this he was surprised to find that it was more than merely held up straight, but really had something of a lodgement in the wood.

"That would have given a man a good jab," he said to himself.   "If a bush could be fixed to do it on purpose it would be a pretty neat little trick."

He looked at the point of the dart, handling it freely, for it was not poisoned, and started to put it back in the sheath.   All at once, as if somebody had laid a hand on his shoulder, he stopped short.

Hop-foot saw him and asked, "Is the dart spoiled?"

With such crude tools as they had, making even a new dart was something to think of. The shafts were usually made of a sort of heavy cane, and of course only the straightest, and of a certain size, could be used, and the head was laboriously worked out of a fish-bone. There was then added a feather arrangement, something like that on latter-day arrows, to steady it in the air.

Sure-dart did not answer for the moment, but put the dart in the case, and started along. Hop-foot saw that he looked serious and thoughtful.

But here Sure-dart roused, and answered, " No, the dart is n't spoiled. I was only — I was thinking of something."

Now, anything like sober thinking, unless it was how to get the next dinner, was uncommon at that day, and so Hop-foot heard his friend's answer, ending, as it did, without explanations, with surprise and a bit of uneasiness. He was a little impressed, too, by the shade of reserve and dignity that the new look on Sure-dart's face gave him.

It was only a few minutes later, however, that they started up another rat, and in the excitement of the new hunt Sure-dart came out of his mood. A better speeding of the dart brought down this quarry, and the rest of the time Sure-dart appeared altogether like his old self.

After supper that night, when all the others had gone for better security back to their old quarters, he slipped around to the rear side of the hill. He was in a brown study again, and this time there was nobody and no happening to jar him out of it. He was not merely thinking; he was busy with his hands, as well. He was sticking a short piece of cane upright in the ground, with a cleft at the top, and a dart stuck horizontally in the cleft. When he had done this he took a broken spear-shaft. Stepping then behind the dart, he struck the end of the butt a smart blow with the piece of shaft. The dart flew a short distance, much as the one had flown from its place in the knot of vines.

He shook his head. " No," he muttered, " that won't do. Even with a better rig it would n't go hard enough, and there's no way of getting a good aim."

He picked up the dart, and stood for a bit, thinking.

Unconsciously he had all but lighted on the discovery of a machine that ages afterwards was to play a great part in war, though not till simpler devices had been invented, and led up to it. It was a simpler device that he was after, and one for direct individual use. This was as far as his farthest groping went, and it was a long step beyond anything the little human world had then thought of.

He failed that night to reach any new ground, and he was gloomy and in an irritable mood when he finally went back to the shelf. He was like many another and later inventor, who finds the keenest pain in his useless thinking and trying, and perhaps one of the greatest pleasures that a human being can know, when he is at last able to cry out, like Palissy, " I have found it! "

For several following days it was the same. He did not, or as yet could not, get beyond the theory that the missile he wished to project must be held in some fixed upright support, while the impelling power must be in the nature of a stroke from behind. To bring this about, and at the same time to improve on the simple method suggested by the original accident, he branched out in a number of experiments, but all unsatisfactory.

But at last — there generally is an "at last," for him who refuses to be beaten — at last he lighted upon the idea that led to what he wanted. It flashed upon him that he could hold the upright piece supporting the dart in one hand, and with the other could release some kind of driving power, perhaps a piece of thin wood, bent back to a point of strong resistance.

This was the germ of the thought; in time the ripe fruit came. Instead of a mere ordinary stick to hold the dart, he cut from a yew-like tree that grew near by, a flat and pliable stave that would spring to a thong of lizard hide. Finally, instead of the original dart, he made a missile a bit longer, but lighter, and with feathers differently placed at the butt. He found they did better flatwise, and upright, instead of in a kind of flange arrangement, like those on the darts. In a word, Sure-dart invented the bow!

It was only then that he told the others of it. He had managed to keep the secret, for he had been careful about it, not wishing to say anything till he was prepared to back it up with something more than a theory.

The astonishment, and then the keen interest that his final disclosure brought out, will have to be imagined. At first, as in the case of all great inventions, there was considerable incredulity, and some ridicule.   Old Stone-arm, looking at the bow and the arrow, and not yet having seen them used, sniffed, and said that when a man's arm became too feeble to throw a dart it would be time to take a stick and a string. Some others, though they said less, smiled sceptically; and a few looked wise, which in fact was a shrewd way to leave them in the right, no matter what happened.   On the other hand, Big-axe, though he looked as if he should prefer to see some proof before he fully accepted the thing as a success, still came out, and unhesitatingly said that he was inclined to believe in it.

The great trial came off.   Stone-arm, at the request of Sure-dart, demonstrated what could be done with one of the present missiles.   He was not over skilful as to aim, but he could cast a long distance, and pride, together with the thought of what he had said, stimulated him to do his best. He made a really wonderful cast.   Nothing has come down to us to show how far the dart went, but it was certainly a considerable number of yards.   Then Sure-dart picked up his newfangled machine and tried.

High and swift the arrow went, and so far beyond the dart that Stone-arm's performance looked like some little child's play.

There was a great roar of wonder and applause, and three-fourths of the crowd rushed off to see just what had become of this most astonishing of all darts, and to measure the distance.   Stone-arm stared, looked around, rubbed his nose, and posted off to pick up his dart.   The sneer had gone, never, as far the bow was concerned, to come back.

It remained to see what the new affair would do as to straight shooting. Accuracy, indeed, was as important as speed and power. There was now silence and respectful waiting, instead of sniffs and sceptical jabbering. Sure-dart lashed a shield to a tree, putting it up at perhaps one-third of the distance that the other arrow had gone. In the middle of the shield he rubbed over with a piece of the whitish chalk so common in the neighborhood, a spot; it may have been of the size of one of our ordinary dinner plates.

He took some pains, this time noting the force of what little breeze there was, but at the end released the bowstring.

Then was more shouting, and even louder than before, for the arrow had clipped the edge of the ring.

This seemed almost like a miracle to the wondering observers, though, in fact, there is reason to believe that the shot did not cover over seventy yards. The long distance shot perhaps reached two hundred yards. But think what this meant to people who had never seen a missile go farther than the comparatively few paces a strong arm could send it, and even then with less accuracy than the arrow.

Nothing could be thought of then but trying the wonderful " dart-sender " — so somebody named the affair on the spot. There was disappointment at first, for bow-shooting is not to be learned off-hand; and Sure-dart had spent many hours at it before he could do what he had just done. Still, even these clumsy trials showed clearly that a new day had come, and that the dart from the hand must give way to the dart from the "dart-sender."

As Sure-dart was trying to answer the questions that still poured in on him, Big-axe, who had been down to the target, came back. He had the shield in his hand.

"The dart not only hit the rim of the circle," he said, "but in spite of the distance it went almost through the shield."

He held the shield up to the light, that they might see it was so. Of course there were more murmurs of wonderment.

"But what this strange machine can do is not the thing we ought to think of," he went on; "it is what we can now make it do. We are just at this time free of our enemies, and not in a bad state, but who can say how long it will last? Who knows when our foes will come back? Besides, this is a hard place in which to get food, and we have seen that it is dangerously near the great hills. Yet where else can we go? The great hills themselves seem to be full of perils, though of a different sort from what we may expect here. Well, what then? I will give you my answer. Sure-dart has made it plain for me. I am for feeding the Fishers and the Islanders out of their own dish. Let us make dart-senders, and learn how to use them; then let us seek our enemies, and so deal with them that always afterwards there shall be peace! When all this is done, we shall know where to go, for we can live again in our old home."

It took the listeners a moment in which to get this new and startling idea into their heads, but when they did there was a tremendous yell of delight and approval.

"Yes, yes," they cried, "march on the man-monsters, and with the dart-senders leave them where we left the Cane-dwellers. Then we can live again in the old home. Begin, chief, begin!"

"Back to the lake! Back to the dear old lake," the women and children and such of the others as had not been near at the moment broke out in echo.

"It is settled," said Big-axe, grimly smiling. "We are going back. To the woods, then, and get the stuff for the dart-senders. That is the first step."

In almost a drunkenness of eager excitement they caught up swords and axes, and flooded out into the woods. Big-axe more quietly followed, his face nevertheless lighted up as it had not been before for more than one anxious day.

CHAPTER XXII

PEACE BY CONQUEST

THE wood of the yew-like conifer, if that was what Sure-dart had made his bow of, could not have been very hard, and though no dull axe of our day could have been so dull as the sharpest of the swords and axes with which the chief and his men were now working, yet it was not very long before the full supply that they wanted had been cut. With this raw material they went back to the open ground, which perhaps might now be called their camp, and all hands, even including the women and some of the children, fell to work to shape it.

This took them longer than they had expected, and as they grew a little tired, and their enthusiasm ran down, they got on more slowly still. Nevertheless, they made good progress, considering the time. Of course Sure-dart and the original bow were in pretty constant demand, and for the time he seemed to be of more consequence than the chief himself.

Several succeeding days saw the work still going on. Then, when the bows were at last finished and strung, and a few arrows had been made, they took up target practice. This was at first a little discouraging, for the bows being of green wood, and clumsily and not very skilfully made, did not perform in the best manner. The archers, too, being as green as the bows, shot at first wildly, and some grew impatient or sulky when Sure-dart tried to explain, or assist them. However, perseverance will accomplish wonders, and after a while the work began to show a clear improvement.

Still later the practice was changed to moving targets, and the shooting party turned hunters, and tried to bag rats, snakes, turtles, the various kinds of small lizards, and birds. They found this rather a set-back, for again they made some discouraging misses. Yet as before, they persevered, and once more began to show encouraging work. They now had the advantage, too, that when they brought down anything they could turn it to use.

At last the day came when even Big-axe, who had been rigid for a standard of good work, told them he was satisfied, and that he saw no need of waiting any longer. As their wants were so few and simple, they were again quickly ready to break camp, and the very next morning they started.

After all, looking at the small number of mature and experienced fighters, the chief did not seem to have waited any too long. They would clearly need all the advantage that the new weapon gave them, and great shrewdness besides, if they were to carry out their plans. There were just eleven grown fighting men, including Big-axe. Besides these were the large boys, numbering twelve, and a small band of women. Only the men and about half of the boys were expected to form what might be called the main line of battle, the others being in the nature of a camp guard and reserve.

Against this tiny army the Fishers, at whom they were to strike first, could show a total muster of over thirty. This would include some old men, boys, and others who would be of use in defensive work. They would be fighting on familiar ground, also, and with the desperation of brave men defending their lives, and those of their families, for thus far in the wars along the lake there had been no quarter shown anybody. On the other hand, Big-axe's little force might be said to be stronger relatively; for aside from the great ability of Big-axe and Bull-head and Stone-arm as hand-to-hand fighters, the mere boys and women, armed as they now were with the new weapons, were nearly on a par with the fighting men.

The plans that Big-axe, advising with the others, had made were these: they would go first to their old home at the head of the lake, and would leave there all the non-fighters, the company of armed women, and half of the armed boys; the rest of the fighting force, being eleven men and six large boys, would march on the Fisher village.

If everything went well here they would make a temporary camp, look after their wounded, leave a small guard, and with the captured Fisher boats would go on up the lake. How far they would have to go to reach the Islander village they had only a vague idea, but, measured by our distances, they must have figured it at least a hundred miles. They hoped, however, to have a clearer idea about this before they finally started, for they thought they could force it out of some of their Fisher prisoners. Big-axe openly said — and his authority was now so great that nobody opposed him — that should any Fishers, without being tortured, give him the information he wanted, he would spare their lives. He took this opportunity also to say, what he had before settled on in his mind, that he should oppose the killing of any of the old people among the prisoners, and any of the women and children. He had softened since the wars with the Cane-dwellers, and, besides, he thought he saw some profit in the new plan. The prisoners could be kept as slaves, except the small children, who could be adopted, and some of the women, who would doubtless consent to marry Rock-men. In this way the prisoners would help to replenish the losses caused by their friends, which Big-axe urged was an excellent use to put them to.

With everything thus elaborated, almost, indeed, to the point of cooking their hare before they had caught him, they pushed along, and made their way to the slopes of what they called the middle hills. Here they halted, and gave the less robust ones a chance to rest; and Big-axe sent out two scouts. They came back, saying they had seen no signs whatever of the enemy, and a little later the party again took up its line of march.

Through all these troubles and hardships Hopfoot had managed to preserve his scamperer; and the little animal was now really of a bit of use:

the boy had broken him to a sort of harness, and had taught him to carry small weights on his back. He was now loaded with a package of fruit and edible roots, and Hop-foot led him by a cord. We may well suppose that this was the first creature of the horse kind that was ever broken to man's use. Some of the smaller children had what we should consider less attractive pets — small, harmless lizards — little rock-snakes, and tortoises. Some of the girls, too, had dolls, and these were doubtless just as precious to them as the wonderfully artistic affairs that our children have.

On the way from here to the lake they saw a few dangerous wild animals, including one thorn-tail, and two of the smaller carnivorous death-beasts, but all were at some little distance, and did not offer to come nearer. They seemed daunted by so large a party, though it might also have been true that they were not hungry at the time, and were not in a savage mood. But it had also been for some little time noticed that even the largest and fiercest of these monsters were not so ready as formerly to attack human beings. Rather they would often keep on about their business, or even would turn aside, as parties of hunters came in sight. We do not know how these things are communicated from one wild creature to another, or whether they are communicated at all, or are anything more than a kind of warning instinct that moves in the different creatures at the same time, making them feel that it is best to keep out of the way of these small, queer animals, which do not seem afraid of them, and which somehow are often seen and smelt about the time that some creature of their own kind suddenly dies.

Yet as those great lizards were, after all, uncertain in their moods, and as they were so mighty in their giant bulk and strength, the chief, on each occasion when one was seen, sent the weak ones of the party back out of sight, and pushed on with the fighting men, till the creature would show that he did not mean to come nigh. It must be borne in mind that even one of these smaller death-beasts was more than half as large as an elephant, and having some of its bones hollow, and being very muscular, was far quicker, as well as more dangerous in every way than any wild creature of our time.

So they came out of the wooded country at last, and to the region of the low and somewhat bare hills. Very soon after this they came to a slightly higher ridge, and as they came out upon the open top, they saw below them the lake.

Savages and barbarians though they were, they had some deep-down sentiment; for at the sight they all stopped, and several of the women and old people broke out in little murmurs of joy and satisfaction. Even the hard faces of the warriors softened, and a light pleasant to see came into them. After all, these caves in the rocks meant home, and so stood for whatever of the gentler things of life those primitive people, their lives so grimly practical, could know.

They had already, as by a common impulse, halted, and after a moment the chief said that they had better put down their burdens and take a short rest. The sun was pouring down fiercely, and the air, even at this height above the lake-borders, was not wholly clear, but had something of the steam and stickiness of the lower lands, though this the inured home-seekers did not so greatly mind. It seemed natural to them, and doubtless they had acquired from generations of seasoned ancestors a certain adaptation to it.

But as this was hardly a time for sentiment alone, Big-axe and some of his experienced men were making practical use of the little interval, for they were using their keen eyes in spying about, and in looking far as well as near for signs of danger. At the end of this careful scrutiny it was found that nobody had seen anything in the least suspicious. The only change from the old times was that the wild creatures seemed bolder, for the men made out two of the great, upright iguanodons near the home beach itself, and some hairy fishing birds were settling on the rocks in which the caves were dug. This made the suggestion of the abandoned homes the stronger, but was gratifying in another direction. From a practical view-point it was cheering and encouraging, for it helped to confirm the idea that human beings had not very recently been in the neighborhood. These iguanodons, or " great stalkers," as the Rock-people called them, were rather shy creatures, and in spite of their bulk and strength, seemed afraid to venture near human beings; and the birds, though less timid, would not ordinarily have taken possession of the caves themselves.

The scouts did not rest very long, for all were anxious, from one cause or another, to push on;

it was therefore immediately after this that they again took up their burdens and started.

There were more feelings and looks of sentiment, when they finally fetched up on the old beach, and ran to look into the caves; but little need be said of this. They found some bats in a few of the darkest of the caves, but beyond that everything was nearly as it had been left. There were signs that the enemy had looked in here and there, but the few articles of household use, such as the pounding-stones, and a few old stone knives and the like, had been left untouched. It was true, indeed, that the careful owners, in spite of their haste, had taken care to leave nothing of mentionable value in sight, burying in other places even the better of the hollowed stones in which the dart-poisons were compounded. The canoes, which they had carefully hidden, were also safe, and nothing showed that a search had been made for them. Here again, however, it was true that the discovery would not have been of great benefit to the finders. The canoes of the Rock-people, as elsewhere stated, were small, and inferior to those of the Fishers in other respects, and might not have been thought worth carrying, or paddling fifty miles. This was about the distance to the Fisher village.

The start of the war-party was set for the next morning, and the remainder of the day was spent in resting and in doing such an amount of fishing as was desirable in order both to have food for the journey, and to leave the home party with an immediate supply. In doing this fishing great care was used not to go far up the lake, and to keep near the shore, for otherwise the men might be seen by some roving party from above. That night there was a heavy thunder storm, but the morning broke pleasant, and at sunrise, after a hearty breakfast, the start was made.

Sure-dart was now fully over his hurt, and he and Wing-foot were detailed as scouts, and sent on a short distance in advance. This was not so much just now on account of human enemies, as to guard against surprise by some dangerous wild creature. Here, in this great low country, was the home of nearly all the giant lizards, and of other monsters not safely to be met without warning. Besides, as matters stood, the tribe could not afford to take even an ordinary chance, for they had no lives, or even limbs to risk. It was not alone that the alert and experienced advance guard could see and give notice of the coming of any of the great monsters, but they could bring back a warning of some of the more subtle, but hardly less dangerous ones. For instance, there were such creatures to be considered as snakes, big and little, some poisonous and some killing by constriction; scorpions, the great bat-lizards, monstrous leeches, and the giant turtles. The leeches were confined, however, to the marshes, though there were several of these to cross; and the turtles were to be looked for only in the shallow pools, some of which the raiders might have to wade. These creatures, it would be well to explain, were essentially deep-water dwellers, and doubtless became extinct no great while after the salt water of the ocean was cut off; but it may be assumed that at this time they occasionally came up some of the numerous small streams, and scrambled their way from there into the neighboring pools and little ponds. They may have acquired this ranging habit in the course of a vain attempt to adapt themselves to the new order of things.

It will perhaps seem that the danger from some of these creatures was small, and should hardly have been made so much of, but the answer to this is that certain of them were much larger and more dangerous than their descendants, that we know.

In the main, it may be said that it was the great number of risks to be run, rather than the magnitude of any one danger, that made this march through the ancient wilderness such a serious matter. It was such a perilous place, in fact, that almost nobody ventured into it any distance alone, and even parties of three or four did not care to go far. When any companies did go they picked their way with care, avoiding, as far as they could, pools and the denser jungle growths, and punching down the reeds and denser ferns with their spears, when they must pass through.

It will now better be seen why the Rock-people and the Fishers, though living so comparatively near together, had, till recently, seen so little of one another. They were never on really friendly terms, and therefore had no idea of running risks in order to become better acquainted. There was, of course, the water route still left, but this, taking into account all the facts, was little better than the other. The water had perils of its own,

including those from sudden and violent gales
(these had been known since the earth had lost
the most of its heat, together with its envelope of
clouds and dense fogs), and the still greater ones
of attacks by the different kinds of hungry water-
monsters. It is true that such attacks were not
common, but neither were they rare, and there
was that about them, when they did happen,
which made them even worse than those of the
monsters ashore. There could be no running
away, for the fleetest canoes were nowhere
against the speed of the giant natives of the ele-
ment; and strong caves and safe trees were
wanting. It was on account of this danger that
fishing, on which the tribe depended mainly for a
living, was generally carried on near shore, and
always with spears and axes handy. In the home
waters there was usually little danger, for the
monsters, like those of the land, rather avoided
the immediate neighborhood of human beings,
and besides, found more to eat out in the deeper
waters.

Big-axe and his party, though none of them
had ever been in sight of the Fisher village itself,
had been about as far as there, and were familiar
with the general lay of the land, and knew just
about what dangers to look out for. It had been
decided to cover on that day a distance equal to
about twenty-five of our miles, to go into camp
then for the night, and the next morning to push
on, reaching the neighborhood of the village that
same afternoon. The dash on the camp would
follow as soon as the moon was up, which would
be no great time after it was dark, for there was

now a new moon. It was the plan to creep into the camp (it is perhaps a loose term to call the rude settlement a camp, and yet it was hardly more than that), shoot down every able-bodied man in sight, and then raise a great yell, taking advantage of the resulting confusion to pour in deadly showers of arrows.

The necessity of spending one night and the beginning of another in the dangerous woods was a drawback to the plan, but the cunning and experience of Big-axe and some of the others were sufficient to overcome this. Before dark, on each occasion, a great pile of a certain kind of thorny bush would be gathered, and this would be made into a high, inclosing fence, the thorns. out. These thorns were tremendously long and sharp, and when the work was made fairly stiff and firm by a lashing of wild vines and creepers, it would make a defence that even the giant lizards, unless in a particularly ugly mood, would keep away from. Against snakes, big and little, it was a perfect barrier, and even the more dangerous kinds of scorpions, despite their shell armor, did not like to crowd far into it. Inside this *chevaux de frise*, then, the trees overhead having been first looked over for snakes and the like, they could settle down and feel reasonably safe.

So much for the planning, over which they were not now spending any time, having the other, and practical part, to work out. With the sun for a guide, together, perhaps, with a kind of instinct, — something that we, without artificial living, have lost, — they pushed on through the wilderness, making nearly a straight course for their destination. The settlement itself was on the head of a tiny peninsula somewhat beyond a point where the lake rather abruptly widened, and therefore they must gradually bear to the south, and so, for the time, away from the water.

The party could make fair progress in spite of the nature of the ground, and the fact that there was no road, or even rough path. This was because there were considerable stretches of what we call open woods, free from much undergrowth, and because they carried substantially no luggage, and were strong and enduring. There were, to be sure, some very bad patches of jungle-like growth, but these they generally managed to avoid; and there were treacherous spots of low ground, marshy, and made additionally dangerous by lurking snakes, leeches, and other creatures, but here, again, they got along without trouble. They kept their eyes wide open, and walked in the light of experience.

The day waned, and still they were doing well, and had come to no harm. The declining sun was giving them only a feeble light, and things not close at hand were taking on a little dimness. The festoons of vines and other parasites helped to cut off some of the vistas, and shroud them with sombreness; in other places the giant brakes and fern-like bushes made walls that the fading light could not pierce. Here and there a palm stood up by itself, its umbrella top lifted high and dark against the paling sky, and its naked bole looking almost dead and stripped by contrast with any lower-branched trees that happened to be in range. In some hollows the plentifulness of water in those days was made apparent, for it had to be but a small depression to be a-glint with it. Reeds and rushes commonly grew here, and sorts of tropical, big-leaved plants that now have retreated many miles to the south. A noticeable thing, as elsewhere, was the entire absence of flowers and grasses. Not in the best-nourished spots, deep with vegetable mould, and reached by the sun, was there so much as one blade of grass or one little appealing flower. Instead were mosses, ferns, onion-like growths, reeds, vines, and creepers. The earth was to wait for its grass and flowers till there were gentler and more attractive things to match them — till there were song-birds, and humming bees, and gentle, darting squirrels. In that grim and harsh world was none of these. Woods and open were flowerless, grassless, and songless. Instead was the bewilderment of a blended forest and jungle, rich indeed, in hues where any shade of green, or tints approaching russet, could make them so, but rank, instead of rare, and echoing to the screams and croaks of monsters and toothed birds, instead of the trills and love-notes of our own little songsters.

Big-axe did not think it best to keep on much longer. He looked for a good place to camp, and when he had found it, he imitated the cry of a certain haired night-bird, and repeated it; and as this was a signal, it called in the two scouts.

There was no more than time enough to get the thorny defence provided before it was entirely dark, but after that they leisurely ate their supper. They had some edible roots, the stalk of a kind of sugar cane, and, for hearty stuff, meat from a vegetable-feeding lizard, and some snails. The snails were big, white-meated fellows, and perhaps were as good and wholesome as those the Romans afterwards ate and praised. The Romans, however, are understood to have cooked theirs.

Though some of the party could not help a little nervousness, which, under the circumstances, was natural, they all got through the night very well. There were disconcerting noises, and flittings of great wings, and once a largish but harmless snake found a hole in the thorny wall, and slipped in; but nothing in the way of a disaster happened. Bull-head saw the snake and speared him, and gave him a fling over the wall, and this ended the bit of real stir there was. Had Hop-foot been along he might have kept up the excitement for a while, for he had a great dread of snakes, and would not have rested till he was sure there were no others coming; but he had been left behind. He was rather too young for work of this kind.

In the morning they again made an early start, and pushed on even faster than the day before. They were feeling more the strain of the suspense, and wanted to have it over; and then they knew that they ought to make sure of reaching the desired spot before it was dark.

They did reach it well before nightfall, and as before, cut and piled up the thorny wall. They had plenty of food, and they had filled their lizard-skin water pouches from a brook, so they were well supplied in those necessary directions. They had taken the pains to prepare the wall, although they hoped not to pass the night there, because they could not be sure just what would happen. They might not find the conditions for the assault what they desired and expected.

These things prudently looked after, it was time to send out a scouting party, and see just how matters stood, and the precise lay of the land. The party had best not be large; Big-axe said that it should consist of two, he himself being one, and Wing-foot the other. The distance to the settlement was short, and communication could be had with the main party, should that be required, by means of bird signals. To enable the scouts to get back quickly into the inclosure, a section of it was left loose, so that it could easily be removed.

Softly the two men slipped away; the others, breathing a little hard, for now the great time was at hand, stood about in silence and waited.

CHAPTER XXIII

THE TEST OF THE " DART-SENDER "

THERE was now such a strain of holding the whole body at the tension of a strong spring, as would have been a pull on anybody's nerves. Even those almost animal men felt it, and, had it been light, would have shown it in their looks.

The minutes went by. Little noises came now and then from the settlement,— the uplift of a man's voice, as if in command, the wailing of a child, and the quick, sharp running together of several voices, which might stand for a party of men at night fishing, with something important struck. Notwithstanding the risks, there was some of this night fishing done, though always well in-shore, and with spears handy, and eyes roving about for danger. This noise soon died down, and there was silence except for the natural night sounds, but these were sufficient to fill the air with what might be called a background of blended noises.

At last the young moon got up in sight, and faintly brought out things around. The scouts could now push on their work, and it must be no great time before they were heard from. But after a number of minutes there was nothing, and the younger men began to stir uneasily, and to whisper around, and the older ones tried to go over mentally the time that they thought had passed, and to see whether it was really soon enough to worry. After a little considering and exchanging of opinions, they concluded not, and passed the word around.

It was not more than another five minutes when, above the other drone of noises, rose the hard, clacking cry of one of the night-flying swamp birds. A start, like a shiver, ran around. Never did men stand more rigidly still, and seem to listen with their whole bodies.

It came again, this time with a little subdued note at the end. There were relaxing and relieved breaths all around. There was a small noise of swishing bushes, and then, after a moment of silence, a low whistle. Stone-arm pushed away the bush-door, and answered the whistle. As he got his head clear where he could see, he made out two dusky figures. One was standing still, and the other moving obliquely toward the right, but as they caught the answering sound they both started quickly that way.

" We had lost you," whispered Big-axe, as they came up. " Yes," he went on, anticipating the question, " we have succeeded. We know what to do, and where to go. There is, though, something else to tell."

He and Wing-foot came inside, and the others gathered close around.

" We shall not have to be very careful in talking," Big-axe first remarked, " for there is nobody about. There are too many big and ugly things abroad for that. It was only by good luck that we did n't run into something. But now for our news. The Fishers and the Islanders have doubled up, and they are both over there. We shall have to fight something like sixty or seventy."

It is a great credit to the pluck of the Rock-men that they stood up stiffly as they heard this news. Though all were surprised, and though there may have been some wooden-feeling legs and sinking stomachs, not a man outwardly winced.

" Well, then," said old Stone-arm, speaking first, " we shall have to make one big job of it, instead of two little ones. On the whole, I am not sorry."

Nor did the others seem to be, judging from what they now said. Bull-head even said that he was glad, for it saved a long, hard journey, with unknown dangers on the way, and afterwards.

" Yes," said Big-axe, " that is true, and as I have thought it over I have not been exactly sorry. Still — not to fool ourselves — we must make up our minds for some hot work. But you all want to know just how the thing stands, and what we found out. Listen, then."

To shorten his account, getting rid of the questions and comments, this was the pith of it:

The camp, or settlement, now covered the whole of the little paddle-shaped tongue of land that the Fishers had originally settled on. The two companies were separate, the Islanders being on the point itself, and the Fishers nearer the shore, on the widest part of the tongue, though a few of their huts stood on the little isthmus itself. Across the shore end of the isthmus was a high barricade of the same kind of thorn bushes that the invaders themselves were using, only it was built higher and wider, and more substantial. In the middle was a hole, to serve as a gate, and this was just now stopped with a great stone. For a guess, it had taken the combined strength of several men to push this stone into its place. The scouts could not make out that there was any guard there, or thereabouts.

As for defences on the water-front, the thornwall, capped on a low one of stones, ran along both shores for nearly half the length of the tongue. Beyond that was nothing but a gravel beach, entirely undefended. The lack of defence here, however, was easily understood, for the defenders had not feared human foes (the only near tribe was the Rock-people, and they were small in numbers, and seemed rather to dread war than to desire it), and what wall they had answered well enough against the wild creatures. The great land monsters could swim, but had not shown themselves disposed to make a bold striking out where there was such a nest of what they probably considered noisy and puzzling, and perhaps dangerous creatures; and the sea monsters could not, from where the wall stopped, come very near the land proper. The beach cut them off. Thus the land creatures could not, without what they seemed to feel was a risk, get a snipping grab at the settlers, and the sea creatures could not get near enough to do harm, even though they had the courage.

The dwellings themselves, the scouts said, were all small huts, and made of boughs and palm stocks. The only difference between the Fishers' huts and those of the Islanders was that the first were round, while the Islanders' were a rough square. As for the estimate that Big-axe had given of the number of fighting men in both camps, it was based on what he had previously known, including what Sure-dart had formerly learned, and what they could both find out now. They could estimate pretty closely the number of huts, and this, put with the other information, formed what appeared to be a good basis for calculations. The total of sixty or seventy estimated included old men and boys, but only such as would be fairly effective in this kind of fight. With women and all, there might be a total of a hundred persons who could handle in some manner a weapon.

With regard to the boats, which were of the utmost importance in the invaders' plans, the greater number of them had been located along the nearer, or west beach, the most being afloat, and secured by short painters to stakes near the water's edge. They were all mere canoes, the largest being intended to hold but six men. The smallest were somewhat like the ancient British coracles, were covered with lizard skin, and would conveniently hold from two to four persons. Such skins were obtained from the great vegetable-feeding iguanodons, and were pretty tough and strong. The large canoes were dugouts.

This was the substance of the report. After all, with the important exception of the presence of the Islanders, it was not very different from what the hearers were expecting.

A brief council of war followed. The old plan

was not now exactly workable, and they must hit on something in place of it. Clearly it would not do to make a direct front attack, trusting to the confusion and the deadliness of the arrows for success. For one thing, the barrier of thorns was in the way of a dash over the little isthmus, and though they could take to the water and swim around it, there would still be the other tremendous risk and difficulty,— they must openly face twice the force they had originally counted on. It was necessary, then, to drop this idea as no longer wise and sound. Something that promised less risk must be thought of.

Bull-head asked why it was not feasible to turn aside at the barrier, wade along till they reached the end of the stone wall, pass around it to the beach, and then make their charge.

Three or four others spoke up at this, and said that they were about to ask the same question.

" It may be the best plan," answered Big-axe, after a little hesitation, " and I had likewise thought of it. At the same time, there are some serious objections. One is that if we do not break them, and they drive us, we are cut off from retreat. By the old plan we had the woods behind us, and could either make a better stand, or run. Then, too, we could probably have made more of a surprise of it, for we could have burst upon them suddenly; by the new plan we should be much longer exposed to discovery."

" Then what shall we do? " said Bull-head, a little impatiently. " I don't suppose we can drop down on them from the clouds, like a big beast-bird."

Big-axe paid no attention to this little outburst, but after a slight pause quietly went on:

"I have a plan, which has only just now come clearly into my mind. I think we could get hold of their boats, and attack them from those. Then we could reach them, while they could not reach us. Such boats as we could not use we could scuttle."

There was some general surprise, for nobody thus far had thought of anything like this, but after a moment first one and then another came out with approval. Even Bull-head joined in with his heavy, commending grunt.

"Then we will get about it," said Big-axe. "The first part will take more care and patience than anything else, for it will be mainly to work along past the side-wall, and cast off the boats. We will do this casting off as nearly together as we can, so that we shall keep things quiet as long as possible. Those who get to the boats first will thus have to wait a little for the others. I will give my bird signal when I think it is time. We may have to pole the boats, or some of them, for we don't know what paddles we shall find, but our spears will answer for that. Of course we shall not have to put off very far, for all we want is to be out of dart-range, and where our friends will have to swim to reach us. I don't know exactly what depth the water just off the beach has, but I think it is pretty nearly what we want. I should guess we could pole clear of dart-range."

This seemed to make everything clear, and as the chief slung his short weapons over his shoulder and took up his spear, they did the same, and all were ready.

By this time the moon was farther up the sky, and though only crescent, was giving considerable light. By its aid it would not be very hard for the men to follow the lighter and more open spaces, till they should be close to the in-shore end of the little peninsula.

Now the test was really beginning, and with new care, and almost crawling on the ground, they turned to the left, and crept down across the little open slope to the water's edge. Here they were partly in the shadow of some small trees, and of the brushy end of the cross wall. So far everything seemed to have gone well, and they stopped, considerably encouraged, and added their last little touch of preparation. This was to tie their quivers of arrows on their heads, so that the precious shafts should stay dry and easily manageable. Their bows they meant to hold high in one hand, swimming, where swimming should be necessary, with one arm and their legs. Every one of them was equal to this small feat.

But by this time the moon, which had favored them in seeing their way, and which would have to help them again if they were to carry out their final plans, was doing a little more than they desired in the way of a supply of light. Not very strong though it was, it still brought out things in the open in a fashion that was disconcerting.

However, there was no time now to stop and weigh chance. They would not turn back, and it was failure, with death on the heels of it, to stay where they were; so they must simply go ahead. Promptly, therefore, as soon as Big-axe gave the word, they pushed on once more.

Almost as softly as so many gliding snakes, they passed the end of the cross wall, and began to creep along the rocky beach at the base of the other. If they should reach the end of this wall in safety they would just about have passed the Fisher camp. The Islanders, it will be remembered, were farther out, from near the middle of the peninsula to its point. They soon found that nobody seemed to be taking the pains to look out through any holes or observation places that might be in this wall, and they accordingly went on more confidently, and faster.

A very little later they reached the end of this convenient road, and were now fronting the open and unwalled beach. Here the only chance was along the highest part of the beach, which was perhaps eighty or ninety feet from the water's edge. At this place a kind of ancient water-mark of scrubby bushes and low rushes almost continued the line of the wall, and extended around the curve of the shore toward the point. The beach here being so much wider than at the beginning, the moored boats, which were not straight down, but obliquely from where they stood, were at least a hundred paces away. The entire fleet of both camps seemed to be anchored here, which was to be accounted for by the fact that the other side of the peninsula was exposed to the rake of winds down the lake. From this point there appeared to be no separation between the two fleets, and they seemed to form a string that began at the wide part of the beach, and extended uninterruptedly to a point about opposite the thickest clusters of the Islanders' huts.

Without a word, for everything was now understood, the party begun to string out, a man stopping every few paces, till the whole company was ranged in a line. Bull-head, acting under the previous orders of his father, had stopped first, Big-axe pulled up near the centre, and old Stone-arm kept on to the end. In this way the chief was where he could best see and direct everything, and a particularly able fighter was at each end. Sure-dart, who was on the whole the best archer in the company, was taken along by the chief, his post being that of aid and messenger, as well as special sharpshooter.

As soon as Big-axe saw that everybody was in his place, and that the line was ready, he raised a low bird-note, and ran toward the water. He crouched as he went, and his dark shape did not come out very distinctly in the imperfect light. The others instantly started, and in a moment the beach was dotted with the dusky figures. They all stooped, the same as the chief, and looked hardly human as they poked out their heads, trying to keep a straight course, and scuttled along.

The faster runners reached the boats, and began to saw away at the painters, and the others spurted, and came rushing up. So far not a sign of trouble. At this distance they could only see, as a few of them whipped glances toward the shore, the humped outlines of the huts, dusky among some small trees, and with everything at the ground-line hidden by the shore-border of bush-growth and rushes.

There was quick work for an instant about

such boats as could not be used and manned. The painters of some of the dugouts were cut, and the boats themselves pushed out, leaving them to float off before the wind. Such coracles as they did not want they punched through with spears. There was now a little more noise, especially some careless splashing, and it seemed impossible that discovery could much longer be avoided.

Nor was it. Big-axe clacked out his second bird-call, and caught hold of the bow of the dugout he was reserving for himself and Sure-dart, but there, for an instant, he stopped. Somebody was thrashing his way through the bushes and other tangle just back of the beach-line, and keeping up a little yelping as he moved.

" Jump in ! " said the chief, quickly. He nodded toward the stern of the canoe, near which Sure-dart already stood.

The boy was over the low side in a twinkling. Big-axe less actively, but quickly followed, and pushed his spear hard into the gravel. Slowly the heavy dugout, which had grounded, slid free. Sure-dart now put his own spear over, and shoved, and as he straightened up again glanced around.

The boats, big and little, were slipping out into the lake, and the dark shapes among them were stooping and shoving away with might and main. The manned fleet and the unmanned were going to sea together. In one or two places figures were on their knees, and these, by their motions, were paddling. Some paddles, therefore, had been left in the boats.

The interval between the first little squawking

alarm and what came next could have been scaled by mere seconds. Sure-dart thrust in his spear again, the squawking on shore rose to a higher key, little yelps from other quarters struck in, and as he got his next full look at the bank, he saw that it was dancing with vague black shapes.

"We shall have to shove a little harder," said the chief, as he spoke giving a powerful thrust.

Their boat was, in fact, a little behind most of the others. Big-axe had meant to be last.

Sure-dart did not stop to look again till he had given a few more shoves, but getting a whisk then he saw that the black shapes were no longer outlined at the top of the bank, but had come into distinctness at the bottom of it, being, in fact, as many as twenty or thirty Islander warriors.

By the increase in the din, and the thrashing among the trees and bushes, about all the rest of the tribe, together with all the Fishers, would soon be on the spot.

"They are awake at last," said the chief, giving still another poke, "and it looks as if we should be busy."

Whatever the carelessness and sluggishness of the creatures at first, they were certainly making up for it now! Even as the chief was speaking, the advance party was at the water's edge, and several jumped into a few sound boats that, in the haste, had been left. They cut the painters in a twinkling, and with their spears pushed out. At the same moment, still others rushed boldly into the water.

"In with your spear!" said the chief, sharply. "Take your dart-sender."

He did the same thing himself as he spoke.

None of the canoes had gained any great offing, and in this respect the movements of the chief had clearly fallen behind his expectations. He had calculated on a sufficient start to carry the party into moderately deep water, where the enemy would be tempted to push after, and where a little stretch of swimming would be needed. At the present moment the water was not over a tall man's head, and a rush and a few strokes would cover the space to the nearest boat. It would be easy, too, to reach the nearest with strongly thrown darts.

Big-axe swept one look to right and left, taking in his whole line. In every boat spears were coming in, and the men were bustling out their bows and arrows. At least they were warned, and would be ready.

There was nothing that their chief could do for them. This time was no narrow battle-front, where a rush of the great body and the crash of the mighty axe might hope to turn defeat to victory; each and every man must be his own hero, and his own rescuer, or take the fearful consequences.

In this emergency the new invention had at last its opportunity. It was a fearful test, and a greater one than had been meant for it.

The chief had turned his face to the front again, but without looking around he spoke:

"Sure-dart, we must not waste our shots. As they come up I will aim at the nearest, and do

you take the next, and so on.   Or, if two or more
come up abreast, I will take the man to the right,
and you the next.   It seems to me," he added,
with a queer, fierce laugh, "that every man,
woman, and child in both their camps is in the
water! All ready!"

CHAPTER XXIV.

A S the chief spoke he raised his own bow, first getting such a balance that the unsteady little craft would not balk his aim, and the next moment he let drive.

He could shoot farther than any other man in the tribe, though he was not among the very best marksmen, but this time he had taken pains, and the target was near. The boat swung of itself a little, taking the chief out of the line of Sure-dart's vision, and the boy saw that the powerfully sent shaft had hit the mark. The tall, tufted fellow wallowing along in advance, dropped his raised spear, and broke out in a yell of surprise and pain. There was light enough to show the outforking shaft of the arrow, which stood obliquely up from the man's right breast. The stricken fellow stopped, took a side-step, turned, and began to wade feebly back to the shore.

The chief grunted with satisfaction, coolly took up his spear, and pushed the head of the boat farther around.

Sure-dart did not need to be told what this meant, and lifted his bow. The whole long row of splashers and waders, like so many people at one of our fashionable beaches, had now opened up.

Some of those nearest the wounded man had stopped, amazed and startled, but the others did not seem to know that anything particular had happened, and still came on. It was now that Sure-dart let fly.

There was no one man that could be said to be "next" to the fellow that the chief had hit, so Sure-dart took for his target a broad-chested warrior, who was almost directly before him. As the bow relaxed, the man lowered his arms, his spear and shield dropped, and he sank gently down and out of sight.

There was a little flurry immediately about where the man had been, but again those farther off did not seem to notice, and continued to wade and wallow along.

But this could not continue, for there were other places in the line now where there were gaps, and, moreover, those in the other boats were beginning to yell and fling taunts. The waders must quickly see that something unusual was the matter.

"We must work fast," said Big-axe, hurriedly. He clapped another arrow to the string, and with an off-hand aim, fired. Then, without looking after the shot, he caught several arrows from the quiver, laid them down before him, and started in again. He now began regular battery work, pulling and twanging away at his bow as fast as he could lay the arrows to the string. The time for fine and deliberate work had passed.

But Sure-dart did not need advice or warning. Even before the chief had discharged his second arrow, he was turning his own work into battery form. He had begun to shoot, and reach for more arrows at a rate distinctly beating the chief's. Now he was working with a sort of weaving motion, shooting, catching up another arrow, clapping it to the string, giving a sharp jerk, and then recoiling, as it were, and swaying down for still another shaft. Like Big-axe, he was no longer stopping to watch results.

It was wonderful how long it seemed to take to get it into the heads of the swimmers and waders that something was wrong. Men yelled, staggered back out of the line, here and there plumped suddenly down, and now and then howled and came to a halt. Yet still the others, seeming hardly to look around, raging at the loss of the boats, and furious at what they doubtless thought was the impudence of the whole affair, — continued to come on. Now those nearest the boats began to let go darts and spears.

" We must fall back," exclaimed Big-axe, dropping his bow and seizing his spear. " Push out! " he roared at the top of his voice to the others.

But strong as his voice was, it was almost lost in what had now become an uproar. The boats' people were excitedly yelling and flinging taunts, and the assailants were screeching and howling in their unearthly way. There was groaning, too, and snarling noises of pain, and splashing and wallowing. Only those in the very nearest boats seemed to hear the chief, and show by their motions that they would try to obey. Setting his lips, the chief gave a powerful shove, and sent the dugout several fect farther into the lake.

Up to this point it was impossible to say how the day was going. The poor light, the general rush and confusion, and the way the fighting lines were spread out, had quickened things out of the first plain and rather slow work to a headlong swirl and tangle that no man could make meaning or end out of! Sure-dart, catching the expression on the chief's face, saw that it was a business now of taking care of themselves till the bloody human knot could be untangled.

The strong shove of the spear had taken their own boat so far away from the few who still ranged toward it that this company stopped, and after a moment scattered and began to move toward some of the other boats. A few of them were already swimming, and the taller ones seemed to be moving almost on tiptoes. In this position they were of course unable to use darts or spears. Some of the other canoes, however, were nearer the shore, and some that were about as far out appeared to be over a shoaly bottom. For an instant the dugout was left to itself.

Big-axe, giving up his poling for a moment, straightened up and looked around. Sure-dart, from the stern, did the same.

They were a little more than in season to make out the beginning of a change. At last even the thick-headed waders and swimmers had found out that something was terribly wrong. They had noticed their falling companions, and had seen, before the final slump into the water, that strange looking darts were forking out of the faces, or bodies. Headlong as the rush had been, and near as it had brought them to some of the boats, it was still clear that it did not and could not account for all those strange and fatal hits. No dart could cover such distances. A few at a time halted, those in advance saw that they were not supported, and even as the chief and the boy looked, the whole irregular line began to fall slowly back. Half a minute later the spatter of out-bound black heads and uplifted arms, had changed to the whole of dusky bodies, and legs showing below the hips, and the raised, or pawing arms had sunk to the sides. There was not a man left that stood in four feet of water.

The noise had died down with the retreat, but now, from the right of the line, broke out a bull-like roar. There was no mistaking it, at least, by the boat people, and on the instant a great answering yell went up.

Big-axe laughed, and with his spear anchored the boat. The breeze, though still light, had strengthened, and the dugout was beginning to feel it.

A look up and then down the line showed two coracles half swamped and deserted; outside of the general line, and drifting slowly off before the wind, was a dugout. Just what this meant in losses, of course there was no way at the moment to tell. There were, very likely, also, some wounded or perhaps dead men in the boats.

As for the work done the other way, it was almost equally hard, in this little lull, to tell. Some had no doubt got back to the shore, but among the dusky figures that now lined a considerable part of the bank, there was no picking out, or identifying. The greater number of those killed or seriously hurt were undoubtedly on the lake bottom.

The only way to make even a wild guess was to note the party that still remained, and to compare it with what had seemed to be the whole original force. On this broad basis there was some shrinkage, and it might amount to a fourth or a fifth. To try to get nearer was out of the question, and there were many reasons why even this guess might be far out of the way.

Big-axe and Sure-dart noted these things, but not many more, for now the little breathing spell was over. The clamor on shore, hardly noticed while the fight was going on, and dropping to lower notes as the assailants drew off, here broke out again, and in the midst of it the line at one point was jostled, and through it broke a bunch of dark figures that fanned out, and rushed almost headlong into the water.

There was time to see some of them more plainly, as they waded toward the fighting party and the moonlight fell on them, and this settled anything that could not have been guessed at. The reinforcement was not great in numbers, for it could hardly have exceeded twenty persons, and the majority of these were women and half-grown boys, but nevertheless, it was a reinforcement of a sort that sometimes effects what mere physical strength and fighting experience cannot. Some of these women were the wives, or sisters, or sweethearts of the hesitating warriors, and some of the boys were the warriors' sons. They could cheer, and encourage, and remind their protectors what defeat meant (death, perhaps with torture, they could not doubt), and at the last could strike with them, and die with them. The reinforcement meant something, then, even when the moon brought out its physical short-comings, and it was not despised by any of the Rock-warriors.

But Big-axe also was thinking of those other women and children that he and the rest of his little band had left behind, and what would be-come of them if victory went the other way; and he thought of the harm these two tribes had done his people, and all without just reason. This steeled his nerves and closed the door to tender and merciful thoughts.

The rest of the pause was short. There was some loud and rapid talk; the newcomers pushed out farther among the sullen and hesitating war-riors; spears and shields were seen to be bran-dished — in another moment the whole com-pany, new recruits and all, were heading out, and splashing swiftly through the shallows.

For some reason the canoe of Big-axe and Sure-dart had again slipped a little out of the irregular fighting line. They both dug their spears into the sand, and began to push it back, but in the meanwhile the assault was on. The canoe that was manned by Bull-head happened to be the nearest to the coming human wave, and on that, accordingly, its crest broke. Bull-head, erect, had thrown aside his bow, and was grip-ping his great club. With it he met the shock. No doubt his arrows were all spent. Big-axe began to pole that way, and Sure-dart, seeing what was in the chief's mind, dug in his own spear.

Bull-head, as Sure-dart saw, smashed the up-lifted face of the first man that reached the canoe, but another swam up behind it, and with a sharp twist all but upset Bull-head, and made him drop his club and clutch at the gunwales. While he was still in this position a tall warrior, his head and shoulders out of water, came over a shoal place just on the other bow, and made a swift jab with his spear.

It must have gone home. Bull-head cried out, started to his feet, and then slumped forward to his knees. The man's head was now hidden by the canoe, but something flashed into sight, and doubtless he had driven in the spear again. But now Bull-head, staggering to his feet, threw one arm defiantly aloft, and once more sent out his deep-throated roar. As the sound died out he sagged at the knees, his body swayed, and he fell like a blown-down tree, over the gunwale.

Both Big-axe and Sure-dart paused as this end came. The boat began to drift outward again. The chief drew a sharp breath, bent down, and drove his spear-point again into the bottom, and with a tremendous push sent the boat bodily toward the floating canoe.

But meantime the tall man had climbed into the canoe, and was using the paddle that it seemed it contained. He was heading it toward a cor-acle, manned by one Rock-warrior, that was next in the general line. As he started, the nearest wader caught it by the stern, and deftly slipped up and into it. Both of the fellows were Fishers, for neither had a topknot, and both carried the distinctive Fisher shield.

Another twist of the paddle brought the canoe a little more fairly toward Big-axe and the boy, and let the moonlight in upon the two men's faces and wet, shining bodies.

" Long-spear! " broke out Sure-dart.

Big-axe did not speak, but slipped his hand behind him, and made sure that his axe was there.

The man who had killed Bull-head, and who was in the bow of the coming canoe, was in truth the wily Fisher chief. He was at the moment intent on the man in the coracle, and did not seem to heed the dugout and its crew.

Big-axe, thinking of his son, and seeing before him the man who had killed him, was in turn heading for Long-spear. He had not uttered a word since Bull-head went over the rail.

Sure-dart drove his own spear in harder, and the boat slipped out of the background obscurity and in front of this part of the line. Long-spear must see the two men now.

Big-axe had evidently marked the Fisher chief for his own, but the other warrior was a proper target, and Sure-dart was about to put down his spear and take up his bow. But something prevented, and that was a snap as of yielding wood, a jolt, a jerk, that made balance out of the question, and then a headlong tumble of the boy into the water.

CHAPTER XXV

SURE-DART FINDS NEW ENEMIES

AS soon as Sure-dart got righted and his head out of water, he looked around. He knew what must have happened, which was that the chief's spear had broken and so upset his balance and the equilibrium of the canoe. Sure-dart now saw that Big-axe was already afloat, and was half turned about, as if to make sure that his companion was safe. As Sure-dart spat out some water, and began to use his arms and legs, the chief swung about, and with powerful strokes made for Long-spear's canoe.

Sure-dart looked after him in surprise and trouble. The weapons had all been spilled out when the canoe canted, and though the bows and arrows were doubtless afloat, their whereabouts at the moment was uncertain. Yet Big-axe was not stopping on that account, but was going straight on, as if nothing had happened. It was a strangely reckless piece of business for him, and it seemed as if his desire to avenge his son's death had overcome his usual patience and prudence.

The boy did not know exactly what to do. He wanted to help the chief, but for the instant could not see how he was seasonably to do it. He glanced around, but there was no other canoe very close, and a man in one some little distance away was having all he could do to keep off a swimmer and two waders. The swimmer was trying to come up behind, and upset the canoe, and the two waders were standing shoulders deep, and throwing darts. The man in the canoe was doing his best to cover himself with his shield, while at the same time threatening his foes with his spear. His arrows seemed to be gone.

There was clearly nothing to hope for there, and Sure-dart next thought of the dugout. To be sure, he had no means of putting it in motion, but if he could find one of the bows, and even a few of the arrows, he might perhaps bring about something. At least, it was all he could think of just now, and time was everything if he was to help the chief.

The canoe, righted again, was not far behind him, but blowing steadily, though slowly, down the lake. Short as the distance was, it looked almost hopeless to chase it, and then expect to accomplish anything. On the other hand, it seemed more than ever the one thing to try, and that on his own account, as well as the chief's. He appeared to have no other haven of refuge. Unfortunately, he was not much of a swimmer.

The dugout, with a sluggish hatefulness, as it almost seemed, dipped along just fast enough to let him gain, but not to make a quick finish, and it was a woful number of lengths clear of all the boats and fighters before he finally came up with it. He scrambled aboard, blowing for wind, and wellnigh discouraged. As far as the chief was concerned, he felt that it was almost certainly too late to do anything. He righted himself in the boat, and looked back. To his great joy Big-axe was still there, but in another direction from Long-spear's canoe, for he had veered out, as if to circle around, and come up on the other side. Long-spear, on the other hand, as if in doubt, had kept the canoe where it was, but seemed to be keeping a close watch on the swimmer.

This, though puzzling, appeared to put another face on the matter. If Big-axe had really lost his head, he seemed to have recovered it again, and might now be counted on to keep Long-spear and the other warrior extremely busy. Forgetting his own situation for the moment, Sure-dart continued to watch, though now his canoe was feeling the wind more, and the distance was perceptibly increasing.

After all, it did not take long to bring this stage of the business to an end. Big-axe continued to swim in a circle, though Sure-dart, had he been nearer, would have seen that he gradually widened it a little. Soon he was on the shore side. All at once he stood up. He was now in no more than five feet of water. Long-spear seemed to think that it was time to wind up matters, for here the canoe shot forward. Big-axe raised his hands, and by his attitude was ready to throw himself upon the canoe. It would appear that he hoped to seize it and overturn it.

Just then Big-axe ducked; evidently the second warrior had thrown a dart. But the chief shot in sight again, and apparently unharmed. It was not easy, of course, to cast a dart very swiftly, and at the same time with good aim, while sitting in the bottom of a cranky canoe.

Now, certainly, Long-spear must get in his work. The canoe looked to be pretty close. Yes, the Fisher chief stands up. He is not trusting to darts; he is swinging back his spear. Oh, Rock chief, death must be a near neighbor to you now! Poor Sure-dart scarcely breathed.

And then the finish came. Big-axe threw up one arm, as if for a shield, and crouched. His other arm was drawn a little back. The spear never came down. Big-axe, instead of parrying, or punching, like a prize fighter, suddenly, and with wonderful quickness, stooped and shot under the water. He did not come up where he could be seen, but at once he made himself felt. The canoe rose at the bow, canted, and overboard, scrambling and clawing, went the two Fishers!

Sure-dart sent up a yell and a laugh combined. He was fairly on his toes, now, and staring, and snapping wide his eyes, in his efforts to follow the dimming scene. He could not certainly tell what happened next. He saw the water fly, and was pretty sure that one man got some sort of blow, and dropped back out of the fight. The splashing went on, and so the man could not be Big-axe, for that would have ended the fight. Big-axe, then, appeared to be having it out with Long-spear. Sure-dart laughed again. If but his leader's mighty arms closed once around the Fisher there could be little more to tell. He had heard of the great strength of Long-spear, and to be sure, the Fisher was a large man, but —

In his excitement he had nearly upset the dugout.

He got a steadier position, and again looked. In vain this time, for now things there were running together, and no manner of staring could bring them out. There were still the vague shapes of the boats and even, in the nearest, the black figures of men, but the little details were swallowed up and lost. In a night like this a certain distance seems almost at once to run things into vagueness.

The boy caught a little breath, and looked around. It was fully time that he were thinking about himself. Yes, it was high time. With neither paddle nor weapon, he was drifting out into the wider part of the lake, with its terrible dangers. Here, especially in the night time, lurked shapes of terror. A crew of armed men would hug the shore, and wait for daylight; or, if some urgent occasion did send them out to deep water, they would watch, spear in hand. Tales were told of fishermen who, perhaps reckless from hunger, had gone out in the night to fish in the broad waters. Catching some small fish, they had eaten what they wanted, and thrown the entrails overboard. Shortly little bumps had come against the side of the boats. Big-headed creatures, with mouths somewhat like a tiger's but far larger, and with stubby, active bodies, were picking up the refuse, and nosing about for more. Then, perhaps, would be the rush of some greater creature, trying for a snap at the tiger-heads. Commotion would follow, the great creature would see the suspended shape of one of the boats, and in curiosity, or anger, would throw himself against it. Then the men in the other boat would hear the water surge and boil, as the giant and tiger-heads forgot their quarrel to get what was going of this new and unexpected feast. Safety for themselves, if that could be had, was all that would be left for the other crew, and they would slip as softly as they could away, afterwards digging in paddles, and driving for the nearest shore. Hours later they would creep into the home cove, with what they had been through written even in their savage faces.

Sure-dart knew about these things, even though the Rock-people themselves seldom went out to the deep waters, and though he himself had never come through such a peril. He was aware that this part of the lake differed from the other, near the home cove, for down there the schools of big-headed fishes, for instance, almost never came; and when they did come, as they got into the shallow water, two or three great fish-snakes were pretty sure to paddle in from outside, and make fierce dabs among them, driving the confused school back to the deeps.

As for another terror of this upper lake region, the monster called by the Rock-people " great killer," he also was seldom seen below. The reason for this was somewhat of a mystery, for, under ordinary conditions, he should be at least a match for the fish-snake. The real reason probably was that the creature was by nature a salt-water dweller, being one of those left to freshen out, as it were, when the great land upheaval cut off the ocean, and that still chiefly haunted those waters which yet, as we may suppose, kept a tang of the original salt. There may have been, in fact, some small openings to the Atlantic still left, or some manner in which the salt water filtered through, though not enough to affect the lower lake. Be all that as it may, it was well known that this monster and the tiger-headed fish ("spear-tooth," the Rock-people called him, but we know him — or know his remains — as *portheus-molossus*) were rare at the west end of the lake, and common as one proceeded east. How numerous they would prove, if anybody dared venture beyond the home of the Islanders, there was no saying, for nobody, as far as tradition ran, had gone so far.

With the gist of this disturbing knowledge in his mind, then, Sure-dart saw the fighting ground fading faster and faster into the shadows, and himself, helpless either to fight or to fly, coming into the region of strange and hideous dangers.

Cautiously, lest there should be another upset, he stood up straight, and looked carefully all around. The light was merely strong enough to give things in large masses, and without distinct outlines. There was in the large little more than a dull, faintly gleaming lake, black, wooded shores, and a pale sky. The thin moon had the company of a wide field of far-off stars, and a faint mist hung low down in the east, dimming the stars that were climbing up there, and helping to bring the horizon sky almost to the pitch of black. The breeze had so far raised no more than a little ripple on the water, so that the boat poppled, and thumped gently, as it drifted along, but kept all the time one general course. That was still almost for the middle of the lake.

In his survey Sure-dart had, of course, included the peninsula, but that was now but a part of the general shore boundary. He could still hear some faint sounds from there, but none of which he could make anything definite, or that told how things were going. He next began to guess at the time it would take to drift across the lake, supposing the breeze to hold as it was. He knew it was a considerable distance, and it seemed to him that it would be well into the next day before he could fetch land. He would then, however, be a somewhat shorter distance from the home cove than from there to the peninsula. This was because, though the distance across the lake was greater than that from the cove to the peninsula, yet the wind was somewhat more than an offset, as it blew diagonally rather than exactly down the lake.

Yet when he should have landed, if he should be as lucky as that, he would still be a long distance from the caves, and in a region as wild and dangerous as that he had just left. The ruined and deserted settlement of the Cane-dwellers was the one spot that showed even the marks of any visit of man.

Sure-dart must have looked pretty sober as he turned all this over in his mind. Wonderfully trained though he had been, for almost every sort of physical trial and hazard, yet this was a heaping up of dangers and ultimate troubles that was almost crushing. The perils themselves were very great, but even if he passed through them safe, he knew not what he must still face. Who could say how the fight over there in the shadows was going, and what would happen if his people lost?

But this would not do to dwell on, for it was shaking him, and pulling down his strength, and he stood to need every nerve and muscle, even in his powerful and rubber-like body. He got down into the canoe again, and determinedly steadied himself. He would simply wait, meeting later troubles as they came.

All this while there had been nothing disquieting in his immediate surroundings. Once a small fish of some kind had broken water, giving him a momentary start; and at a distance a few birds, or small bat-lizards, which looked like birds, had skimmed and dipped past; but that was all. If the monsters from the upper waters were cruising down here they had not as yet made any sign.

Just then the breeze came in a little puff, and he raised his head quickly, for it brought a faint new sound with it. With every delicate nerve of his trained hearing at top pitch, he listened. The sound had no individuality — nothing that could be set down as any one note, or that meant anything distinctly. It was not a prolonged sound, like a wail, but was made up of short, jerky notes, almost like the far-off and very faintly heard barking of a dog.

That was what we might compare it to, but at that time there was not a dog in all the world. Sure-dart was puzzled, but he knew that it was a noise made by human beings, and that it came from the scene of the fighting. What could it mean? He could hardly make it into cries of victory, and it was less like the wails and groaning cries of despair and defeat. Once more the wind brought it to him, and it was the same as at first. He could make no more out of it.

The puffs of wind ceased to come. Instead there was almost a calm. The boat, nevertheless, with a little way on before, continued to drift. He listened still, and even put his head over the side, that he might catch the travel of the sound, if it came again, along the surface of the water, but nothing came. Nothing came, either, after he had listened for several minutes more.

He gave it up, but he still puzzled and anxiously wondered. It was almost a torment not to know.

At last, as he could not know, and as he was now feeling all he had been through, he thought he would lie down and get a bit of rest. He would not go to sleep, for then he might stick an arm up in sight, and some prowling monster might see it; or he might even give a sharp roll, and once more upset the cranky boat! no, he would merely stretch out, and ease his hard-worked body and limbs.

He was already sitting, and had merely to tip back and stretch out his legs. He did so, and felt a bit more at ease. Nothing so far had come near to harm him, and, after all, the noises from the fighting might well mean victory for his friends. Perhaps they were yelling in triumph, and the distance had deadened the prolonged part of the notes. He would try to think so, anyway.

Now that he was down in the boat, and everything below the level of the sides shut off, he could not well help noticing the sky. It seemed strangely serene and out of all the dealings of the earth. The moon, too, whatever the strange thing really was, had a quiet, safe, and far-removed look. He began to find it all a little soothing. He was really getting a comfortable rest, and a much better one than he had counted on.

But the woods, strange as it may seem, had crawled up till they were not a great way from the moon. That was queer. The moon had moved a little too, though the other way, and was far up the sky for the time of night, though, to be sure, it was a young moon. But there was another queer thing: the moon was green, instead of pale yellow, and the dead Bull-head's great war-club was hanging by a thong to one of the horns. Now that was strange, and he was certain that he had never heard of anything like it before.

A few of the stars dropped out of the sky, and made such a commotion in the water that the boat rocked. Now they rolled over and hit against the boat. It jarred. He woke suddenly, and with a start. There was indeed something bumping against the boat. With a leap of the mind back to full consciousness, and a sickening little shock of fear, he quickly, but carefully, sat up. As he did so there came another bump. It was almost under where he sat, and had the sharp, rather than solid, feeling that he thought he had noticed in the last one. He worked over upon his knees, and from there to his feet. He would know, at least, with what he had to deal.

It was no mystery. Flashing dull white and dark gray in the moonlight, a big spear-tooth was rounding up to the top of the water. Just behind him, and under the surface, but all too plain, were five or six others.

He got some of his steadiness back. He had never heard of a charge on a substantial boat by these creatures. It was only if a man fell overboard that the great, tooth-filled mouths meant sure death. Or it was very unwise to put a hand over the rail, or at close range to stick one's head over. If only, then, no other and bigger monsters felt a call to look the boat over, he should not particularly worry. It made him feel a little cold, and queer, though, when he thought of what he might have done while he was asleep,— what would have happened if he had thrust a hand, or a foot out. He wondered now how he had relaxed to such a pitch that he could sleep.

The fish appeared to see him, for the school increased and crowded closer, and two or three great, terrible heads came almost out of the water. Sure-dart began to feel a little troubled, and all at once concluded that it would be fully as well to give the creatures less of his company. If only they knew their strength, they could easily upset the boat. Yes, it was surely better to sit down and be less of a temptation. He lowered himself to his old position, and finally lay flat. In this way he was the least exposed, and he could the better balance the boat, should there be an earnest bump into it. But though he was lost to sight of the creatures, he was clearly not forgotten, for the bumps came harder and oftener than ever. Something appeared to be working through the thick, fierce heads that a supper was up here, if only they could find a way to reach it.

A most uncomfortable fifteen minutes or so went by. Then his heart gave a little jump, for he thought he heard a heavy, rolling splash. Was a killer, or some other bulky and headstrong monster coming?

As before, he determined to know the worst. He got to his knees and looked.

CHAPTER XXVI

HE could make out nothing strange at first, for only the spear-teeth were in sight, but just a few yards off a hump of water was going away in a suspicious undulation. He turned his head, and looked the other way. There was no hump of disturbed water there, but there was the thing that had made it.

A huge, long, bony snout, that was greatly like the crocodile's of to-day, was poking out of the water, and a broad flipper, somewhat like a seal's, but vastly larger, was fanning out on the surface of the water. Back more than fifty feet, the tip of a lizard-like tail trailed along in sight. It was the " great killer," such a creature as had more than once upset boats, and whose doings afterwards made a very short story.

The boy's fingers clenched hard on two little brackets, or cleats, that were designed to support a thwart. The movement was perhaps instinctive, though it might have been from the doing the right thing that had come from long training. At least, he could now stick better to the boat.

He never knew how long it was after this before the next thing happened. It was long enough to make his fingers stiff and weak. What did happen was as sudden and nerve-shaking as most of the other things during this eventful night. It came while he was staring at the great fish-reptile that now was swinging lazily around on another tack. The small fish had gone.

Up from the smooth water came a snake-like head, softly, and as if pushed from some substantial base below. The head was not much bigger than a python's of to-day, but it was longer and slimmer. A dusky and scaled neck, still with a silent and frictionless motion, rose steadily after the head, till at last that head looked down upon the water from a height of more than a long spear-length!

But the neck had finally come to an end, and now it was seen to spring from a great, broad-backed mass, that was somewhat like the body of an enormous, shell-less turtle. Yet the body, for size, might better be compared to an elephant's.

The boy sat silent, and not more shaken than he was before. Rather he was less so, for now he had a dim, new hope. He wanted whatever might be in it to come soon, however, for he would not have that long, inquisitive neck lifted beside the boat, and that deadly head hang in air over him.

The first investigating monster turns farther around, and now he sees the other. He lifts his great head a little, drops it rather quickly, and straightens out his vast length. Then, with his head, as we say of vessels' decks, barely awash, he gets in motion, and with a smooth speed that he has not before shown makes straight at the fish-snake.

As he comes nearer the long neck of the fish-snake drops almost level with the water, and the thin jaws open. The moonlight strikes on a mouthful of long, strong teeth such as no true snake ever had. The crocodile head suddenly goes under and out of sight, and the mighty tail throws flirts of water and spray into the air. He is for the under hold in that titanic wrestle.

The poor boy had all he could do to keep in the boat, and to steady it on its keel, and he lost the run of the fight. He had to do almost the work of a performer on a tight rope. Of course the commotion had raised a little sea, in the midst of which his unsteered craft was pitching and rolling. All he knew with certainty was that the two monsters were in some sort of death grapple, and that they were tearing at each other when their heads were under water, and hissing like great snakes whenever their heads came out.

The boat continued to dip and roll, and great splashes of water came aboard, and still the duel went on. Sure-dart happened to be now, as the dugout rode partly around, almost back to the fighters. Just here he heard a great crunching noise, something beat the water, as a mighty flail might, and the hissing stopped.

The boat began to ride more steadily. He looked over his shoulder. The fish-snake was in two parts, — the neck and head (which seemed now, indeed, to make an independent snake), and the great, cushion-like body. Into this body the victor was fiercely and hungrily tearing. The blood was running out in streams, and the flesh, as the mighty jaws ripped and rent, showed white in the moonlight.

The boat steadied yet more. Sure-dart could see everything now.

And then — all at once there was nothing more to see. The waves around began to dimple, hundreds of bull-dog heads and humped backs rolled up in sight, and victor and vanquished broke into mere slabs and strips of bleeding flesh!

Then the legion pulled what was left of the two bodies wholly under; they fairly covered them with snapping and gobbling heads.

A breeze sprang up, blowing sharply in the boy's face. It was nearly from the old quarter, but stronger than it had been before. The boat began to get headway, though yawing from lack of steering. The battle-ground was already some little way behind.

Minutes passed, and still other minutes. The boat was now far out in the lake. No other monsters had thus far appeared. In spite of all, the boy was again growing drowsy. He shook off the feeling, but it came back. On the boat swung and dipped, the wind luckily keeping down to its moderate pitch, and showing no signs of increasing.

Something jarred on the boy's senses. After all, he was losing himself again. The boat had given a new sort of jerk. He started up. The wind was changing, and beginning to come from the southwest. What if it got around still more, until — ? He was wide awake enough now. He wet his fingers and held them up, noting which was the cold side.

Little by little the wind worked its way to the

north. It might bring in a gale, but he would take chances of that. The blessed truth was he was going back toward the starting point. If his friends had won, as he had come to believe, he would be safe; and if they had lost he would find it out soon enough, and take to the water. With the wind in his favor, he was good for a short swim, and he would take the chances of fish enemies. On the main shore, and in the wilderness, he would be in a bad way, certainly, but better off than his poor friends at the caves, who would be sure to fall into the hands of the cruel victors. For himself, he was almost a child of nature, and he knew all the ways of the wilderness. He might manage to get along, and perhaps ultimately work his way back to the less dangerous region of the hills. At any rate, he hastily thought of these things, as his boat blew along.

A few minutes later he had a bit of good luck. A piece of a small tree-branch floated near him; he picked it up, and made a sort of steering paddle out of it.

And now, after all this long time and mighty strain, he neared the old battle-ground. What was he to see? What find out? The moon was going to its decline now, but there was still light enough to show the point, and the nearing things upon it. At last he could dimly make out the water-front.

The boats were again inshore, but now mainly pulled up on the beach. All at once the water about him began to popple again, and some unknown things broke water near him. He peered at them and saw that they were spear-teeth. And they were very, very busy. They were tearing in pieces and fighting over what was left to show that a battle had been there.

Yet a little nearer. Ah, there was a man! He was standing on the beach, and his figure came out against the light-colored up-slope of the sands. Was he friend or foe? How was Sure-dart to find out? It would not do to wait very much longer, although, with the steering-stick, there was a little more control of the boat. On the other hand, here were the spear-teeth.

Desperately, and setting his lips together, the boy kept on. Ah, there were voices! Some were calling out commands, and others seemed to be wailing, as in despair.

A little nearer yet. One voice rises above the others. It is in a shout of command, and is as if spoken to a person or persons at a little distance. Sure-dart, forgetting everything, jumps to his feet. He cannot be mistaken. The voice is the deep, far-reaching one of Big-axe! He takes all chances. He tries to help the wind by paddling. He draws in at last to the beach.

The man hails him, *and the tongue is that of the Rock-people.*

It is enough. The boat grounds on the beach. Old Stone-arm, almost stunned with wonder, helps him ashore. He is not weak now, though, but only stiff.

"We beat them, then?" he finds himself saying. It sounds almost strange to hear his own voice.

"Yes, we beat them, but we had a pretty hard

time. Toward the last we fell into a streak of luck, for a school of spear-teeth came in, called, I suppose, by the blood that was flowing, and began to make grabs at them. They could n't stand that, and made for shore. They yelled loud enough to be heard half-way across the lake." The remembrance made the old man smile.

"I guess I heard them," Sure-dart said, "but I did n't know what to make of the noise. I hoped, though, it meant something good for us. But how about our losses? How did Big-axe come out? I left him fighting with Long-spear."

"Big-axe held Long-spear under till he was quiet, and rather.full of water," the old man said grimly. "He will never bother us any more. As for our losses," he went on, "four of the grown men were killed, and one severely wounded. Three of the boys were killed."

"That is a heavy loss," said Sure-dart, sadly.

"But not quite so big as theirs," said Stone-arm, with exultant fierceness. "Every one of their fighting men was either killed or disabled. But they won't have so bad a finish as we should have had if they had whipped us," he went on, "for we have not killed any since the fight was over, and are not going to kill any. We shall take what are left alive back with us, and adopt them into the tribe. That is Big-axe's idea."

"What became of Strong-back?" Sure-dart next asked.

"We found out that he had died some time ago," answered Stone-arm, "and that was why the Islanders had doubled up with the Fishers. They had lost their chief, and some of their best men, and concluded to move the rest of the tribe down here. Besides, it seems the lake is a good deal worse for fishing up there, on account of the water monsters."

"We are to go back soon, I suppose?" asked Sure-dart.

"Yes," said Stone-arm. "We have decided to go by water, as it will be easier. We can start by day, and with such a big party it will probably be safe enough."

By this time they were coming into the camp, and Sure-dart had stopped asking questions, and was using his eyes.

Again the mists of one of those ancient mornings are rising from the little cove. Once more Sure-dart and Hop-foot are looking down on the lake from the hill-side, but this time with no strain of worriment in their faces. They have not come up here to spy out something; they have merely come out for a stroll.

Indeed, there are no monsters now lurking beyond the crest, and there have been none for these five years. Their day is past, and they have shrunk back into the remote wilds, to finish there what remains to them of life on the earth. That will not now be long. There are coming new times and new conditions.

Neither is it now a common sight from here to note the snake-necked fish-lizard, or even the giant but harmless "great stalker." These, too, have gone from the neighborhood of the destined conquerors of all the earth.

But there are some new sights, to take the place of the vanished ones. The strangest is a fire on the beach, and fish roasting on spits over it. Yes, the people have scraped acquaintance with fire at last, and it has begun its long but rather treacherous service as the slave of man. The discovery was an accident; it grew out of the burning of a tree by lightning, and the experiment with some of the coals that were left in cooking a fish. Since that at least one fire has been kept alive. Sometime the art of kindling fires will be added to the other discoveries.

And these two young heroes that are talking together have likewise had their share of change. Ten years have brought them from boys up to men. They have taken their places now as regular warriors of the tribe; and it is understood that when Big-axe gives up the reins of chieftainship the tried Sure-dart will take them. The sturdy Scar-face is still living; she and One-ear, now grown to be a large boy, live with Sure-dart in one of the best caves. Stone-arm, though no longer fit for war, is still in good health, and likes to stand around one of the great beach fires in the rare times when the weather is chilly (which it is, however, oftener than it used to be), and fight over again his old battles.

Best of all, there are few real battles to fight, and for the present, at least, none at all with human foes. When the Rock-people conquered the Fishers and the Islanders, they established peace in all this region of the lake. Their remote descendants were to have wars on their hands, and were to have their brute foes besides, though of another and very different kind. Perhaps we may yet take up their history, and see what their struggles, triumphs, and defeats were.

But in the days of the monsters there are left in the little cave village peace and contentment, as well as the safety and quiet for which they had so long hoped and so bravely struggled.

THE END